Enough!

Akarr moved to the empty copilot's seat, his balance unhampered by the shuddering ship. He took one look at Riker's grim expression—these humans were hard enough to read, never mind the fact that this one had unusually patterned hair on his face—and demanded, "What's happening?"

Riker didn't look up from the shuttle console; his fingers flew over controls that meant nothing to Akarr. "Trouble," he said shortly, and then swore, abruptly shifting to reach the console in front of Akarr. The shuttle lurched, straightened, and lurched again.

Akarr drew back just enough to keep from hindering his pilot, but not so far that he couldn't see out the viewport, where the trees seemed to be rising at an alarming rate. Something scraped the bottom of the shuttle, tilting them.

"Sit back," Riker said, intent on the controls as the craft somehow straightened. "And hang on."

STAR TREK
THE NEXT GENERATION®

TOOTH AND CLAW

DORANNA DURGIN

POCKET BOOKS

New York   London   Toronto   Sydney   Singapore

This book is a work of fiction. Names, characters, places and incidents are products of the author's imagination or are used fictitiously. Any resemblance to actual events or locales or persons, living or dead, is entirely coincidental.

An *Original* Publication of POCKET BOOKS

POCKET BOOKS, a division of Simon & Schuster, Inc.
1230 Avenue of the Americas, New York, NY 10020

STAR TREK is a Registered Trademark of Paramount Pictures.

A VIACOM COMPANY

This book is published by Pocket Books, a division of Simon & Schuster, Inc., under exclusive license from Paramount Pictures.

ISBN: 0-671-04211-4

First Pocket Books printing February 2001

10 9 8 7 6 5 4 3 2 1

POCKET and colophon are registered trademarks of Simon & Schuster, Inc.

Printed in the U.S.A.

For Strider, who would have loved the hunt

With thanks for help with the details
(and any errors, of course, are entirely mine):

Lorraine Bartlett, Dana Paxson, and Nancy Durgin—
and to Lucienne, who helps me to go boldly!

Chapter One

DEEP IN THE TANGLE of night-blacked foliage, slick fur slid between thickly leafed branches, making no more than a whisper of sound beneath the clamor of myriad insects crying out for the company of their own kind.

A shriek ripped through the chorus, startling it to silence.

Bones crunched.

Night in the Fandrean jungle.

"Lions and tigers and bears," said Geordi La Forge, more or less under his breath.

Entirely without inflection and without missing a beat, Lieutenant Commander Data said, "Oh, my."

Silence fell over the conference room. Geordi, who had not intended that his comment garner quite so much attention, winced.

Data faced that attention without any apparent con-

1

cern. *"The Wizard of Oz,* MGM 1939. I believe Geordi was making an analogy between the imagined threat of the beasts in the movie, and the very real beasts on the planet . . ." And finally he trailed off, taking in Captain Picard's thinly veiled impatience, Deanna Troi's quiet amusement, the spark of humor in Will Riker's eye. "But you knew that," he concluded.

"They knew that," Geordi confirmed. The movie was, after all, still popular enough to list in the holodeck programs.

"We did," Troi confirmed, as solemnly as possible.

"Ah," Data said. "My apologies for the unnecessary digression." But he hesitated, as though he might say something else. In the end he decided against it, but Geordi knew that expression. Data's insatiable curiosity—about *something*—had been triggered.

Worf stared intently at the creature on the viewscreen—an indistinct image, captured from beneath the creature as it swooped from one tree to another in the dense growth of the Fandrean jungle. Even blurred, the two barbed and prehensile tails were evident, along with the teeth gleaming in that long-snouted face, and the impression of size and strength. An arborata. Typical Fandrean jungle fare, according to the notations, right along with half a dozen other oversize flesh-eaters. "What does this have to do with the Ntignano evacuation?" he asked, with much interest.

"The Tsorans control this part of space," Troi said, "and we want to talk to them about the evacuation. They want to go hunting. Attending to their wants in this matter may well grease the wheels when it comes to *our* wants."

"Grease the wheels," Data repeated, as if he'd made some discovery.

Geordi glanced at him and decided now was not the

time. He returned his attention to his padd, which held the details of the Ntignano evacuation—not that he didn't know them by heart. One prematurely doomed star system—thanks to a doomsday cult with inappropriate out-system technology on its hands—and not quite enough time to evacuate the moderately populated planet within it. He'd known that the Federation had an ambassador on Tsora, trying to obtain the charts for the hard-to-navigate area—but why the *Enterprise* had ended up here, he had yet to figure out. "We've got to concentrate on getting those people out of there, Captain, not on hunting with the Tsorans. And that means getting—or making—maps of that graviton-free corridor they've surveyed. It'll cut evacuation time in half."

"Some of the more sensitive Ntignano people are already showing signs of damage from exposure to the star's fluctuations." Beverly Crusher, her long-fingered hands loosely entwined and resting neatly on the table, reflected none of the challenge in her eyes as she looked directly at Picard. That *do something about it* challenge she always seemed to have the leeway to make.

This time, Picard just gave her a short shake of his head, nothing more. He paced to the end of the conference table and rested a hand on his empty seat. Not a good sign, Geordi decided. He'd be sitting if he were pleased with the course of things. "Counselor, perhaps you can summarize the situation for us."

"Ambassador Nadann Jesson has done an impressive job with the Tsorans," Troi said. "Theirs is a society based on physical prowess . . . survival of the fittest, one might say. They are not impressed with the Ntignano plight, and the Federation has little influence on them as nonmembers. Ambassador Jesson has been on the planet for a month now, learning their ways and trying to introduce these negotiations; she's done well to have held their attention for this long. When they learned that the Federation flagship was in the area . . . Well. They are a people who are impressed with titles. They have not been willing to discuss seriously the use of the graviton-free corridor with Nadann, but they've indicated an interest in a dialogue with the flagship's captain."

"They are," Picard said, tugging absently at his uniform jacket, "significantly invested in matters of prestige. They have a term for it—daleura. And, as you would expect from a society that places so much pride on their hunting and achievements of aggression, they are also a bit prickly."

Worf shifted in his chair. After his alert stillness, the movement might as well have been a shout. Picard took quick note. "No offense meant, Mr. Worf."

"None taken. Unless the captain implies that Klingons are merely . . . *prickly.*"

"In point of fact, I find most Klingons to be downright contentious."

"Thank you." Worf settled into satisfied silence.

"That explains why we changed course," Geordi said. They'd been headed for doomed Ntignano until only the previous watch; now they orbited Tsora, a planet with sporadic forestation showing like green jewels against the brown continents, surrounded by a system full of invisible graviton eddies that kept a pattern all their own. "But not—"

"The hunting," Riker said. He'd been the one to present the information on Fandre's main preserve, the one who seemed to know the details.

"The hunting," Geordi agreed, hiding his impatience—and more concerned with recent reports that the results of the probe-induced singularity at the core of the Ntignano sun were far less predictable than expected.

Fandre and its preserve seemed more than irrelevant.

He'd rather be introducing his plan to use a probe-web to make their own charts. Such webs were complex and needed constant monitoring and adjustment, but with a dozen probes relaying high-speed data to the co-ordinating probe, a preliminary star chart could be available in a fraction of the time required for standard charting procedures. True, the most complex probe-web used successfully to date employed only eight probes, but Geordi felt he'd solved the logistics issues involved in adding another tier. All he needed was a chance to try.

None of which Picard was aware of, nor likely to become aware of just yet, since he now looked at the image of the arborata and said, "Fill us in, Number One."

Riker leaned back in his chair, swiveling it slightly. "Fandre is a big-game hunter's delight, with several species of massive carnivores, all cohabiting a relatively small and tightly managed preserve called the Legacy. Since the Tsorans reestablished diplomatic and trade relations with Fandre fifty years ago, they've been traveling to the preserve for their ceremonial rite of passage, in which the participant tranquilizes his prey and harvests a token from it. The prime kaphoora, they call it."

"No doubt a ceremony of much . . . prestige," Worf said.

"Exactly," Riker said. "And when they heard we were in the area, they decided that the ReynTa—what we might call a prince—would benefit from a Federation escort to his kaphoora. Everything else aside, we're certainly faster, even in these rough waters."

"His name is ReynTa Akarr," Troi said. "But here's

the crucial part—while he's hunting, his father, the ReynKa Atann, will discuss terms on delivery of the corridor map, and permission to use the corridor itself."

So *that* was it. "What if they don't have any intention of coming to terms?" Geordi frowned. "It sounds to me like they're using us, Captain. The prince—the ReynTa—might come back from his kaphoora and that'll be the end of it. They'll have their prestige and we—and the Ntignanos—will have nothing."

"There is that possibility," Picard agreed. He glanced at Troi. "The counselor and I will do our best to see that it doesn't happen. And meanwhile, Commander Riker will pilot ReynTa Akarr to Fandre, along with an escort of senior security personnel and—"

Ensign Gage burst into the room, her expression warring between annoyance and chagrin. "Captain, I'm sorry, I—" Alarm won; she threw herself to one side of the door, clear of the impending and intractable presence of—

"ReynTa Akarr," Picard said, unruffled. "We weren't expecting you just yet."

The ReynTa barreled through the door and drew himself up to examine them all critically, with no pretense of doing anything else. Though he was short, his stout and muscular nature left no doubt about his strength, and his bearing reflected a confidence in that strength. *He's only a kid,* Geordi reminded himself, feeling himself bristle under the scrutiny of the Tsoran. Then he took a look at the Tsoran's hands, where four fingers and two opposable thumbs came equipped with thick, clawlike nails. *Yeah, a kid who could rip my face off, VISOR and all . . .*

He suddenly had no envy for Commander Riker, who would be stuck in a shuttlecraft with the ReynTa all the way across the graviton-eddy-sprinkled system to Fandre. A look at the commander revealed that, aside from one distinctly raised eyebrow, Riker wore his poker face.

"I chose not to wait," the ReynTa said, his translated words partially lost in the throaty under-purr that accompanied them. With his severe overbite and a diminutive chin covered by a pouch of flesh, he probably couldn't articulate English if he tried. His lower lip looked flexible enough to cover his overbite, but at the moment he displayed his wickedly sharp incisors in all their glory. "I chose to see that arrangements have been made to my satisfaction."

Geordi exchanged a quick glance with Data—it wasn't easy for other people to tell when Geordi glanced at them through the VISOR but Data could do it—and he noted Data's keen interest in the nuances of the personal exchanges taking place. Earlier in his career on the *Enterprise,* Data would have interrupted to query the participants on the fine points, but he'd learned better.

Geordi hoped.

Riker stood, a respectful gesture, and nodded at ReynTa Akarr. "We were just finalizing those arrangements," he said. "If you'd like to wait outside, we'll be ready to discuss them with you momentar—"

"I spoke to Captain Picard," Akarr said, making no attempt to soften the interruption. "I wait for his words."

In the utter silence of response, Riker drew himself up—lifting his shoulder, adding the tilt of his head that sent wise ensigns scurrying for cover. *Trouble brewing.*

"Commander Riker's words are to be considered as my words," Captain Picard said, staring directly at Akarr, his gaze implacable and unrelenting—but his austere and astonishingly hairless features without aggression. Not that he had the means by which to back it up. Too lean to carry Tsoran strength, no claws, no fangs, only one thumb . . .

Akarr considered the rest of the humans. They, unlike him, had no decency of fur to cover their naked skin; they might as well be the youngest younglings. At least they all wore clothing over their arms, unlike the Federation ambassador Nadann Jesson, who often went about with her arms bared as if she were the coarsest flesh peddler—oblivious of the way Akarr's honored mother, ReynSa Tehra, averted her eyes. As if any Tsoran would avert her eyes for less!

Otherwise, the humans were not remarkable. He'd never get used to their faces, and the short distance between their eyes and mouth. Or the way their jaws met neatly instead of allowing their upper teeth to thrust forward for proper food handling—and fighting, if it came to that, although in modern Tsoran society, it seldom did.

Soft. It described Ambassador Jesson, and it described all the rest of them, too. Even now, they just sat around the table, looking to their captain for guidance. Except for Commander Riker—an imposing human, Akarr would give him that, and with eyes of startling, unnatural blue—who maintained a subtly different posture than the rest of them, but not one that meant anything to Akarr.

All that mattered to Akarr was taking proper advantage of this opportunity he'd been given—to build more prestige with his prime kaphoora than any ReynTa before him . . . than his brother Takarr, after him. He smoothed the fur on his arms—an absent, anxiety-betraying gesture that his father Atann would have corrected, had he seen it—and said, "But it is you, Captain, that I will be dealing with on the kaphoora. I see no reason to involve these others."

"*These others* are valued members of my crew." Picard stood by the flat, amazingly detailed wall image of the arborata, and spoke with quiet assurance, unmoved and unaffected by Akarr's formal dominance posture. His father would be pleased; this human would be worth dealing with.

"Commander," said the big one, the near-human with the interesting face and the low, growly voice not so unlike a Tsoran male's, "permission to—"

"That won't be necessary," Commander Riker said, calm despite his interruption.

"Very well," the big one said, but he gave Akarr a meaningful look. Akarr blinked without thinking about it, a subtle offer of subservience. No matter. The big one would not know; none of them would know.

Akarr advanced to the table, disdaining their chairs. "The ReynKa has advised you of our requirements. I only wish to confirm them."

"On this ship," Captain Picard said, "we follow certain procedures. In this case, we are discussing your requirements among the officers who will be most affected by them. You're welcome to stay while we complete our discussion, at which time we'd be grateful for your comments."

The golden-skinned being gestured at an empty chair and said, "Would you like to be seated?"

Akarr hesitated. He wasn't sure how these humans would view a choice to sit, especially not since the captain and his favored officer were both standing. As if reading his mind, Picard sat, crossing his legs in a move that Akarr could not hope to duplicate, but which looked casual enough. Riker, after a brief hesitation, also sat.

Akarr discreetly rearranged his stiff formal vest and followed suit, displeased to discover that his feet barely touched the floor.

"Since the ReynTa is here, we'll forgo discussion about the Ntignano situation and concentrate on the kaphoora arrangements," Picard said. "ReynKa Atann has requested that we transport the ReynTa and his private security to the planet Fandre, along with an accompanying honor guard from the *Enterprise*. Mr. Worf, that will include you and six of your most appropriate personnel. The ReynKa has also requested that we provide assistance in solving a problem with the Fandrean forcefield that encloses the preserve, and which keeps the civilian population safe." He glanced at Akarr. "We, of course, are glad to do so. Mr. La Forge, acquaint yourself with the forcefield specifications and prepare to join the away team."

The smaller, darker human with the strange facial assembly stiffened—in chagrined surprise, Akarr would have said, had he known the species better.

"I was thinking I'd deal with graviton mapping issues," the human said. Mr. La Forge. "Barclay's got a good feel for field diagnostics—"

"You think this is not worth your time?" Akarr said, staring hard at La Forge despite the disconcerting realization that he couldn't tell when he was looking the human in the eye.

"No, that's not what I meant at all," La Forge said, somewhat hastily, and looked to Picard.

Pathetic.

Picard gave a simple shake of his head. "Ambassador Jesson, who has made the arrangements and forwarded the forcefield details, informs me that the fields, while in some ways technologically more basic than our own, are formed from complex interlocking frequencies;

they're also combined with a technology damper of some sort. With the safety of the Fandreans at stake, I think it's best that you handle this situation."

"Yes, sir," La Forge said, and Akarr had to give him that much; he was as obedient as his lower rank dictated he should be. He liked Picard's confidence in the man, as well.

If the forcefield on Fandre failed, the beasts—freed from their huge preserve—would have the chance to kill only an insignificant number of Fandreans before they were slain. But without the forcefield, without the preserve, the Tsorans would lose the opportunity to experience kaphoora under such challenging conditions—conditions that Tsora itself could no longer replicate. The older, more established civilization of the two, with untold generations of kaphoora and daleura building behind them, the Tsorans had managed to eradicate the dangerous species on their own planet. Until they'd developed renewed trade relations with Fandre and agreed to Fandrean restrictions regarding the hunt—that the animals were not to be killed, that the Tsorans could gather only a token trophy of hair or claw and spine tip, that they could use none of their technological hunting tools to do so—the Tsorans had faced a rising daleura-based dueling rate despite strictures against the same.

On Fandre, behind those technology-damping fields, the daleura waited for Tsora's bravest. And now Akarr, alone of all on Tsora, had acquired as escort and pilot the captain of the *Enterprise,* flagship of the Federation.

Not that the Fandreans truly understood. But that was irrelevant.

In fact, it was hard for Akarr to believe that their two species were related, despite the obvious similarities in appearance. The soft Fandreans had initially created the forcefield and the carefully balanced ecological environment within simply so the beasts that called Fandre home would have a place to live, and so that the Fandreans would not be forced to eliminate them to insure their own survival. Absurd. Only the Tsorans saw the true worth of the place. The challenge of tooth and claw.

"Due to the number of people involved—the ReynTa's own Tsoran escort, and our security personnel, along with Mr. La Forge—we'll be using two modified cargo shuttles. Geordi, will you see to it that both are specially appointed for this purpose?"

"Consider it done," La Forge said, with no hesitation that Akarr could see, and even a certain amount of cheerful willingness. Interesting. He would have to take careful note of this human. How, while clearly remaining under the command of the ship's captain, did he maintain that air of independence? A useful tool to cultivate . . . at least, until Akarr was assured of his appointment as ReynKa, and no longer bowed to anyone. This trip would help insure that the ReynKa did not adopt the obscure decision to pass his reign on to his second-born.

The engineer, however, did not appear to be finished. "Captain," he said, "given what I'm hearing about the forcefields and tech dampers, I have to express some concern about shuttle integrity. Do we even know if our shuttles will function in that environment?"

"Starfleet has worked with the Tsorans and Fandreans to be sure that they will, and Admiral Gromek has forwarded the details regarding shuttle operating parameters while under the forcefields."

"I don't suppose we can delay long enough for me to examine these calculations myself?" La Forge asked.

Akarr didn't give Picard a chance to respond. "Absolutely not," he said. "There can be no delay." Not with the kaphoora fete behind him. Any delay at this point would look like hesitation on Akarr's part, and would forever cast doubt on his prime kaphoora.

Picard did not acknowledge Akarr's statement. "I'm afraid not, Geordi. Nadann Jesson suggested that the kaphoora might come into play some weeks ago, before we knew the *Enterprise* would be involved; there's been time to check it out. I'm sure Admiral Gromek had her best people investigate the matter."

"I'm sure she did," La Forge said, sounding unconvinced. "I just think it's wise—"

"And I do not disagree. But we don't have the luxury of following through. We'll use the figures that the Tsorans have provided."

La Forge gave a short nod and leaned back in his seat—almost a defiant slouch, Akarr would have said, except that the human was too relaxed. Still disagreeing, perhaps, but accepting.

As long as he did as was required, Akarr didn't care how much he disagreed.

"Geordi will pilot one of the shuttles," Commander Riker said, speaking up after enough personal silence that Akarr had assumed he wouldn't. "I'll take the other. With Fandre in its oppositional orbit and the system's graviton eddies to avoid, we can expect a trip of seven to twelve hours—"

"You are in error," Akarr said, trying to hide his sudden panic as he realized just what Riker had said. "My pilot will be Captain Picard. It is arranged."

Riker glanced at the captain, but it didn't seem to be in supplication, or to garner permission for any words or behavior. "There must be a misunderstanding," he said. "I'll have the honor of piloting your shuttle. The captain has obligations to the ReynKa and the Federation."

Speechless, Akarr looked at Picard, his fur ruffling up and his nostrils flaring in distress he knew these humans—*hoped* these humans—would not recognize. The flagship captain, *not* his pilot? Unacceptable! But . . . should he negotiate, play their game until he could gain enough sense of the human daleura to turn it to his advantage? Or startle them with a full daleura display here and now, demanding that which had been promised him?

But Riker watched him with wise eyes—blue human eyes—and no alarm. As though he knew the decision that Akarr weighed, and had no concern about dealing with it either way. And . . . very few Tsorans ever fully recovered from a failed preemptive daleura display.

So even though there were no other Tsorans in the room—his escort waited outside the conference-room door, blocking, as he'd been given to understand, the bridge privacy facilities—Akarr chose the safer way.

No matter. He'd make up for it on Fandre.

Chapter Two

"HERE'S THE THING," Geordi said, avoiding the temptation to raise his voice against the backdrop of the thrumming warp core, though it was the reason he'd chosen this spot to chat with Reg Barclay and Lieutenant Duffy. "This isn't exactly official. Not yet."

"You don't mean . . . that is, the captain doesn't—" Barclay stopped, took a breath, and said, "We're not—launching the probes behind the captain's back?"

Startled, Geordi said, "Of course not!" and glanced around the engine room to see just who might have overheard Barclay's unfortunate phrase as Duffy gave Barclay a pointed jab with his elbow. "What I mean is that this is an option I'd like to have ready *in case* we need it. But *until* we get the go-ahead, no one else needs to know about it. Is that clearer?"

To judge from Barclay's expression, not terribly.

"You want to *prepare* to launch the probes behind the captain's back," he said, his voice much lowered.

"I—" Geordi started, and then raised his hands in a gesture of defeat. "Yes, Reg, something like that. And I won't be here to handle it. Which is why I want you and Duffy to go ahead and modify and program the probes. Basic class-five medium-range reconnaissance probes."

Duffy gave him a doubtful look. "That's a pretty complicated program, sir. I mean, we can do it, but I'm not sure if we can pull it together before you get back—"

"I've taken care of that." Geordi handed Barclay a padd. "I've been thinking about this possibility ever since I heard the Federation was having trouble getting the charts. All you need to do is prepare the probes themselves, and then—if the orders come down—send them out and run the program. Do it from cartography—their input feeds are designed to work with this probe. But find a quiet corner for it, okay?"

Duffy brightened considerably, some of his normal cockiness returning. A good balance, these two—Barclay's innate caution versus Duffy's occasional attack of youthful enthusiasm. "That, we can do. Prepare the probes, keep it quiet. No problem."

"It shouldn't be," La Forge said. "Just keep in mind—it's not the captain you have to worry about if this becomes general knowledge, it'll be Admiral Gromek. This evac is *her* baby, and if the Tsorans somehow get wind of this, you can bet they won't be understanding about it. Our goal here is to *avoid* using these probes, and to hope that no one other than the three of us ever knows we were ready to do so. Got it?"

"G-got it," Barclay mumbled.

Duffy bounced on his heels once, and under Geordi's stern look, settled. "Understood." And then the blood flow to his cheeks increased considerably, a fact La Forge was easily able to discern with the VISOR; he turned around to see the cause. Data.

"What is happening in this neck of the woods?" Data asked.

"I, uh, I've got a holodeck glitch to check out," Barclay said, and ducked away around the warp core before Geordi could so much as lift a hand to slow him; his gesture hung, incomplete, in midair, until he let his hand fall back to his side and shrugged at Duffy.

"You, too," he said. "Dismissed."

"Yes, sir," Duffy said, with perhaps a tad more volume than he might have used.

Geordi waved him off with a sigh, watching as he bolted after Barclay. "What's up, Data?"

"Skulduggery, from the looks of it," Data responded in his most conversational tone.

"How's that?" Geordi asked, surprised . . . and thinking he wasn't much cut out for skulduggery. Not if even Data could discern the human signs of it.

"Do not be alarmed, Geordi. Whatever it is, I am sure your intentions are honorable. I have no plans to stick my nose into it."

"Well . . . thank you," Geordi said, full of caution. "Is there . . . anything else going on?"

"Such as what?"

"You just don't . . . seem yourself."

"If I wished, I could quite accurately reproduce the voice and speech patterns of anyone on the ship," Data said. "But since I am not doing that, I am not sure who you might think I seem like."

Geordi looked at him a moment, then nodded slowly. "That's more like it," he said. "Can I help you with anything?"

"Ah. You are wondering why I am here."

No beating around the bush with Data. "You could say that."

"The science officer on the *Curie* is providing me with constantly updated data about the state of Ntignano's star. I plan to tie the input into the bridge science station, and need to make sure you had no plans to use that station during our time here."

"Well, since I'm not going to *be* here . . ." Geordi said, and let the words speak for themselves. He didn't mention the probe work; those could be run straight from engineering, or patched through one of the auxilliary bridge stations.

"Excellent," Data said. "See you later, alligator."

Geordi looked at Data's briskly retreating back with a frown that hovered between puzzled and concerned. "In a while, crocodile," he heard himself mutter.

Great. Whatever was going on with Data, it seemed to be infectious.

Riker strode into Ten-Forward with more than the usual amount of purpose in his gait. He'd read Nadann Jesson's lengthy report on Tsoran customs twice, and the extra file on the Fandrean preserve—the Legacy, they called it— one more time. The Legacy didn't concern him, despite its arborata, cartigas, skiks, and giant ictaya; he hadn't been invited on the kaphoora, only to play chauffeur. And while the notion of a token hunt didn't faze him, the company of this *particular* hunt put him off entirely.

Meanwhile, Akarr was tucked away in a guest suite somewhere, the shuttles wouldn't be ready until late enough to delay departure for the next duty cycle, and Riker . . .

Riker was off-duty with a vengeance.

He eyed both the bar and the empty table in the back, and opted for the bar. Back tables were for brooding, and he wasn't interested in brooding. He wanted to contemplate precision phaser practice. Perhaps drilling a new belly button for Akarr.

Or maybe an initial belly button, if the Tsoran didn't yet have one.

"I think I have just the thing for you," Guinan said, appearing at the bar in that way she had of just suddenly being there. She held a tall, violent-looking drink, a murky concoction of barely compatible liquids swirling around to produce a sticky foam. "To judge by your expression, it suits your mood, don't you think?"

Riker gave it a dubious look. "I, ahh, think I'll stick to something more basic. Whiskey, double, neat."

"Whiskey it is." The tall glass disappeared, and in moments a stout tumbler with the air bubbles of hand-blown glass sat before him, cradling a dark amber liquid. "Our best single-malt." She eyed him from beneath a hat of imposing stature; on anyone else it would have looked ridiculous. On Guinan, it looked right at home, the color bright against her dark skin. "Think it'll help?"

Riker lifted the glass to the light for a moment of appreciation. "No," he said, and took a sip, closing his eyes to follow the burn all the way down. When he looked at Guinan again it was with a glint of humor. "But I'm sure going to enjoy it."

"There's always that." She produced a bowl of bar peanuts to match the whiskey, filled two more requests, and cleaned up after a spill without ever apparently taking her attention from him. "Not easy, is it?"

"What's that?" he said, thoughtfully sucking the salt from a peanut.

"Working with someone so important to your goals who's also so rude."

He raised an eyebrow. "All over the ship already?"

"No," she said, and smiled a most serene smile.

Riker sighed, giving up. This was Guinan. She'd get it from him sooner or later. "It's nothing I haven't dealt with before." He sipped the whiskey, let it settle. Could hardly tell it was synthehol, at that. Bless those Ferengi. "Nothing I can't handle, now."

"Of course not," she said. "But does it ever really get any easier?"

He lowered the glass to look at her. "Is this supposed to be helpful?"

"Maybe." She doled out another set of drinks and then regarded him with one elbow on the bar and her knuckled forefinger thoughtfully at her full lower lip. "Sometimes," she said, "just because you get used to something, doesn't mean you should ignore the way it makes you feel."

And then she was gone again, at the other end of the bar and leaving him to stare at the spot where she'd been, the words of question and protest unspoken on his lips.

Never mind. He had the whiskey, he had the peanuts . . . and his bearing—which did rather match Guinan's unpalatable-looking drink, at that—kept away anyone who might make inquiries to his mood and especially to his latest assignment.

With one exception. "Commander," La Forge said, spotting him at the Ten-Forward entrance and coming straight to the bar.

"Problem?" Riker asked.

La Forge shook his head, then hesitated, and shrugged. "The shuttle refit is right on track, but . . ."

"Geordi," Riker said, "I don't blame you for wanting out, but I have to back the captain's decision on this one.

We have to keep these people talking to us, and that means keeping them happy."

"It's not so much wanting out," La Forge said. Guinan planted a drink before him and he picked it up without even checking to see what it was. "I'll just have a couple of Tsoran security guards in my shuttle; *you're* the one who'll share space with Akarr and Worf and the main body of the security detail."

"Thanks for the reminder," Riker muttered.

"I really think it would be wiser to have someone here start the mapping process, just in case negotiations fall apart."

Riker gave him a hard look. "If the Tsorans found out we were making an effort to map the graviton eddies in their restricted space, you can *believe* that negotiations would fall apart."

"There's no reason they ever have to know. Lieutenant Duffy'll be holding down engineering; he and Reg Barclay work well with one another. Let me put them on it—at least get a *start.*"

Riker shook his head, staring down into the drink. "These Tsorans are too . . . prickly. We can't afford to take the chance."

"With all respect, Commander, the Ntignanos can't afford for us *not* to take that chance."

He was right, of course. That the Tsorans had put up this much resistance to merely talking about use of the mapped corridor spoke of their disregard for other species in trouble. There was no assurance that, even placated by Federation kaphoora escorts and technical assistance, they would agree to the kind of traffic the evacuation would cause. In the end, it might well come down to mapping that space as quickly as possible, and commandeering the space corridor for the duration.

Not exactly the Federation's style. The delay involved before such a decision could be made—and the maps charted—might well mean the death of hundreds of thousands of Ntignanos.

Riker lifted his head. "I'll talk to Captain Picard, see that he gets your assessment of such a project."

"Thank you." La Forge lifted his drink for a careful sip—it was a teal-blue fizzy creation—and behind the VISOR, his eyebrows rose in appreciation. "Guinan, you never cease to amaze me. Where did *this* one come from?"

"Well," Guinan said, imparting an air of confidentiality as she moved in closer, "there's this little planet just to the left of Sardia III—you know the one I'm talking about?"

"Lieutenant La Forge!"

Riker groaned silently, instantly recognizing that rough voice and the under-purr that garbled it. Who'd told Akarr about Ten-Forward? He'd find out, and he'd—

He'd turn around with a cordial expression on his face, that's what. "You must mean Lieutenant *Commander* La Forge," he said. "Welcome to Ten-Forward."

"Are the shuttles prepared?"

La Forge hesitated, glancing at Riker. "The modifications are under way."

The short being readjusted his stiff vest and made a face that Riker hadn't ever seen before—a manipulation of his mobile lower lip, which had to be quite flexible indeed, to meet his protruding upper mandible. A pinched-looking, disagreeable look. For all Riker knew, Tsoran to Tsoran, it was a smiling pleasantry.

But he doubted it.

"Is it wise to leave such things to your underlings?" Akarr asked, confirming Riker's suspicions about the expression.

"I trust my people," La Forge said simply, and left it at that. Wise, indeed.

Guinan leaned over the bar, her hands folded neatly before her. "This must be ReynTa Akarr," she said with enthusiasm, and Riker gave her a startled look; seldom had he heard Guinan . . . *gush.*

"Guinan," he said, by way of formal introduction, "I'd like to present the ReynTa of Tsora, Akarr." And to Akarr, "Guinan is our hostess here. If there's anything you want, she'll get it for you."

"Well, by way of food or drink, anyway," Guinan said. "And I think I have just the thing for you. You're the adventurous type, I hear. The bold explorer, yes?"

Akarr's words came more garbled than usual by the underlying purr. "You have heard rightly."

"I have this drink . . . I'm looking for someone to try it and give me their honest opinion. Problem is, I can't get anyone interested; it's too *different*-looking. Do you think you might . . . ?"

Akarr didn't hesitate. "Of course. I would be glad to help you."

"Wonderful." She nodded to the other end of the bar. "Come this way, and I'll fix you right up. You know, this drink has a long history of use by warrior cultures . . ."

Riker listened long enough to hear Akarr's confident noise of reply and turned away, his back to the bar and his warming whiskey in hand. He had a good idea which drink Guinan had in mind, and he didn't want any part of it. Given Akarr's propensity for challenges, he didn't want to be in evidence if the being decided to facilitate Guinan's data-gathering by daring others to drink the thing. *Double dare,* he thought, just about able to imagine Akarr saying it.

No, double trouble. And come morning, he and La

Forge would take it with them to Fandre. But for now—there was throat-warming synthehol and good company. He caught La Forge staring glumly at his own fizzy drink, and arched an eyebrow at him. La Forge gave him a wry grin and hoisted his glass; Riker matched the move, and simultaneously they declared, "To the Ferengi!"

Chapter Three

"SORRY I'M LATE," Beverly Crusher said as the door to Picard's quarters opened to her. "One of the evacuation doctors wanted to consult on the specific wavelength variation affects from the Ntignano—" She stopped, looked at him sitting by the morning teapot, at the steeping tea, at the single, stark bloom offset on the low table, and shook her head at herself. "Never mind. You don't need to know all that. Not the details, anyway, though you should be aware of our concern for the refugees. That sun simply isn't reacting as predictably as we've been told."

"Beverly," Picard said, sitting back on the firm cushions of the couch, tugging his uniform jacket down, and . . . waiting. Then, "Why don't you come in? Have some tea. It should be just about ready."

"Yes," she said, her expression sheepish. "Of course." And came in to sit beside him, shedding her turquoise lab coat and resting it neatly at her side. "I'm sorry. I got off to much too fast a start today."

"Then here is your chance to remedy that." Picard handed her a teacup—one of the modern ones, this morning, sleek and perfectly insulated—and she accepted with a smile.

After a sip or two and a few moments of companionable silence, she said, "What do you truly think of your chances of talking to the ReynKa, Jean-Luc?"

"My chances of talking to him are excellent." Picard offered her a small smile and admitted, "My chances of communicating *with* him seem less certain. If he's anything like his son . . ."

"Akarr is a child, trying to get what he wants. Surely the ReynKa will deal with the larger issues, the lives at stake? Especially since we're offering him and his son all the . . . daleura we possibly can?" But she shook her head. "Did you *see* the look on Will's face in the conference room yesterday?"

"I could have seen that look with my eyes closed," Picard said. "And I'm not making any assumptions about Atann. I have great respect for Nadann Jesson, and the best she's able to do is keep their minds open to continuing discussion—as far as I can tell, she hasn't directly broached the subject of using the charted corridor, although certainly the Tsorans know that is why we're here. And Atann . . . you know, I had the distinct impression that his intense interest in acquiring our assistance with the Fandrean shields had more to do with the future of the kaphoora hunts, and not much at all to do with Fandrean safety."

She stared at him over her half-lifted cup. "Then . . . he won't be much impressed with the fate of a planet he knows nothing about."

Picard shook his head. "That is quite likely so. But if I can find some way to couch the issue in terms that he understands, that he respects . . . well, *then* I might have some chance."

"And let's hope this kaphoora goes well, if that's what they care about." Crusher sighed, her breath making little ripples in the surface of the tea. "I don't envy Will this one. How many hours is he going to be stuck in a shuttle with Akarr?"

"Six to twelve, depending on the graviton eddies. In system, the eddies are of smaller duration but greater frequency; the patterns often change. They'll have to check against the charted eddies every step along the way." He regarded her a moment, the faintest amusement on his austere features. "I have every confidence in Will, Beverly—you know that. He'll not only be fine, he's likely to end up saving a small civilization along the way."

"You're right, of course," she said. "He'll be just fine."

"Stand down!" Riker bellowed above the noise of the fight, charging into the back section of the opulently modified cargo shuttle to haul human and Tsoran apart from one another. He took a quick assessment of the situation—Worf, thrown in front of the uninvolved Tsorans, keeping them uninvolved and holding the two *Enterprise* security crew members in their seats by dint of his glare alone. Akarr—standing on the seat of his padded, double-wide chair and snarling Tsoran imprecations—and the remaining Tsoran, facing off against Ensign Dougherty, both of them bristling and bearing marks of the first clash. "I said *stand down,*" Riker repeated, feeling not a little like snarling himself as he inserted his shoulder between them.

Both participants took a fraction of a step back; Riker

scowled them back another as the Tsorans behind Worf subsided and Akarr himself finally stopped shouting orders. "What happened here?" Riker asked it of them all, but it was Worf to whom he looked.

And Worf could only look uncomfortably vague. "I do not know," he finally admitted. "It started behind me."

True enough, Worf had been placed in the front port seat, opposite the ReynTa's extra-roomy accommodations. Three of his security crew sat behind him, and one sat copilot with Riker, spelling him regularly over the long and tricky journey—and for those unexpected moments when the ranking officer felt compelled to bolt from his seat and stop the brawling in the back.

The roomy cargo shuttle allowed more space in the aisles between the seats than the medium-range personnel shuttle, and had an additional two seats in the back, along with a reasonably spacious head—not to mention Akarr's special seating. Eight passengers on a long journey . . . Riker had hoped the extra space would keep the inevitable tensions low.

Apparently not.

"Mighty sybyls! This is little honor, to travel with such an escort. Can you not keep your people in line?"

"We still don't know what happened," Riker said, and eyed the now shamefaced ensign before him. Her long blonde hair had come loose from its restricting clip; tendrils of it hung askew along the side of her cheek. "Dougherty?"

"I . . . I'm not sure, sir," she said, sneaking a glance at her opponent, trying to tuck her hair back. "I was just sitting there . . . I wasn't doing anything in particular. I guess . . . sir, you could say my mind wandered."

"It's a long trip, Ensign," Riker said. "But that doesn't explain what happened." He turned her head aside to confirm that she did indeed bear the light marks of two claws near the back of her jaw, oozing but not dripping blood.

Akarr snapped something, too fast for the universal translator to decipher, and the Tsoran beside Riker— taller than most of them, and with an unusual cinnamon cast to his coat—shifted, looking away from Akarr. Finally, his words more difficult to understand than Akarr's, he said, "She was staring at me at an improper time. It was a great rudeness. She would not look away."

Riker glanced at Dougherty, who still didn't seem anything more than puzzled. "Did you," he said carefully, "*ask* her to look away?"

"I did," the Tsoran said with great dignity.

"I couldn't understand him," Dougherty said. "So I looked at him to ask him to repeat what he'd said—"

Ah. One Tsoran, in some private moment that happened to fall under the gaze of a human whose mind had wandered off and didn't even know she appeared to be staring. And then, in misunderstanding, she really *had* stared . . . .

Riker was suddenly reminded of childhood territory disputes. *He put his finger on my side of the shuttle!* Wonderful. "It appears that both parties bear equal blame," he said, to Akarr as much as anyone else. "Ensign, didn't you read the contact protocol?"

"Yes, sir, but—"

"No *buts*," he said sharply. "You clearly didn't read it closely enough. Go wait for me up front, and I'll provide you with another copy." To Akarr and his security force—all males, as far as he could tell—he said, "I apologize for the misunderstanding. I hope in the future you'll understand that we have little experience with your species, and that any error in manners is an inadvertent one." He looked at Akarr in particular and said,

"As far as we're concerned, nothing has changed; this was merely an unfortunate incident that no one else needs to know about. We'll disembark on Fandre as your formal honor escort, as planned." Whatever the hell a "formal honor escort" was . . . but it sounded good.

Akarr must have thought so as well. Although his lower mouth was pouched up in the same distinct but hard-to-read expression he'd worn in Ten-Forward, he made a motion with his hand—and then, as an after-thought, nodded in the equivalent human gesture.

Good. And only a few more hours to go before their "full formal honor escort" arrived at Fandre, after which Riker alone would pilot Akarr into the preserve, and happily wait in the shuttle for the Tsoran to complete his prime kaphoora, snag his trophy, and present himself for a triumphant return.

Worf stood in the narrow entrance to the shuttle conn, and Riker hesitated there, murmuring, "Do you have any idea what that was about, Mr. Worf?"

Worf's murmur was more like a bass hum; Riker tilted his head to catch it. "I am afraid not, sir. However . . ."

"Share, Mr. Worf. Don't keep it to yourself."

"Shortly before the . . . incident, I noted an annoying noise. I believe it was one of the Tsorans scratching. From the far back seats," he added, in case Riker hadn't caught the significance.

But Riker had. "Probably not something they prefer to do in public," he said. "But there's nowhere else to go." He sighed. And then some wicked little spirit made him lean conspiratorially close to Worf as he said, "You know what this means, don't you?"

Worf hesitated. "Do not stare at them if they are scratching?"

"Watch where *you're* scratching," Riker said, and raised a meaningful eyebrow at Worf before slipping past and into the front cabin.

There. At least his tactical officer had something to think about for the rest of the trip. And as for Dougherty . . . she waited next to the pilot's seat, stiffly at attention. "At ease," he said, sorting through the modest stowage for . . . ah, yes, the padd. He extracted it and put it in her hand. "The contact protocol for the Tsorans," he said, ignoring the ill-concealed dismay on her face. "Don't bother reading it; there's not a thing about staring when they're scratching. However, I do believe there are several of the captain's Dixon Hill novels in the padd's library, and you might apply yourself to them. Whatever you choose to do, try to look appropriately studious while you're at it, will you?"

She stared at the padd an instant, and then quite obviously decided not to question her good fate. "Yes, sir. Studious, sir!"

"And get cleaned up—have those cuts taken care of, too. See if there's anything that'll hide them. I suspect that Akarr would prefer us to look undamaged."

"I'll do my best, sir." She was doing her best to hide her relief, too, but without much success. Riker couldn't help a grin at her retreating back.

And now . . . maybe he could get back to the comparatively easy job of guiding them through the rippling graviton eddies that could easily tear this shuttle apart, luxuriously modified appointments and all.

It seemed the shuttle's occupants were willing to do that all on their own.

They did somehow manage to make the rest of the flight with no more excitement than one close brush with graviton forces, which left Riker's copilot—one of Worf's men, security with a pilot rating pulling double duty this time around—white around the lips and Riker grinning at him, more exhilarated than anything else. Give him a good piloting challenge any day . . . it was diplomatic assignments that turned him pale.

Fandre presented itself as a much greener planet than Tsora, with smaller continents mostly concealed by thick banks of clouds—and, over the ocean, several swirling storm systems. Riker and La Forge brought the shuttles down through a thick and turbulent atmosphere, breaking through the clouds to land the shuttles in a precision lineup on the wet and puddled Legacy preserve tarmac, a space lit to startling brightness by large banks of lights looming at the edges.

Before them sat the Legacy museum, the headquarters for all preserve activity—of which there was plenty of evidence. A hangar, open along its entire front length, grew off the east side of the museum; at the moment, it held only a few small personal transport devices and the beings responsible for maintaining them. Short and stout like the Tsorans but with more of a waddle to their movement, the two at the closest end of the hangar barely glanced away from their energetic argument to look up at the descending shuttles.

Riker sat in the pilot's seat for a moment after landing, staring at the great gray arc of the forcefield rising to the left of the shuttle. The artificial light slid smoothly off the field perimeter, but nothing about the forcefield seemed to discourage the jungle-like growth climbing the sides several stories high, heavy and healthy and still reaching upward.

The Fandreans might not be able to sort out their field problems, but they certainly had green thumbs.

Well, there was no putting this off. Riker stood and had the shuttle occupants arrange themselves as dictated for the ReynTa's entrance at the Legacy museum, where a reception, attended by Tsorans and Fandreans alike and rife with media and newscasters despite the late evening hour, waited only on Akarr's presence. Akarr, flanked by Riker and followed by his six personal escorts—who were in turn followed by Worf and his six security officers, moving with as much precision as possible given the differences in the Tsoran and human stride length—led the way, under the scrutiny of innumerable data recorders pointed in their direction.

Riker, much as he hated to admit it, was impressed. Whatever his diplomatic deficiencies, Akarr had not exaggerated the importance of this event. When the museum doors opened, a crowd surged around Akarr—and so did his escort. At Riker's nod, the Federation escort closed the distance.

It was a losing proposition, but Akarr didn't seem to mind; he also seemed to consider Starfleet's job completed, and after some moments of being jostled and ignored, Riker drifted aside. The noise in the crowded museum made it impossible to engage the interactive displays, but there were plenty of stills and holos to look at. Life-size holos.

It was quite a big museum.

Riker studied the gliding arborata hologram, finding it even more impressive than the viewscreen image in the conference room—its size truly apparent, matching his own torso even without the span of the thick skin between its bat-like forearms and heavily clawed back legs, and its teeth gleaming in an opossum-shaped muzzle. He took special note of the action of its barbed tails; most of the animals highlighted here had two tails in some configuration—like the sholjagg, a broad-chested, barrel-legged ground-hunter that had a long primary tail with a shorter secondary tail riding the spine of the first. Looking at its wide, copiously toothed mouth, Riker couldn't imagine it ever had occasion to employ the tail barbs. What, after all, would be so foolish as to chase *that?* Skiks, maybe. He circled around a holo of skiks in action, a large, darting flock that attacked in strafing runs, spitting digestive poison as they flashed overhead.

He found Worf eyeing the cartiga display. Its shoulders came to Worf's midsection, and at intervals in the display, the animal's rocky territory phased into sight, proving the worth of its patterned, rippling fur; the creature all but disappeared.

Worf seemed not to notice. It was the cartiga's teeth he looked at, and the massive, semiretractable claws.

"Mr. Worf," Riker said, "you look like a man with a certain gleam in his eye."

"I only regret that I am not to join this hunt," Worf said, seeming almost mesmerized as he added, "The honor of combating such an animal . . ."

"Aside from the fact that there's no room in the shuttle"—for the ReynTa, his six men, and their supplies in case the hunt should last a number of days filled the shuttle to bursting—"I'm sure that's exactly why you're not coming."

Worf tore his eyes away from the cartiga for the first time. "Commander?"

Riker leaned in, not that discretion was necessary in this noisy celebration. "The competition, Worf. He doesn't need the competition. He wants all the glory for himself this time out." And probably the next time out, for that matter, for Riker understood that any time a ranking politician on Tsora lost popularity, he'd stage a kaphoora to earn daleura . . . and approval.

Hmmm. Not a bad idea, come to think of it. He could think of a few Starfleet admirals . . .

La Forge squeezed through one last set of Fandreans into the relatively open area around the cartiga. "Finally!" he said, straightening his uniform. "I'm all for getting to work on those forcefields, but to discuss the fine points of harmonics in *this?* No, thank you!" Then he seemed to realize he was all but between the paws of the leaping cartiga, and moved aside. "Nice kitty."

"Mr. Worf shares your opinon," Riker said. "I think he's considering stowing away on the *Rahjah* to join us tomorrow."

"I would do no such thing," Worf asserted, frowning with much disapproval.

Riker sighed. "It's a joke, Mr. Worf."

"Well, you sure wouldn't get me inside that preserve, not without a pretty powerful projectile weapon," La Forge said. "Phasers aren't any good in there, you know. Nothing is. These people may have some trouble with their forcefields, but the technology dampers they're tied to are something else again. Limited engine function under heavy shields, no energy-based weaponry . . . no tricorders, for that matter. The shuttle will run, but only with its own shields at full capacity—and, of course, there's no way to communicate through the fields. Once you're inside that preserve, it's man against . . ." He glanced up, and up higher yet, to the leaping cartiga's snarling mouth. ". . . that."

"Not strictly true," Worf said. "They use tranquilizing darts."

Riker nodded. "Short-range propulsion devices, just

enough to let the Tsorans gather a trophy from the animal. Actually harming any of them is forbidden."

"Emphatically. Why do you think those shields are so complex?" La Forge said. "They don't need that much technology to protect the people from the jungle. They use it to protect the jungle from offworld poachers. And from what I understand, they *need* it. There's quite an underground market for furs like the one that would come from this fellow." He shook his head. "If you ask me, there's plenty enough daleura to be earned just by surviving long enough in there to track *anything* down."

"The Tsorans must feel the same, or they wouldn't include security teams to take down unexpected attacks." Riker stared up at the animal, taking in its eerily feline-like gaze, and unaccountably reminded of the time—the one and only time—he'd played baby-sitter for Data's cat, Spot. Not something he ever planned on doing again. "Nice kitty," he murmured. "You can stay right where you are. I don't have any intention of becoming *your* feline supplement."

A cough sounded behind his elbow; it sounded suspiciously like amusement. Riker found Akarr there, escaped from the throng and all but incognito without his escort. Although he stood out from the Fandreans present—for as similar as they were, the Fandreans appeared to be an entirely different branch of the species, with gentler features and longer, silkier pelt hair—there were enough Tsorans, all dressed in stiff, naturally colored leather vests, for Akarr to hide among if he chose.

Apparently the opportunity to goad Riker was too much to ignore, for here he was. "I thought that might be your feeling," Akarr said. "But don't worry. We don't expect you to come out of the shuttle. We each do what our courage allows of us."

Riker narrowed his eyes, only half-aware of La Forge's uneasy shifting and Worf's sudden deadpan expression, the one that meant you didn't *want* to know what he was thinking. "I have found," Riker said carefully, "that there is a difference between having courage, and having courage and also the wisdom to know when to challenge it."

Akarr didn't seem the least affected. "Those are pretty Federation words," he said. "But until one has proven the first, does the second matter?"

Riker stiffened, lifting one shoulder. *Does it really get any easier? Thanks a lot, Guinan, for putting that thought in my head.* Beside him, he heard La Forge murmur his name—just as a concerned question. *It's nothing I haven't dealt with before.* So he turned to Akarr, and looked down, and smiled a reasonably genuine smile. "Maybe someday you'll have the chance to find out."

Waves of pleasant heat from the morning sun washed against La Forge's dark skin, reflecting from the paved staging area behind the museum. To the left sat the shuttles; several Fandreans loaded supplies into the back of the *Rahjah*. Soon enough Commander Riker would be on his way . . . and La Forge wished him luck. Plenty of it.

He also hoped that the kaphoora went slowly, given what he had to accomplish here.

He refocused his attention on the shield controls, a small station at the back of the museum, enclosed in its own environmentally controlled booth. Not room for two of them, but he was only here to watch, anyway—the guts of the system were on a lower museum level. Soon enough, that's where he'd be, out of this beautiful day and into the exacting work of finding a way to get communication signals through the shields. Two layers of interlocking shielding with fluctuating frequencies, meant to foil any poacher, no matter how sophisticated.

La Forge wasn't sure but that it would foil him.

He sighed, rubbing the back of his neck. Just to make things interesting, the Fandreans admitted that for the past several days, they'd been experiencing unpredictable surges in the technology damper; they thought it was interacting with the shields, but weren't sure how. They wondered if La Forge might possibly take a look at that little problem, while he was at it. "Sure," La Forge muttered to himself, looking out at the opaque forcefield dome arcing up and away from the edge of the staging area. "Why not?"

"Did you say something, Lieutenant Commander La Forge?" His Fandrean liaison, Yenan—La Forge had the feeling he was of middling rank, but the Fandreans didn't seem to go for titles—pulled himself out of the shield booth. Like most of the Fandreans, he came only to La Forge's chest, but given the muscle on that stout form—and Yenan was stouter than most—La Forge wouldn't want to get into a wrestling match with him. He'd stick to wrestling with the shields.

"Just talking to myself," La Forge said. "And call me Geordi."

"Geordi." The Fandrean . . . well, La Forge supposed that was a smile; he drew his mobile upper lip down to completely cover his normally exposed teeth. And whether it was meant to be a smile or not, a smile was certainly the reaction it invoked in La Forge.

"So you're telling me," La Forge said, picking up on the conversation they'd been having before Yenan ducked into the booth, "that out in the shield perimeter somewhere, there's a device that will generate a fixed-dimensional portal *within* your shields."

The Fandrean nodded. "It nullifies the shields, in effect. Only because for that moment, we assign a stable frequency to the shields—which we change every time, so none of the poachers take advantage of that moment." Yenan had an under-purr with a less gravelly tone, and it made him much easier to understand than Akarr—a fact for which La Forge had been instantly thankful. "But the procedure uses an enormous amount of power, and we can only trigger it a few times before we must recharge the system." He gave La Forge a flutter-fingered gesture ... chagrin? A shrug? "You can see why we have such need of communications. We cannot see through the shielding to know when someone needs to come out; we can only arrange intervals at which we open the portal. This often leaves our Legacy specialists out in the field much longer than we'd like them exposed."

"Yeah, I can see that would be a problem," La Forge said. He scanned the shield along the perimeter line, looking for variations in the neat energy patterns his VISOR showed him. "There," he said, pointing. "Is that the portal?"

"That is where it will be," Yenan said, surprised. He gave La Forge a curious look, and then smiled again. "That is an impressive device. If we have time, you will have to tell me more about its function."

"If we have the time," La Forge said, not expecting to have any such thing. Right now, he wished Akarr would get a move on. He couldn't start work until after the portal had been invoked and closed again, and he needed—

There, finally. Akarr came strutting out of the museum. Unlike several hours earlier, this was a private moment, and one without excessive data recorders. La Forge saw only one, wielded by one of the museum officials. Riker walked just behind him, and the personal escort followed them, in formation. But once they reached the shuttle, the escort broke formation and entered first to see that all was to their satisfaction. Riker angled over to La Forge. After a hesitation, Akarr followed him.

"Any progress?" Riker asked La Forge, nodding a greeting to Yenan.

"We're ready to get started, as soon as you're under way," La Forge said. "This is a pretty severe shielding arrangement—it has to be, to protect these animals—so you'll be flying a lot of seat-of-the-pants. None of your sensors will work; you're going to have to navigate by speed and course. I've got it logged in for you. And don't shut the power down completely upon landing—keep some trickle of energy to the shields, so you can go live again."

"Much advice," Akarr said. "Maybe we should have had Picard pilot the shuttle after all."

Beside La Forge, Yenan made his fluttery hand gesture again. Definitely some kind of chagrin, Geordi thought. "No, you've made the best choice," he said. "Commander Riker is the best shuttle pilot we've got. Even Captain Jellico had to admit that."

"Admiral, now," Riker said, somewhat darkly.

"This Jellico is no one to me," Akarr said.

"Let's just say he doesn't offer praise lightly." La Forge nodded at the *Rahjah*, where Akarr's men were now clustered around the shuttle door. "And I think you're about to have an opportunity to find out for yourself."

Akarr rested a hand on his much-decorated trophy knife, and pondered Riker for another moment longer. "Of course," he said, "flying in is not the hard part. The hunt . . . you are, Commander, welcome to join us on the hunt. But, given our conversation yesterday, I expect that you'll choose to stay with the shuttle."

"I would happily join you on your hunt," Riker said, snatching the challenge before the words even had time to settle.

"Uh, Commander—" La Forge said. "The shuttle . . . someone really needs to be there to monitor—"

Riker glanced sharply at him, and La Forge fell silent. His point had been heard, no need for more words. The ReynTa glanced between the two of them and gave a short laugh, a strange noise of which La Forge hadn't been able to discern the origin. "As I thought," Akarr said. "A shame. We would have liked a Federation witness to the kaphoora. So be it. Commander, shall we depart?"

And Riker, giving La Forge one of those looks, chin at its most contentious angle, turned on his heel and stalked for the shuttle, overtaking Akarr on the way.

Yenan seemed to come out of hiding. "I wouldn't want to be on that shuttle," he said, smoothing down the fur of his arms.

"You and me both," La Forge responded under his breath. "Now, how about we look at those shields? I don't want to miss my chance to see them in operation."

Yenan straightened. Unlike Akarr, he didn't strut; his gait was more of a lurching waddle. But it took him where he needed to go, into the booth with La Forge looking over his shoulder, trying to keep an eye on Yenan's activities with the controls and the portal area at the same time. As the shuttle lifted, hovered, and then moved smoothly forward, Yenan made a few lightning adjustments to the frequency inputs, and then thumbed a sickly green switch that would have said *don't press me unless you mean it* in any language.

With a painful whine of power, the portal opened— starting at the ground in a semicircle, and expanding evenly outward until it was large enough for the modified cargo shuttle. The shuttle slid through with remarkably little fanfare, and the portal snapped shut behind it.

La Forge transferred his attention back to the controls, where Yenan made a series of quick adjustments, then pointed at a timing indicator on the display. "There, you see? The countdown for the scheduled openings starts automatically. If the shield booth is not manned shortly before, the console will contact me, and I'll make sure someone is here."

"Good system," La Forge said. "But what's this?" He pointed to one of the normally static readouts, and the glut of Fandrean number icons tumbling past. Just as quickly, it was over; the Fandrean didn't even glance up in time to see them.

"I'll recall them," Yenan muttered, jabbing at the controls. "Probably another one of the strange surges we've mentioned—ah, yes. Just that. Lucky we are, that you were right here for one. When we go back inside, we'll call up the data and compare it to the previous surges. Maybe your outsider's perspective will give us the answers we need."

La Forge shook his head. "That may well be, but I think we'd better let your people continue to work on that while I tackle the communications challenge. That is the one you want given priority, isn't it?"

Yenan made a face with his lower lip, similar to the one La Forge had seen on Akarr, but less extreme. "You are right," he said. "Come, let us go inside." And he suited action to words, nudging past La Forge to leave the booth.

La Forge hesitated, looking at the spot in the gray, coruscating shield through which the *Rahjah* had vanished, shaking his head. "Good luck, Commander."

Chapter Four

THE TSORANS CERTAINLY DID like their receptions. And Atann, who couldn't pass up either the opportunity to attend a reception on the *Enterprise* or the daleura of playing host, was no exception. Once Nadann Jesson explained the situation, Picard offered the only possible solution: a request that Atann share with the *Enterprise* a sampling of Tsoran delicacies. Under Atann's guidance the occasion quickly turned into a full-fledged social affair, for which Picard provided only a token supply of Federation favorites on a small, plain table set to the side. The two spoke briefly with one another—in person for the first time—as Atann commenced preparations in one of the larger function rooms; Picard could get no feel for the ReynKa's character whatsoever.

Shortly before the late-afternoon reception—and from all reports, Chief Brossmer had performed heroically at the transporter console during the preparation, both in dealing with the Tsorans and in the number of direct precision transports performed in the course of a single shift—Picard beckoned Troi into his ready room.

"Any words of advice?" he asked, seating himself behind his gleaming black desk and gesturing for her to sit.

She tucked herself into the couch and crossed her legs beneath the flowing skirt she'd adopted for the reception, looking comfortable—and, as was usual in the aftermath of such a question, as though she were searching inside herself for the answer, her black eyes distant. "I've read Nadann's report, of course," she said. "I have great respect for her work, but she's barely had time to skim the surface. The Tsorans are a complex people. On the one hand, they appear very much prone to surface emotions—they don't seem to hide either their feelings or their opinions about us. We certainly saw some of that between Akarr and Will in the conference room."

"But on the other hand?"

She came out from inside herself to look at him again, and to give him a rueful little shrug. "On the other hand, Nadann has plenty of evidence that despite these apparent behavior patterns, the Tsorans have plenty that they *do* hide. For instance, a male Tsoran will do anything to avoid scratching in public; and if caught doing so—especially by a female—both Tsorans instantly turn their backs on one another. In the next moment, it's as though they've forgotten it ever happened; neither will ever acknowledge the moment. If one Tsoran offends another socially—in manners of etiquette, one might say—they both similarly ignore the situation. For instance, Nadann has worn sleeveless or short-sleeved tops for most of her stay in the capital, in Aksanna—showing the flesh of her arms in a way that the Tsoran society sees only in females who sell their bodies. No one's ever said anything to her."

Picard steepled his hands before his chin. "So if they are communicating with you, it's likely to be . . . blunt."

"Or too subtle for a human to perceive," Troi agreed. "It adds up to this, Captain—if you annoy or offend Atann, or do something that he interprets as daleura one-upmanship, you'll hear about it in no uncertain terms. If you embarrass him . . . you're not likely ever to know."

"Until the negotiation for the use of their charted space fails," Picard said dryly. He glanced at the replicator but decided against the tea that would go down nicely with this conversation. He was already late for the reception. "Counselor, I would appreciate it if you stayed close while I'm talking to Atann or his ReynSa, Tehra. I don't expect to get past preliminary comments about the charted space during the reception, but if I can get a feel for their reaction to me . . ."

"Of course," she said, uncrossing her legs to stand in one fluid movement. "Shall we?"

Picard hesitated on the way to the turbolift long enough to say, "Mr. Data, the bridge is yours," and then to add, "though you should feel free to attend the reception if you wish."

"Sir, unless that is an order, I would prefer to monitor the increasingly unpredictable behavior of the Ntignano sun. I have one of the science stations tied into a feed from the Federation vessel *Curie,* and am maintaining contact with their science officer."

"Very good, Mr. Data. I'll make your apologies to the ReynKa." Picard headed for the turbolift, and turned back in an afterthought. "Data, I would like to see a summary of your findings, if you would."

"Yes, sir." Data settled into the captain's chair. "Paint the town red, sir."

"Excuse me?" Picard said—no, almost said, and then decided against it. They were late enough as it was.

How apt, then, to walk into the reception room, Troi beside him, and discover the pleasant gray, maroon, and slate blue color scheme replaced with bright red. Or perhaps not replaced, but covered. Red curtains along the walls, red tablecloths, red throw rugs over the utilitarian floor covering. Four tall poles grouped together in the center of the room, all bearing identical red flags with a complex, jagged black and orange device. Both Picard and Troi stopped short.

"Oh, my," Troi breathed. "I'm not sure I can even think in here, much less pick up impressions from our guests."

"We'll get used to it," Picard said, with more hope than assurance. "As I recall, the Tsorans don't see color quite like we do—perhaps to Atann this is a subtle effect." He stepped aside from the door—no point in blocking someone else's overwhelming initial sight of the room—and tried to get his bearings.

The food, at least, smelled wonderful. By that smell, it leaned toward meat dishes and spices, although Picard also saw an entire table devoted to desserts. He spotted the Federation's token offering against the wall and nearly engulfed by one of the curtains, the food mostly untouched. Well, that would probably make Atann happy. He noted, too, that despite the pleasantly cool air, almost everyone was sweating. His officers dabbed their upper lips with their napkins, their cheeks flushed; if the Tsorans showed any similar signs, Picard couldn't discern them. And thankfully, the Tsorans—dressed in plated leather uniforms and loose flowing trousers, with their females in unusual combinations of leather and flowing silks—seemed to be mingling freely and happily enough.

Atann himself stood at the center of one of the larger groups, entertaining them all with a tale that took wide gestures and exaggerated expressions requiring much display of tooth—a hunt, no doubt. Nearby, the ReynSa had her own collection of listeners. Dressed much like the other Tsoran women, she nonetheless bore an unmistakable air of authority, and unless Picard was mistaken, she, too, spoke of the hunt.

"Captain Picard!" the ReynKa bellowed, breaking into the middle of his own story and walking away from his gathered listeners without even appearing to take note of them. "What do you think of your ship now? An improvement, don't you think? Have you tried the heessla?"

Every sweating crew member within earshot stiffened, shooting desperate sidelong glances their way.

"I've only just arrived," Picard said, not quite prepared for such a casual greeting. "I have to say you've made some amazing changes here."

"Just so," Atann agreed. "It is not, of course, as regal as my own fete room, but I did my best."

"I hope the view helps to make up for anything the accommodations might be lacking," Picard said, trying out the line between holding his own and treading on Tsoran daleura.

Atann smiled—at least, Picard thought it was a smile. "I find myself much too taken with the sight of my own ReynSa," he said, gesturing at Tehra. "I recall the hunt she describes; she was magnificent. After the death of my first ReynSa, I had convinced myself I would never find another with her daleura, but that hunt changed my mind."

"Did it?" Picard said, trying to remember if the information had been in his mission brief.

"Indeed. Tehra offers all things—beauty, an acute sense of daleura, the skills to thrive in the ReynSa's competitive life . . . not only has she raised Akarr as if he were her own, she honored him by naming her own son—my second son—Takarr." He looked back at Troi. "But I am rude, to so praise another woman while enjoying your presence."

Troi gave him a genuine smile, and Picard took note—the Tsorans could turn on charm as well as the brusque daleura tones Akarr had thrown at them.

"Please," said Atann, "let me expose you to the advantages of living on Tsora." Without waiting for a response, he turned away to lead them to the food.

Picard glanced at Troi, and found her exotic features tinged with alarm. Was it something he'd said? Some reaction she felt from Atann? Or—he glanced again at the *Enterprise* officers around him. They had plates, he noticed, but no one seemed to be going back for seconds. Or finishing what they had.

When he met Troi's gaze again and saw her eyes widen slightly, he knew he'd guessed right. Apparently those spices were just as strong as they smelled.

"This is the heessla, " Atann said, picking up a stylish Tsoran serving utensil and scooping a steaming meat entree onto an equally stylistic plate. "One of the favored foods of my region. This vegetable is from the southern continent—you'll want to try it, too." And he applied some to the plate. *Picard's* plate.

"I want to be sure to sample everything," Picard said, resigning himself to an evening of gastrointestinal upset. "Smaller portions would make that easier, don't you think?"

"Eh?" Atann twisted back to look up at him. "Mighty sybyls, you humans have a puny appetite."

There was a stir at the doorway as Beverly Crusher entered, attracting more attention than one might expect; *Enterprise* personnel immediately gravitated toward her, as though she were some sort of pied piper. She was dressed for the reception in flowing slacks and a tunic of subtle greens and blues that were a soothing balm to Picard's eyes in contrast to the rest of the room. And—odd—she carried a small matching satchel. In another time, he would have called it a purse. Her fair cheeks carried a fading blush not unlike the one the rest of the room's occupants sported.

She scanned the room, spotted him, and swooped in just as Troi put a hesitant scoop full of heessla on her oval plate. "Good afternoon," she said breezily, not at all like herself. "Glad you made it, Jean-Luc."

"Where else would I be?" Picard said, somewhat taken aback.

But she didn't answer; instead she nodded respectfully at the ReynKa—and while she was at it, she pressed something into Picard's hand, a wafer of some sort. To judge by the look on Troi's face, she had received a similar offering.

"You *were* late, Captain," Atann said, no more or less belligerently than usual; Picard would have said he enjoyed the chance to point it out, though he didn't hesitate in his self-appointed task of heaping Picard's plate with food.

And while Picard sought a suitable reply, Crusher leaned over to his ear and murmured, "Chew that *very* well before you put one bite of that food in your mouth!" Then, rather more brightly than her wont, she said, "Oh, there's the ReynSa. I brought back that little token from Risa she was asking about a moment ago."

"Surely not," Picard managed, but she was gone—and if she was on her way to the ReynSa, she was taking the long way around, and surrounded all along the way by crew behaving like beggars imploring a tourist for coins.

Troi, he noticed, had already consumed her wafer. He slipped his own into his mouth, nodding at Atann's enthusiastic endorsement of the pureed . . . whatever it was. Good Lord, the wafer tasted awful.

Picard glanced at the crowd of discomfitted, red-faced crew members . . .

And chewed.

Akarr clutched the edges of his padded, extra-wide seat, feeling a quick flash of annoyance. They'd only just started their short journey when the *Rahjah* shuddered; the engines shifted pitch. It didn't matter, he told himself. They were through the forcefield . . . there was no one to see the man's clumsy piloting. No one but his men.

They sat behind him, in padded seats no less comfortable than his own. Special seats, installed by the flagship just for his kaphoora. He'd seen the pleased looks on his men's faces as they inspected their conveyance. Nothing like the minimalist Tsoran space vehicles they were used to . . . although of all his men, only Gavare had been on kaphoora before. The others were his own personal security, those who had trained hard to protect Akarr in all aspects of his life. Pavar, the light-coated and curious one, Regen, Ketan, Takan—all had started out with him when he was merely a child and they were young men barely past kaphoora. Rakal ranked them all, Rakal who had been caught scratching by the Starfleet woman. A disgrace that she had not immediately looked away; Rakal no doubt still felt the shame of it.

Now Rakal moved to the other side of the shuttle, the side consumed by stowage compartments and a fancy head. The stowage held their food—enough preserved rations for an extended hunt, if that's what it took. They couldn't judge the length of this kaphoora by any others . . . it was not only *his* first, it was a first for all Tsorans to go so deep in the Legacy . . .

The stowage also held their trank weapons and darts, shelter-building materials, and medical supplies. With all of that, there was also much empty space; on the trip from Tsora to Fandre, these compartments had been stuffed with engineering components, and had been sized for those needs.

Rakal, lurching in the shuttle's turbulent progress, double-checked the stowage latches, giving the doors a good thump for extra measure. Shifting back to his place, he lost his balance entirely, falling into the padded chair instead of sitting with dignity.

Enough! Akarr moved to the empty copilot's seat, his balance unhampered by the shuddering ship. He took one look at Riker's grim expression—these humans were hard enough to read, never mind the fact that this one had unusually patterned hair on his face—and demanded, "What's happening?"

Riker didn't look up from the shuttle console; his fingers flew over controls that meant nothing to Akarr. "Trouble," he said shortly, and then swore, abruptly shifting to reach the console in front of Akarr. The shuttle lurched, straightened, and lurched again; Riker responded too quickly to be doing anything but randomly punching at controls.

Akarr drew back just enough to keep from hindering

his pilot, but not so far that he couldn't see out the viewport, where the trees seemed to be rising at an alarming rate. Something scraped the bottom of the shuttle, tilting them.

"Sit back," Riker said, intent on the controls as they somehow straightened. "And hang on."

"What kind of superior technology is this?" Akarr demanded, ignoring the command, feeling nothing but offense at the fact that the Federation flagship would put him on a faulty shuttle. "The Fandrean scooterpods have never failed us!"

"Technology that wasn't built to function within a tech damper!" Riker hit a few controls in quick sequence, and made a satisfied noise; Akarr knew only enough to guess it had something to do with communications—even though Riker hadn't said anything. Then Riker glanced at Akarr, sitting on the edge of the human-sized seat, and gave a jerk of his head, a commanding gesture. "That seat is built to protect you when we hit—sit back!"

"Hit?" Akarr repeated, even as the shuttle dipped wildly, barely recovering to level flight. Behind them, his men stirred; a glance showed Pavar rising from his seat to come forward.

"Crash. Wreck. *Smash into the ground.*" Riker didn't even look at him, intent on the controls as the engine whine faded almost to nothing, fingers dancing as the shuttle bobbled and straightened, one arm braced against the edge of the console.

Akarr couldn't believe his ears. His prime kaphoora, ruined! "You're supposed to be the best pilot the *Enterprise* has!"

Riker lifted an eyebrow at him. Cocky. "Then you'd better hope I'm good enough to keep you alive."

* * *

"Whoa," La Forge said, jerking his head away from the communications console as a blast of static burst through. "What was *that?*"

Yenan looked just as startled as La Forge felt. Deep in the building, where few people worked and even fewer made any noise while about it, only the constant hum of the shield generators in the background served as a reminder that this was indeed a crucial nexus of Legacy management. But a background hum was all it was, and it in no way ameliorated the brief, startling cacophony of the incoming transmission.

"I don't know," the Fandrean finally admitted. "We have no expected communication of that type coming in on this board."

La Forge finished the job in which he'd been engaged—installing a translator module into the Fandrean system so all its blinking displays appeared in Federation Standard at request—and stared thoughtfully at the resulting console. Getting the lay of the land. There were only so many logical ways to organize a communications board, after all, and the Fandrean sense of order suited human needs quite well. This entire complex—squared-off cubbies of spartan design, not quite large enough for human comfort; Worf or Riker would bounce their heads off the ceiling—could have been enlarged and fit neatly within a human facility. Of course, that somehow made it twice as disconcerting when he ran into something uniquely Fandrean . . . .

Ah. There. "Looks like it came from within the Legacy," he said. "Thought you couldn't get anything through?"

"This is so," Yenan admitted, bobbing his head with a strange twist that also exposed his throat. "On occasion we have received partial transmissions from within the preserve, but none more than a few seconds. As with that one. A word, maybe half a word . . . and that is with special equipment built for use behind the forcefields."

La Forge frowned at the console. "Is there anyone else in the preserve right now? Besides the shuttle that just left?"

"There are always Legacy rangers at work," Yenan said. "We monitor the preserve very carefully."

"But . . . they would be using the special equipment—the transmitters that provide clear signals if they get through."

"Yes."

La Forge tapped his way through a series of hesitant commands, still getting the feel for the Fandrean system and possessed of a foreboding that it would be a while before he was truly able to work on the actual problem he'd been sent to address. "There's no way to tell just *where* the signal originates?"

"Not through the forcefields," Yenan said, bobbing his head again. "Please don't distress yourself over it, Lieutenant Commander La Forge."

"You can call me Geordi," La Forge said, pulling up the band the communication had used.

"It's probably a random transmission, possibly caused by the energy surge you yourself witnessed."

Not one band. *All of them.*

At least, all of the bands of communication—from sublight to obsolete radiowaves—that were readily available to a Federation shuttle.

La Forge shook his head. "No," he said. "I don't think this was a simple noise burst. I don't think that's it at all."

Thanks to Beverly's foresight, Picard made his way through the reception with his taste buds intact and his stomach without need of heroic repair. He spoke to as many of the Tsorans as possible, trying to build on Ambassador Jesson's reports and on Troi's comments, and finally found himself in front of the ReynKa, in a position to mention the negotiations. "Just over to the right," he said, pointing out at the starscape before them after he and Akarr had stood before the viewport for a moment of contemplation. The noise of the reception bubbled on behind them—somewhat more active than before, thanks to the addition of several theremin-like instruments and the Tsoran musicians who mastered them. There, to the right—the Ntignano system. A bright, perfectly normal-looking star.

"The fools who destroyed their own sun?"

"Only a handful of people took the action that instigated the sun's impending nova," Picard said. "A few members of an extremist doomsday cult, reacting to a significant religious date."

"That still makes them fools."

"You and I might think so." Picard looked away from the stars and held Atann's eye just long enough—as far as he could tell—to indicate the utmost polite emphasis to his words. "But that doesn't mean the entire population of the planet deserves to die." And then, before Atann felt cornered into an immediate response, Picard made his posture more casual and looked out to the stars again. "Amazing things, those graviton eddies. One can hardly perceive them from here—only a faint rippling in the stars. And yet right now they control the fate of all the Ntignanos." He glanced back at Atann, who seemed not to know what to say, but whose expression didn't look promising. "As do you," Picard told him. "That kind of responsibility must carry much prestige with it. As does how one manages the responsibility."

Atann made a noise that Picard couldn't interpret one

way or another, but the pursed shape of his mobile and considerable lower mouth looked no more promising than before.

Still. It was a start. Now, to find something to put the conversation on more casual terms, so Atann wouldn't feel he'd been challenged.

"Data to Captain Picard."

Blast. "What is it, Data?"

"Incoming message from Lieutenant Commander La Forge, sir." And, as Picard hesitated, Data added, "I suggest you take it outside the reception, Captain."

Not for the casual ear. And not a transmission to delay. "Understood," Picard said. "I'll get back to you momentarily." He looked down at Atann and quickly away, a deliberately submissive—and hopefully placating—gesture. "If you'll excuse me, ReynKa—"

The ReynKa turned away with no further ado; Picard's final words may or may not have been lost on him. It was hard enough to read the Tsoran's facial reactions, never mind his stout, stiff back. Picard made a final effort before taking leave. "I'll look forward to resuming our conversation at your earliest possible convenience."

Troi, never far, moved in to join him as he wended through the reception—and a much happier contingent from the *Enterprise,* since Crusher had returned—and toward the door. "That last," she said, "was embarrassment."

"I thought as much," Picard said. No one likes to be told you have more important things to do.

And this had better be *that* important.

Picard headed for the nearby bridge, nodded to Data on the way by, and ended up in his ready room, Troi still at his side. He sat behind the desk and touched the computer console. Data had already routed the transmission through, and La Forge waited. "Captain," he said immediately, and then hesitated. "Are you alone?"

"Counselor Troi is here," Picard said, somewhat brusquely. "What's happened?"

"Trouble, I think," La Forge said. He seemed to be alone, in a control room of some sort. The wall behind him sported a variety of screens, monitors, and input devices; the ceiling loomed low over his head.

"You *think?* Mr. La Forge, either there is trouble or there isn't." Crabby. Picard definitely found himself feeling crabby. By-product of the Tsoran food . . . or, more likely, the Tsorans themselves.

"It's not that clear-cut, Captain." La Forge appeared unfazed. "We've just received a broad-band transmission from within the preserve—more like a burst of noise than anything else. It's not a transmission event the Fandreans have experienced before, and . . . Captain, I have a hunch that it came from Commander Riker."

La Forge's hunches about such matters were not to be ignored. Picard exchanged a glance with Troi, and saw from her concern that she'd come to exactly the same conclusion as he. And Riker would hardly take such a desperate gamble unless the situation were . . . desperate. "I see," he told the engineer, while his thoughts raced ahead. *How to tell Atann. How to determine the situation inside the preserve. How to get Riker out of there.* "Assuming you're right—that there's trouble—what are our options?"

"If it were as easy as contacting the *Rahjah* to check it out, I wouldn't be here working on their communications board," La Forge said ruefully. "I haven't had a chance to discuss this with the Fandreans, and Worf is on his way—some of Akarr's staff insisted on showing him how Tsoran goods are improving the city, but I finally tracked him down. I have some ideas . . . but I'd like to confirm them with our hosts and get back to you, Captain."

"Make it quick," Picard said.

"Understood." From the look on La Forge's face as his image blinked out, no doubt he did.

Picard pinched the bridge of his nose. "Counselor," he said, his eyes closed, preparing himself for the scene to come, "I think it best if you accompany Atann and Tehra here. If there's one thing we can't afford to do—"

"It's to offer them inadvertent offense," she finished for him. "I'll be right back."

The Tsoran ReynTa, under Federation escort, in trouble in the Fandrean Legacy preserve—while negotiations with his father held the fate of a world's people in balance.

And Will, right there in trouble with him.

Chapter Five

THE SILENCE FILLED HIS HEAD SO completely that Riker momentarily wondered if he were deaf . . . or dead. And then the shuttle settled, creaking and groaning, and he knew he was neither.

He'd navigated the plummeting shuttle with a mere scrap of power at his command, doing no more than trying to aim *between* the trees, to keep the nose up, to allow them to skim to a stop along the rugged earth . . . .

In reality, they'd skipped more like a stone across choppy water. Unpredictably. Bouncing. And striking hard, that one, final time. Now, as Riker pried his eyes open and took in the sights, sounds—and smells—of the shuttle, he found the cabin dim and tilted, no flicker of power in evidence. Someone gave a throaty Tsoran groan, but subsided again. Riker took a deep breath of his own and decided that although everything hurt, nothing was significantly damaged. He ran his tongue over the sharp taste of blood on his lip, and disengaged himself from the console, glancing over at Akarr. The Tsoran lay draped half over the console, half over the seat, and was just beginning to look around in a dazed way. No blood in evidence; no obvious injury.

But there'd been that groan. And there was that . . . smell. Someone was hurt, all right. Slowly, still not quite trusting his legs, Riker slid out of his seat onto the unnaturally sloping deck. Individual battery-powered emergency lights painted the back of the cabin in soft shadows, but he saw the blood clearly enough—splashed across the deck and wall and even the ceiling. Not quite the color he was used to, but ominous enough. There had been six of them, he thought, realizing then that among the tangle of limbs, among the mostly seated Tsorans leaning against one another like dolls, and just now coming to life—there were only five heads.

Touching a wall here, a seat there, he made his way back and found the sixth Tsoran, the one who'd gotten up at the last minute, more or less splattered against the back of the shuttle. *Breathe slowly,* he told himself. And then he was past the momentary reaction, switching to problem-solving mode. He gripped the shoulder of the Tsoran nearest him—the fellow looked as whole as any of them—and said, "What's your name?"

The being looked around as if seeking Akarr's guidance, and—upon seeing his ReynTa still dazed in the copilot's seat, though clearly stirring and as alert as any of them—said, "Rakal."

"Rakal, check on your friends. I want a report of the injuries." Back to the front of the shuttle, then, to assess Akarr for himself.

The ReynTa looked up at him, a thin smear of purplish blood running from his nose. "This was not what we expected of the Federation," he said, although for the moment his tone lacked its usual edge. He rubbed a double-thumbed hand over his arm, apparently dismissing whatever pained him.

"You're alive, aren't you?" Riker glanced out the front viewport, into the thick jungle, remembering the holo of the cartiga, the size of the thing . . . and wondering how many of them were between here and the way out of this preserve. "Are you hurt?"

"No," Akarr said, futilely attempting to stand not once but twice.

Riker came to the sudden realization that the ReynTa had not quite figured out that his stiff vest was caught on the edge of the seat, and fought the impulse to simply reach over and release it. That would be too easy . . . and it would only cause trouble later. He'd read Nadann Jesson's report often enough to know that. So instead he turned away, looking back out the viewport and into the jungle. "It would seem that the Fandreans were mistaken when they said the shuttle's shields would allow us to navigate safely within the technology dampers."

Akarr grunted; Riker heard the scrape of leather against fabric. "They overestimated your shuttle, obviously. Or your piloting skills."

Breathe slowly. For an entirely different reason this time. As mildly as possible, Riker said, "Or underestimated the effectiveness of their dampers." He glanced down at Akarr. "It's not important, not now. What's important is getting us back to the museum in one piece."

Rakal approached from the back of the shuttle. "It's already too late for that." He moved to the down-tilt side of Akarr, and twisted his neck in a quick gesture that showed a flash of throat. "ReynTa, Pavar is dead."

"Dead?" Atann's nostrils, set down close to his mouth, flared; he looked accusingly at Riker.

"He got out of his seat," Riker said, keeping all judgment out of his tone.

"Several of us are injured—broken limbs, among those of us who were sitting next to the wall. Regen's arm is broken; Ketan is badly hurt in the upper arm and shoulder. Gavare hit his head and is still bleeding. He is not yet sensible." The Tsoran was hard to understand, and while Riker first blamed the being's harsh and obtrusive under-purr, he quickly realized that the Universal Translator in his combadge wasn't quite as seamless as usual with its response.

"And Takan?" Akarr asked.

"Takan and I are bruised, only."

"As am I." Akarr gave Riker a dismissive glance, as if to indicate that Riker's condition, though obvious, was hardly important.

"First things first, then," Riker said, as though he hadn't noticed. "We'll treat your men as best we can. Then we need to decide the best course of action. We made it about two-thirds of the way to our destination, as near as I can tell—that's three days of walking in *easy* terrain. Meanwhile, the shuttle may not fly again, but it's still shelter—and Worf will be looking for it."

"Not until we are long past due," Akarr scoffed.

"I sent out a Mayday of sorts. I'm betting La Forge picked it up. If he did, they'll figure it out; they'll send someone out to look." There was a good chance. La Forge was there, after all, to work on the communications equipment. If he hadn't noticed it directly, he was in the perfect position to hear about it. And if he heard about it, he'd figure out it was no accident. Once he'd done that . . . nothing would stop Worf from mounting a rescue effort.

Akarr merely made a snuffling noise of sorts. Not anything Riker made an attempt to interpret. First things first, he told himself. Retrieve the med kits, see what was functional and useful.

The med kit contents turned out to be his first good news of the . . . well, for several days, now. Someone had replaced the highly technological components of the kits with basic supplies. Bandages. Cut-glue. Antibiotic salves and antivenom patches . . . even insect repellent, a water-purifying plug for the canteen, and incendiary tablets. And once he was through poking around Riker was sure the changes were Worf's doing— for the small weapons locker held not useless phasers, but sharp-edged knives with thick, sturdy blades from a Klingon forge. And even better . . . a *bat'leth*.

Not that he intended to go hand-to-hand with anything—neither with his passengers, as much as he might be tempted, nor with the creatures prowling the jungle around them. But . . . it still felt good when his hands closed around the wrapped grips of the *bat'leth*. And the knives would replace the phasers as tools. *Worf,* he thought, *once we get back to the* Enterprise, *I'll owe you one hellacious holodeck hunt.*

Riker replaced the *bat'leth* and strapped one of the knives snugly into place along the outside of his calf. What, he wondered, did the Tsorans have in the way of weapons? He hoped, suddenly and fervently, that they had broken the strictures placed upon them by the Fandreans, and had more than a few short-range projectile dart weapons.

If not, they'd deal with it. It was folly to leave this shuttle for anything but burial detail anyway. Well, and . . . he glanced at the shuttle head. With nothing but individually powered emergency lights functioning on board, he didn't expect the head to be usable, so maybe there were *two* reasons to leave the shuttle.

"Once my men are attended," Akarr said, standing just behind the pilot's seat and contemplating Riker as Riker contemplated the head, "I'll begin the kaphoora."

"What?" Riker forgot to be diplomatic. He forgot to be anything but astonished. "You're going ahead with the *hunt?*"

Akarr pouched his lower lip in disapproval. "We cannot put this shuttle back together; we cannot fly out of here. Therefore we'll do what we came for."

"We can concentrate on *survival.*" Riker braced his arm against a canted wall; that the movement made him loom over Akarr only meant it served him twice. "We can assess our supplies, our position, and decide on the best course of action."

Akarr seemed to turn thoughtful—it was still hard to tell, but his lip relaxed and he idly rubbed the end of his nose. "We will hunt, as well," he said after a moment. The Universal Translator offered a garbled word, then shifted into perfect operation. "—Pavar is honored, we will gather what we need to walk out of here, and we will hunt along the way."

Not a chance. But he didn't say it. If nothing else he knew better than to throw a challenge like that at an adolescent Tsoran bent on earning daleura. So instead he said, "We'll talk about it then. Right now, your men are bleeding." He gave the med kit meaningful heft, and Akarr, smiling—his teeth fully covered—moved out of his way.

"What if you're right?" Yenan said, his normally smooth under-purr now harsh with tension as he reacted to La Forge's short presentation about the signal burst. They—several highly placed Fandreans, Worf, La Forge, and a Tsoran representative—had gathered around a table in a brightly lit museum meeting room of clashing decor and random preserve holos . . . almost like a classroom with the teaching aids left scattered around. La Forge certainly felt like he was sitting in a child's classroom, given the Fandrean scale of the furniture. Beside him, Worf must feel even more out of place; his knees hit the underside of the table. And these chairs . . . definitely not designed with the human posterior in mind. Yenan looked directly at him. "If you're right, what do we do next?"

"Find them," Worf said, simply and immutably.

Yenan waved his arms in a complicated gesture; the three Fandreans with him—the museum head, the city leader, and the preserve ranger commander—hummed in agreement. "Find them? That is not so easily done! And even if we do? Then what?"

The single Tsoran, a permanently stationed liaison named Kugen, clamped his mobile lower lip firmly over his mouth and left it that way, stiff and disagreeable.

"Look," La Forge said. "Let's start with this: the signal was from Commander Riker, and it means they're in trouble—there's no other reason he'd send what amounts to a broad-spectrum burst of noise in conditions under which he couldn't really expect it to get through. And it stands to reason that whatever else may have happened, the shuttle is inoperable—or they'd have returned, waited by the portal, and blasted those same signals at us until we let them out."

"You know your people so well to say all of that?" the ranger commander—Zefan was his name—said.

"Yes, I do," La Forge said.

"As do I," Worf rumbled. "We must go in after them."

"Oh, no, it's not as simple as that," the museum expert, Chafar, said immediately.

"*I* think it is," Worf replied.

"No, he's right, Worf," La Forge said, earning a glare from Worf. "There are a lot of things to think about. We can't just send the *Collins* in—whatever damaged the *Rahjah* might just leave you as stranded as the commander."

"*And* the ReynTa," Kugen said pointedly. "And what *do* you think happened to the shuttle? If the machines are so vulnerable, I'm surprised you would risk the ReynTa's life with one."

"They're *not* vulnerable, not under normal circumstances," La Forge said, letting the Tsoran's attitude wash over him, hiding his fierce regret at the lack of opportunity to scope out the shuttle operating parameters himself. Anyway, Kugen wasn't nearly as bad as Akarr, and La Forge had more important things on his mind. "One of the things I've been asked to look into is a random surge effect in the shield output, one of which the preserve experienced shortly after the *Rahjah* entered. If that surge somehow interfered with the shuttle's systems, made it more vulnerable to the technology dampers . . . well, it could cause a cascade of failing systems."

"If we cannot send the *Collins,* then what about the Legacy scooterpods? Those are reliable within the shielding, are they not?" Worf glared around the table as if daring anyone to disagree.

"They are," Zefan said with complete certainty. Of all the Fandreans, he was the fittest, the most outwardly assured; if he'd had to go into the preserve, La Forge would have preferred his company to all six of Akarr's city guards. "But they carry only two people each—in this case, one to pilot the scooterpod out to the crash, plus a passenger on the way back. It would require eight of them to effect a rescue—and we do not have eight of them available at this time. They are being used by our rangers, at work within the preserve."

"Furthermore," Chafar added, not meeting Worf's gaze or looking anywhere near it, "the scooterpods are slow compared to your shuttle. Even if the shuttle made it only halfway to the intended landing, it would take several days to get there and back."

"That's one of the reasons the ReynTa wanted the use of the shuttle," La Forge said. "It allowed him to start his kaphoora more deeply in the preserve than any Tsoran before now."

"We cannot allow this to take that long," Worf said. "They may be injured."

Zefan showed a little tooth. "It is irrelevant, since the scooterpods will not be available for a matter of days. We must wait for the rangers to return on their normal schedules—there is no way to contact them."

"That's why I'm here in the first place," La Forge said, more or less under his breath. And a good thing he was, too, given the way things had turned out. He found himself surprised at the Fandreans' apparent unfamiliarity with the shuttle systems despite their work with Admiral Gromek's people, and more than a little annoyed. No one had been of any help at all when he'd tried to discuss his theory that the forcefield surges might cause trouble.

Worf shifted impatiently; his knees knocked the low table, shifting it as well. "We cannot use the scooterpods. The shuttle is not safe within the forcefield and technology dampers. There is no other option—we must shut down the technology damper so the *Collins* can function within the forcefield even if it experiences another . . . surge." He kept his own teeth well covered, but his regard for the twitchy field—or lack thereof—came through clearly in his voice.

The city manager, Elen—up until now a quiet observer—spoke up quite sharply. "That is not possible."

"You might say otherwise if it were *your* ReynTa lost in the preserve," Kugen snapped, staring directly at Elen.

"None of our ruling family would choose to enter the preserve in such a manner, with such a purpose." Although his words lacked the habitual edge of a Tsoran challenge, Elen easily met Kugen's challenging gaze. "It is not our way. And we will not risk the entire city of Legacy for one being who did make that choice."

"What do you mean?" Worf said, frowning. "I would never suggest you risk your city—I spoke of shutting down the technology dampers only."

La Forge came to his rescue. "The dampers are intrinsically tied to the shields themselves. There's no way to shut them down without removing the entire protective dome around the preserve. Not only could the poachers get in—and they're always lurking just out of orbit, as I understand it—but the Legacy animals could get out." He glanced at a miniature holo of the same cartiga he'd seen during the reception, rested his finger on the base. "I don't know about you, Worf, but I can sure understand why they don't want *these* fellows roaming among their families."

"I see," Worf said slowly. "With regret, I agree."

"Then what?" The short fur on Kugen's neck and arms had risen, subtly, until all of a sudden it was standing nearly on end. His lips peeled back from his teeth, revealing an imposing set of double canines, the gums flushed deeply purple with his rage. Full daleura display, La Forge thought suddenly, flashing on his mission prep and glad to be at the end of the table. Chafar, who was opposite the Tsoran, inched sideways and backward. Worf, who was next to him . . .

Well, Worf ignored him.

"It sounds like you all plan to do *nothing!*" Harder than ever to understand with his lips rigidly withdrawn, Kugen worked up a good bit of foamed spittle to go along with his exposed teeth. "You've talked yourselves into impotency! Do you really value his life so little? Do you value your own associations with my people so little? If you think we're interested in trading with a society of such pitiful regard, prepare yourselves to learn otherwise!"

"Hey, now, hold on there," La Forge said, impressed if not immediately alarmed. "We're not out of options yet. And we don't abandon our people when they're in trouble. Just because it's not easy doesn't mean we can't do it."

"You see, this is why we wanted a Federation engineer here for our forcefield problem," Yenan said. "We've heard that you're like sculper on the trail of problems such as these."

"I'll take that as a compliment," La Forge said, while Kugen, his display ignored, slowly subsided—into, as far as La Forge could tell, intense embarrassment. No one had run screaming, after all.

"What did you have in mind?" Worf asked.

"We've got what we need—the shuttle. As long as we make sure we protect it from any field surges."

"And do you know how to do that?" Zefan asked.

"Not yet," La Forge said. "But I've got some ideas. . . ."

Picard appended his initials to yet another report and called up the next, a second mug of tea by his hand; the other hand came to rest at the back of his neck, rubbing gently and ruefully.

Deanna Troi had not "been right back." She had, in fact, contacted him shortly after her departure to inform him that she didn't know how long it would take to get the Tsorans to his ready room, and that it would not help matters any for him to reappear at the reception—that it would, in fact, only cast a spotlight on the current situation.

Which was that Atann, embarrassed by Picard's sudden departure, was taking him at his very word. *"I'll look forward to resuming our conversation at your earliest possible convenience,"* Picard had said, and Atann had not yet found it *convenient*.

"Perhaps if we explained the situation," Picard suggested over the comm link, unable to keep the frustration from his voice.

"I don't advise it," she said, regret clear in hers. "I think it best to let him maintain control, Captain—at least for a while. All we can do is wait. I don't honestly think it will take long. He just needs to make the point."

"Very well, then," Picard had said, waiting for Troi to sign off before releasing the waiting sigh. After a moment of staring at the padd an ensign had left on his desk, he decided perhaps Atann had done him a favor. The reports *did* have to be read, after all . . . and until Geordi got back to him, there was very little to be done.

Except drop everything and take the Enterprise *to Fandre.*

With an entire race of people waiting for him to talk Atann into a humanitarian gesture? Not likely, no matter how it called to him. *Will can take care of himself. And Geordi is the one who can deal with the complications caused by the preserve shields. Worf is there.* All Picard himself could do was sit and watch, whichever planet he orbited.

The thought drew him to the viewport. They held a synchronous orbit above Atann's palace in the city Aksanna, but it wasn't the planet that called to him. It was those stars, the ones that held among them the Ntignano sun—and the slow waves of distortion that blurred them. Slow and subtle; if you didn't *know,* you might just think you had something in your eye.

Without those graviton eddies, the evacuation efforts would already skirt the edge of the Tsoran system, instead of following the edge of the wide eddy field at reduced speed. Without the eddies, Nadann Jesson would have been left alone to learn the Tsoran culture—and accustom them to Federation cultures and ways—at an appropriate rate. The *Enterprise,* with Will Riker aboard, would be far from here, participating in the evacuation.

He'd seen images from Ntignano IV, the only inhabited planet in the system. Before and after images of a moderately stable population with no out-system travel capability and a technology level equaling twenty-second-century Earth. Until now, they had been left to develop further on their own, not quite ready for Federation contact—and they'd done well. Until this, they'd been nurturing a thoughtful, environmentally friendly plan for their own growth. The planet itself had remained remarkably integrated in terms of its civilization and its natural ecosystems and fauna.

How ironic, then, that disaster came in a form that first destroyed that delicate balance for which they'd fought so hard, before killing the civilization itself.

Before: Entire cities almost invisibly situated within natural forestation and geological formations. Abundant birds and wildlife in each community. Remarkably unpolluted air considering the technology level.

After: Withered vegetation, buildings suddenly stark against the landscape, small corpses littering the ground—the smaller species, the delicate ones. The first to go in the increased solar activity and quickly skewing ecosystems.

Not everyone in this galaxy favored the Prime Directive.

In this case, no one knew just who had provided the doomsday group with the apparatus they'd altered to become a sun killer. Heavy odds lay on the Ferengi.

But at this point, it didn't really matter. What mattered was the slow ripple of the stars before him, and how they interfered with everything. The journey to Fandre, twelve hours instead of several. Even briefly diverting to check the situation there, to try to help, meant an entire day's absence from Tsora . . . and Atann had already been deeply embarrassed at the interruption of a single conversation.

The door chimed for attention; Picard twisted to look at it in surprise. Troi would have informed him, had the Tsorans been on their way up—and everyone else on the bridge knew better than to bother him just now. Even Data. "Come," he said, maintaining his position.

"Captain!" Atann boomed, as if they were long-lost friends and there had been no embarrassment, no waiting. The spicy scent of the heessla floated into the room with him, and Tehra followed, looking as pleased as her mate. Behind them both, Troi entered, flashing Picard a quick apology from her expressive eyes. He gathered, then, that the lack of warning had not been her idea.

"ReynKa," Picard said, trying to match the Tsoran's enthusiasm. "I'm so pleased that your obligations allowed you some time here."

"Of course, of course. I came as soon as I could. But only to find you looking at the stars again. Do they draw you so?"

"Often," Picard said, seating himself behind the desk and gesturing for Atann and Tehra to sit before it, if they chose. Troi waited until they were settled, and quietly took the corner of the couch. "As it happens, I was watching the graviton eddies between here and Ntignano. But that is not why I needed to speak to you."

"Isn't it?" The ReynSa said, startling him; she had not made any effort to speak to him at the reception, but now she acted as though she'd been part of each of his discussions with Atann. She was, he thought, certainly privy to them. "It's what you spoke of at the time your other conversation took you away."

"Yes," he said, with no idea where to go with this line of thought, other than that he wanted badly to avoid it—and from Troi's face, she thought he should do just that. "In a way, that interruption is why I've asked to speak to you now."

"How is that?"

"I received some disturbing news in that conversation . . . about your men, and your son. And my first officer."

"What has happened?" Tehra sat very straight in the human-sized chair, filling it with her dignity if not her body.

"It seems possible that the kaphoora party has had some trouble."

"What manner of trouble?" Atann asked. "And how has it been discovered? If they've started the kaphoora, they're behind the forcefield. No one communicates through that field."

"Not directly, no, but Commander Riker seems to have gotten some sort of signal through." At Atann's skepticism, Picard added, "His resourcefulness in difficult situations is one of the reasons I was confident to send him in my stead. He's also a better pilot than I."

"But you don't really know what happened," Tehra said, in more of a challenge than a question.

"Not yet," Picard said carefully, having been prepared

to handle her concern, and not quite sure what he'd gotten instead. "I'm waiting for a report on the situation."

Not that any report was likely to shed light on whatever might have happened beyond those shields.

Tehra didn't seem to be affected by his words. "Akarr is on his prime kaphoora. He is a nobly raised Tsoran son. Whatever has happened, whatever he must do, he will acquit himself well."

Picard said nothing. It seemed safest.

Atann didn't reflect his ReynTa's certainty. "If there has been trouble, what will you do about it?"

Another question with no answer. "Our options will come clear when we have a better understanding of what happened."

"You don't really know anything, then, do you? Except that you want us to give up our charts to this important area, when in return you've lost our son!"

An unavoidable development in the conversation. Picard didn't flinch from it. "These are really two different issues, ReynTa."

"How can you say so?" The hair on Atann's arms rose slightly. "We can only judge you by what we know of you. And all we know of you is that you have lost our son!"

Picard hesitated. Whatever had happened within the preserve, he could confidently state it had nothing to do with Riker's actions or the normal operating status of the shuttle—that some outside force had intervened to create the problem. Atann, at this point, did not seem likely to make that distinction. With another human, his instinct would have been to back off, to offer emotional space for the other in which to react. But a glance at Troi—at her intent expression, her rigid, almost edge-of-the-seat posture—confirmed his inclination to hold his ground with Atann. "We *don't* know that," he said firmly. "We take the safety of our passengers and associates very seriously, and do not allow anyone to impugn us in this regard."

Atann hesitated, and behind him, Troi relaxed slightly. Good. Picard held his gaze evenly on Atann's, not upping the stakes, just holding his own. No doubt the Tsoran had never run into that particular combination of diplomatic verbiage and aggression before.

Fortunately, before maintaining the locked gaze became too onerous, Data's disembodied voice startled Atann into looking around the room. "Captain, there is an incoming transmission from Lieutenant Commander La Forge."

"Just a moment," Picard said, even as the ReynSa rose from her seat, her face pinched. "Please stay," he said. "This is my chief engineer contacting us from Fandre, and it is he who will have our options for proceeding." He leaned back in his seat. "Of course, if you don't care to stay, I would be glad to inform you of our decisions."

Direct hit. The ReynSa sat. The ReynTa leaned forward, attentively. Picard swiveled his desktop viewer so the Tsorans could also see it; Troi came around to stand at the side of his desk. "Put him through, Mr. Data." As soon as La Forge's image appeared on the screen—a different room, this time, a colorful place littered with freestanding holos and unidentifiable tools—Picard said, "Mr. La Forge. We've been waiting to hear from you. The ReynKa and ReynSa are eager to hear what news you might have." There, if Geordi didn't know he was onstage after that . . .

La Forge took it in stride. "I wish I had more definitive news for you," he said. "We did confirm that no similar signal has ever been received at the museum."

"And you still believe it was from Commander Riker."

"More strongly than ever."

"But you have no direct evidence," Atann said, prodding.

"No."

"There, you see?" Tehra said, gesturing dismissively. "Akarr is probably starting his kaphoora this very moment."

"He may be at that, ma'am," La Forge said. "But we think it's too important to leave to chance."

No, we're not going to leave it to chance. Picard glanced at Troi. "Counselor, it's my understanding that you often have an impression of Commander Riker's feelings."

"Yes," she said, glancing at the instantly curious Tsorans, hesitating, and responding candidly anyway. "There's a small number of people I can receive a sense of at any given time. Will is certainly one of them."

An understatement if he'd ever heard one, Picard thought. He didn't know exactly what had happened between those two, and he suspected he'd *never* know . . . but he did know the strength of the connection it had left behind. "I know we're some distance, but—"

"All I can tell you is that he's not experiencing any extreme crisis emotion at this time. Earlier, when we first heard from Geordi, we were at the reception. I was too . . . distracted to feel anything from outside the room. Now, I . . ." She hesitated, briefly dipping all her concentration within herself, and then shook her head. "I sense some annoyance, some anger; definite worry. But that could also be echoes of what I felt from him in the hours before he left the ship."

"Is your commander of a foul temper, then?" Tehra asked.

Picard decided to concur with Nadann Jesson's observations that the female Tsorans played the daleura games just as avidly as the males. "He is a man of strong passions, whatever might suit the moment. Do you think, then, Counselor, that you would have detected it had Commander Riker experienced any . . . say, life-threatening moments?"

"I'm sorry," she said, and hesitated, then shook her head as if she'd rethought the question and come to the same conclusion. "I really don't know. The distance is a factor, and I have no idea what effect those shields might have. I *believe* what I feel is an accurate reflection of his current state. But I can't be certain."

It would have been too easy, anyway. Picard turned back to La Forge. "We'll proceed on the assumption that your concerns are correct. What are our options?"

"Pretty limited, I'm afraid. The Legacy's scooterpods are built to work within the shields. They're small, and eighty percent of their function is geared toward their own shields—light ones, for the pilot, and heavy shielding around the engines. "

"Then what's the problem?"

La Forge made a wry face. "Not enough of them. And they're too slow to use in shifts. No, the scooterpods are tempting, but . . . what I'd like to do is spend some time modifying the *Collins*'s shields. I think the reason the *Rahjah* had trouble is related to the strange field interplay surges. But it hasn't bothered the scooterpods, so I want to see if I can modify our shields to more closely resemble theirs. Then Worf will take the *Collins* out and follow the *Rahjah*'s course. If they went down, there'll be a pretty clear indication of it in the trees. If they didn't, they'll be at the planned landing site."

"Just Worf?"

"And a couple of the Legacy rangers."

"We have people on the planet," Akarr broke in. "We would like to include some of them."

La Forge hesitated, then shook his head. "There's no room. Commander Riker was flying a full shuttle on the way out; we need to make sure there's room for everyone on the way back, if we're right about the *Rahjah* going down."

"Mr. La Forge," Picard said, and then he, too, hesitated. He knew the answer to his question . . . but he had to ask anyway. "Those fields . . . is there anything the *Enterprise* can penetrate with her scans? Any way in which we can help?"

"Captain, those fields are meant to keep orbiting ships from doing just that," La Forge said ruefully. He shifted; his next words were chosen with obvious care. "There is something the *Enterprise* can do, though. Captain, before I left, I spoke to Commander Riker about a project I'd requested. He said he'd discuss it with you. I was wondering if you'd made a decision about implementing it."

The charting project. "I had not," Picard said. The project would offend the Tsorans beyond measure, and probably destroy any chance of pleasant discourse between the Tsorans and the Federation for years to come.

If they found out about it.

"I'm still considering it," he said, after a moment. "The factors are complicated."

"I understand." La Forge stepped back from the viewscreen, distracted by something out of sight. "They've got a scooterpod ready for me to tear down, Captain. Unless you have any other questions, I'd like to get right to work on this."

Picard glanced at Atann and Tehra. "Have you any final questions?"

"No," Atann said. "But we know no more than we knew before."

That was something to get into later—not with which to delay La Forge. "Let me know when you have the *Collins* ready to go," he said by way of dismissal, and cut the connection at La Forge's already distracted nod. Troi, although she remained standing, moved back from the desk slightly so as not to unduly intrude on the conversation. "ReynKa, ReynSa," he said. "I realize that you must be preoccupied by the events on Fandre, but I would like to at least open discussions about the charted territory."

"Yes," said Atann, but both Tsorans were out of their chairs. "We will be in touch, Captain."

And they left. With no more fuss or explanation than that, they left.

Picard glanced at Troi, who lifted both shoulders in a mild and eloquent shrug. "They weren't easy to read," she said. "Distressed by the potential situation on Fandre, but not entirely convinced there *is* a situation on Fandre. My guess is that they simply couldn't switch gears quickly enough to discuss the charts. They'd already gone from hosting an historical reception to hearing that their son may have crashed in an isolated area filled with that world's fiercest predators." Another shrug. "Give them some time, Captain. It seems to be important to them."

Time. Time was one thing of which he had too little. The desperate Ntignanos, trying to flee their planet, could not afford to wait on intransigent Tsorans, or even to afford the distraction of the *Enterprise* captain. The Ntignanos needed help *now*.

Maybe it was *time* to think about La Forge's request for probe-assisted, high-speed charting.

Chapter Six

RIKER PEERED OUT the front viewport, glad to see that the Legacy inhabitants didn't seem to have recovered from the crash; there was no sign of movement in the dark green foliage surrounding the shuttle.

Which didn't mean there wasn't danger. As far as Riker could tell, the place was teaming with carnivorous life just waiting for juicy, defenseless humanoid morsels to expose themselves. He could well understand how a hunter could take six men to watch his back and still gain prestige from the kaphoora. From what he'd seen at the museum, even the Fandrean rangers avoided exposure—for as much time as they spent within the preserve, most of it was in the air, or behind the scooterpod shields . . . making observations, charting changes, and collecting data for Legacy management. Only occasionally did they venture into the jungle on foot, and any adjustments to the preserve—culling a species that was beginning to unbalance the managed ecosystem, seeding more prey species, thinning the forest to allow for the growth of certain plants to feed the prey species—were carefully planned, always involving just as many rangers on watch as those who did the actual work.

And now Akarr wanted to go out there with only two guards. Well, plus two wounded guards, one addled guard . . . and Riker. Three days of walking, by Riker's calculation, to get them back to the forcefield portal. Four, perhaps, if Akarr insisted on hunting along the way.

On second thought, that probably wouldn't slow them down. No doubt the hunted would assume the role of the hunter, closing in on them often enough for Akarr to gather all the trophies he wanted.

Think of the Ntignanos, Riker told himself. He was doing this for the Ntignanos, in the hope that Akarr's father would then negotiate use of the charted space. A bribe, they might have called it, in another day. Maybe that was still the best term for it in this one. *Just trying to get your attention, Atann, so we can save an entire sentient species.* Staring out into the dimly lit forest — no light to speak of came down through these thick trees, although the shields were calibrated to let sunlight through despite their opacity from the other side—Riker grinned wryly to himself and shook his head. It would get Atann's attention, all right, when he learned his son had gone down in the Legacy.

If any part of that transmission had made it out past the forcefield . . .

If Geordi had then noticed the nonsensical burst of noise . . .

If Atann learned his son had gone down in the Legacy.

"Riker!"

Somewhere along the way, Akarr had ceased to use

Riker's rank. Riker had no qualms about returning the favor. He straightened, stretched a bruised kink in his back, and responded to the overloud hail in a more moderate voice that knew it only had to go from one end of the shuttle to the other. "Akarr."

"We are done here." Patching, bandaging, wrapping . . . licking their wounds. "It is time to go outside and honor Pavar."

Riker moved to the center of the twisted shuttle to take in the triage area in the back. Rakal and Takan had done most of the initial sorting, tossing aside those goods damaged beyond reason and keeping close tally of those things that could yet serve them well. Riker had been right in there with them to start, working with the wounded. Suture glue and a protective patch took care of Gavare's head wound, but the blow he'd taken had left him dazed, wandering in thought and likely to wander in body. After Regen's broken arm had been set, Akarr assigned him to stay by Gavare's side, for Gavare had taken to heading for the shuttle door at every befuddled opportunity.

Not that he was likely to get it open, not when it required a manual release and manipulation, and not in his condition. But no point in taking chances; there was plenty of reason for Gavare to want out, what with the blood of his fellow guard drying to deepest violet along the shuttlecraft walls.

Ketan remained the most miserable of them. Whatever injury he had taken to his shoulder and upper arm, it was not obvious. In a human, Riker would have called the joint dislocated, but none of the Tsorans seemed to recognize what he was talking about; either the Universal Translator was glitching again or their anatomy differed too significantly for the analogy. The best they could do was bind the arm tightly to Ketan's body. They dared not use the painkillers—who knew how the human medicines would affect the Tsoran's system—and the minimal Tsoran med kit did not include them. Whatever the kaphoora generally presented in terms of challenge, the Tsorans clearly had not expected significant injuries.

Or else they knew better—one either avoided close encounters, or one died . . . that, too, would alleviate the need for medical care.

Akarr had not gone unscathed in the crash—his nose was swollen and still leaking blood. But he made no complaint—only stood impatiently by the door, waiting for Riker to tackle the manual release.

With no little effort, Riker did just that. The door did not open easily—definitely stressed by the landing—but eventually it cranked open far enough that Rakal and Takan could carry Pavar's body, sheeted by the rich maroon fabric from several denuded seats, out in search of a place to bury it.

Fresh air flooded the shuttle—or what passed for fresh air on Legacy. Hot and humid—thickly humid—it was ripe with humus, the odors of rich foliage and exotic flowers, even a strange musk. A large, bold insect flew in, bounced stupidly off the back wall, and came to rest, unfazed, on the dead navigation console. The first of many, no doubt. Riker left it there and stepped out of the shuttle onto a ground spongy with thick mosses and fallen leaves. *Big* ones—for the brush here at ground level consisted of huge leaves to catch the heavily filtered light, some of them rubbery, all of them gleaming with dampness that spoke of recent rain. *Daily thunderstorms,* Riker recalled suddenly, and unimpeded by the forcefields in any way.

In the humid air, he smelled again the blood on his lip, and that which had trickled into his beard; he swiped a hand across the damp foliage and scrubbed it across his face several times. "You might want to do the same," he told Akarr, who was gazing about himself as if he'd just entered the largest of cathedrals.

"Blood is honorably worn," Akarr told him, barely taking his attention from the preserve. He crouched and ran his claws through the ground matter down to the dirt, and stood even as he contemplated the substance on his fingertips, rolling it between fingers and thumbs. "Ah," he said. "Deep-jungle scent—the promise of rich hunting. There is no other smell like *this.*"

"There's *blood,*" Riker suggested. "Which, if you *don't* wash it off, will make you all the more tempting to any number of the creatures who live here."

"I'm not concerned about that. I want them to come to me."

"Then think about Gavare—right now, he probably doesn't even know where he is, or the danger he's in. Even if we wash him off"—no small effort, the way that head wound had bled——"he'll still be with you, and *you'll* still be drawing them in."

"ReynTa," Rakal said, steadfastly looking away from Akarr and tilting his head to expose the side of his throat, "maybe you should pick and choose your own time for the hunt, and maintain control over it—not bring it here where our honorably wounded have no ability to protect themselves."

Maintain control over it. There *was* no controlling this place, or anything in it. But Riker stayed silent, suspecting that any single thing he could say at this point would cause trouble—especially given the glare that Akarr had tossed his way as Rakal spoke.

"It is true that a leader must protect his men," Takan said, in the most offhand of manners, also looking away from Akarr. He, like Rakal, looked some years older than Akarr, and seemed to have a relationship of long standing with the ReynTa.

Akarr stared hard at them both, examining their postures, mulling their words. Finally he said, "Then you two may see to cleaning up Gavare. When you're done, scout for a place for Pavar."

The two guards briefly tilted their heads aside, and then set about their task with alacrity that poor addled Gavare couldn't understand or appreciate.

Rather than take any part of a chance that Akarr would interpret his watching as gloating, Riker set off to walk around the shuttle, wincing at the damage—who would have thought that duranium would twist and bend like that—and more grateful than ever that his aches and pains were only that. They were lucky to have lost only one.

But that didn't mean the others were capable of walking out through *this*. The ground foliage grabbed at his ankles, and hidden roots snagged his toes. Within a short distance, the damp leaves had soaked his pants from the knees down; he squinted up at the all-enveloping treetop canopy and considered the strength of the rain that could get past it. An image of the steaming, heavily puddled landing pad outside the museum hangar came to mind.

At this rate of going, even if they traveled right through whatever rain fell, it would take days longer than his original estimate to walk out of here. Even as he thought it, Riker stumbled, grabbing a vine to keep himself from going down—and then jerked to a stop when he couldn't unwrap his hand. With a concerted effort and the ticky-tacky noises of something coming unglued, he pulled his fingers away from the vine. A closer look showed it coated with sap—already fresh liquid oozed to fill the gap he'd created—and covered thickly with insects.

Not your basic Alaskan taiga. *Remember that.*

The shuttle's flight path left a scar of loamy brown against the green undergrowth—a darker green than seemed natural to Riker's eyes. He followed it a short distance. Easy going, this, and directional as well. If he couldn't talk Akarr out of walking out, this was the place to start. And ahh . . . he remembered *this* bounce, the biggest during their final plunging descent. He stood at the edge of a particularly deep gouge, well through the thin soil and into light, chunky clay-and-rock layers, and contemplated their almost-fate . . . how if he'd come in at a slightly steeper angle . . .

None of them would have survived that one.

Something flittered above him; of the creatures they'd scared off, apparently some were bolder in returning than others. The silent jungle had begun to rustle and chirp again. Riker felt the weight of the knife at his calf, and wished for the weight of a phaser in his hand. Time to return for the *bat'leth.*

He met Takan and Rakal at the back of the shuttle; already they panted slightly in the heat, their short, cupped ears blushing a bruised color and fanning thin to distribute heat. "Be careful," he said. "Whatever we scared off is coming back."

"It was expected," Rakal said. In Akarr's presence he had taken no special note of Riker; now he raked him up and down with a dark and scornful gaze. Riker had not paid much attention before, but he suddenly recognized the cinnamon cast to Rakal's coat, the pattern of his vest . . . this was the Tsoran who'd scuffled with Dougherty on the shuttle. Wonderful. Of the two uninjured guards, one of them bore Riker a grudge simply for being embarrassed in his presence.

"We've gone beyond *expected*." Riker looked into the trees as something let loose a raucous cry. "We're running headlong into *now*."

Takan lifted his weapon—a short-barreled, extremely short range dart-propulsion gun. "We are prepared to deal with them. If you are not, then you should return to the shuttle."

I'm about to get prepared to deal with them. But of course he didn't say it. He returned the Tsoran's stare and said, "No, Guinan, you win. It doesn't get any easier." That baffled them completely, which was almost as good as shedding his good-guy Federation Officer face and taking these Tsorans down a peg or two. Never mind that those teeth jutted out for slashing in a fight, just like a boar's. And never mind that they had stout, sharp claws on all four fingers and both thumbs of each hand.

Stop it. Survival, that was the goal here. And to do it in such a manner that the Tsorans weren't alienated beyond allowing the Ntignano evacuation to traverse the edges of their space. So, trying to take the belligerence out of his posture, he added, "Looks like a good spot to bury Pavar back there, if that's what you want to do with him. We dug it out on the way in."

They didn't reply. But they did start down the crash path. Riker returned to the shuttle door the way he'd left, and tried not to smile at the sight of Tsoran fur running the length of the sticky vine.

Akarr sat at the shuttle entrance, sitting on the ground and shoving darts into the chamber of his own tranquilizer gun. Gavare, damply clean, seemed to have ceased wandering, but Regen kept a close eye on him anyway. Ketan simply sat at the side of the shuttle looking miserable. Akarr looked up at Riker, closing the chamber on his little weapon by feel. Like the other Tsorans, he also had a knife at his side, and unlike the other two, he wore a highly decorated, ceremonial trophy knife jammed slantwise in the front of his vest. "No other Tsoran has hunted so deeply in the preserve."

"You're not hunting yet," Riker said.

"Soon." Akarr seated the gun into the holster in front of his knife. Far overhead, something screeched; Riker couldn't tell if it was in warning or dismay. "Takan, Rakal, and I have assessed our status. We have food enough. We have tranquilizer guns for all who are uninjured plus one; the others were damaged. You, of course, were planning to stay in the shuttle, so I doubt you have any weapons of note—"

"Don't worry about me," Riker said. "I've got what I need."

"As soon as Pavar is honored, we will begin our journey to the portal."

Riker shook his head. "We're better off staying here. We don't have to worry about how much food we can carry, and we'll have shelter at night." Behind him, Rakal and Takan quietly returned; Riker glanced back to see that they'd hunkered down in the flattened foliage, and were listening with great interest. "I got a signal off; Geordi will make sure we get help."

Akarr made a face. "Your Lieutenant Commander La Forge wouldn't even be on Fandre if it were possible to communicate through the forcefield."

"I didn't say I'd communicated. I said I got a signal off." He hoped. "Geordi will know it's from me. They'll send someone in after us."

Akarr stared at him a moment, in astonishment rather than his usual challenge. "What makes you think we *want* to be rescued at all, never mind by your Federation? We will rescue ourselves."

"By offering yourselves up to every predator that lives here? Akarr, a hunt is one thing. Prolonged exposure to the dangers of this place is another thing entirely. Are you *determined* to die here?"

Akarr smiled at him—not the socially appropriate smile of covered teeth, but a curl of the lip that left nothing to the imagination. The Ferengi would envy such teeth. "There is much daleura in such a death, if it must be. But no, none of us have any intention of dying."

"Have any of you been here before? Had experience with this place?"

As one, they glanced at Gavare.

"Wonderful," Riker said, not caring if they understood the sarcasm. Too much courage, not near enough wisdom.

Akarr stood. "Your opinion is not important here, Riker. You got us into this situation, but we will decide how to get ourselves out. For now, we care for Pavar—you will wait here, as it is a private matter. When we return, be ready to leave. Or stay here alone, as you please."

There was nothing that Riker could come up with in reply . . . nothing, that is, that it would do for him to say. As Akarr led the Tsorans away, with Pavar suspended between Rakal and Takan and the injured guards more or less staggering along behind, the creature above them screeched again, circling lower, rustling in the foliage just overhead.

Something splatted to the ground; Riker couldn't see it, but he could smell it well enough. He couldn't help but offer a sardonic smile. "I couldn't agree more," he said, and went into the shuttle to gather up his supplies.

* * *

Picard paced from the viewport to the food replicator, decided against taking supper until the tingle of afternoon heessla faded from his tongue, and returned to the viewport. The ready room seemed smaller with every passing moment. *Give them time,* Troi had said. Well, he was giving them time. Time during which, despite the padd-pushing, he could do nothing but think of the *Rahjah,* bent and twisted on the jungle floor—along with all its occupants. And of Geordi La Forge, working without support from the *Enterprise,* trying to suborn Fandrean technology to effect a rescue.

If the *Enterprise* were there, surely her sensors would be able to tell them something. Surely Geordi's finely honed engineering staff would brainstorm quick answers to the shielding and communications problems. Surely they'd all make short work of finding Will . . . of finding the ReynTa and therefore successfully completing their mission to expedite the Ntignano evacuation. . . .

If the *Enterprise* were there—instead of sitting in orbit above Aksanna, Atann's sprawling capital city, waiting for Atann to comprehend how many people would die if he didn't put himself in the mood to chat—a development which was by no means assured.

Picard turned away from the viewport, an abrupt move. "Picard to Data—would you join me a moment, Mr. Data?"

"Certainly, sir," Data said; almost immediately, the door chimed.

"Come," Picard said, just shy of impatience, and when Data entered, gave him no chance to inquire. "Mr. Data, given the *Enterprise*'s superior scanning ability, how long would it take us to reach Fandre?"

Data didn't hesitate, didn't blink the way a human might have, tripping over the implications of the question. "As compared to a shuttle? What time we save with our scanners, we would lose to our size and the need for precision manuevering. Sir, may I ask—"

"No," Picard said.

"Sir, if you are considering leaving orbit, I think you should be aware of the latest reports from Ntignano—straight from the horse's mouth, so to speak." He ignored Picard's blink of surprise. "Theoretically, the massive singularity carried by the doomsday probe *should* have resulted in predictable, incremental increases in the sun's fusion rate, until it reached the point of nova. However, that has not been the case. There have been several surges in the fusion rate; the star is enlarging more quickly than anticipated. While the current evacuation procedure will remove all refugees from Ntignano before the nova occurs, the solar flares and other artifacts of the increasing fusion rate will kill them long before that."

"I see," Picard said. Not good news. But there was, at the moment, nothing he could do about it, regardless of the *Enterprise*'s position.

Except . . . Geordi's mapping project. Perhaps it was time to consider the suggestion more seriously.

"Thank you, Mr. Data," he said, his mind already returning to Geordi's written request, and the details of the project. "Dismissed."

As Data left, Beverly Crusher breezed in, back in her uniform and med coat. Crusher breezed everywhere, light on her feet, creating enough of her own wind to ruffle her fiery hair on a regular basis. Always intent on something.

At the moment, that *something* seemed to be him.

"Jean-Luc, I need to talk to you," she said, dispensing with any preamble.

He gestured at the couch, and seated himself behind his desk. "What is it?"

She hesitated a moment, as if suddenly realizing she hadn't thought out how to tackle her concern. "I understand that discussion with the ReynKa isn't going well."

Picard gave a genteel snort. "The discussion with the ReynKa isn't *going* at all."

"And . . . Will? Have you heard anything about Will?"

Of course she knew about that. Picard hadn't told her directly, but the suspected shuttle trouble was far from classified information. "I'm afraid not," he said. "Geordi is hoping to modify the *Collins*'s shields so that it can safely enter the preserve and locate the *Rahjah*. Local time is several hours behind ship time; they still have some daylight with which to work. And let us not forget the possibility that the transmission isn't from Commander Riker at all, but is just another symptom of the problems with the Fandrean forcefields."

"But you don't think that's the case." It wasn't really a question.

"No," Picard said, answering anyway. "I don't think that's the case. I'm considering taking the *Enterprise* to Fandre to expedite the rescue."

Alarm crossed her features. "You can't do that!"

"I beg your pardon?"

"Jean-Luc . . . the Ntignanos . . ."

"I'm aware of the Ntignano situation." Overwhelmingly aware. Flagship captain, sent in to accomplish crucial negotiations, and thus far, a resounding failure. At this rate, the *Enterprise* would have done better to join the convoy of ships transporting the Ntignanos. "I also know that as things stand—until the Tsorans are willing even to *talk* to us—there's nothing I can do to affect it!"

"Then find a way," Crusher said, fierce and undeterred by his vehemence. "Jean-Luc, they're already dying. Between the injuries they're sustaining in the panic, the stress placed on those who are already ill or elderly, the radiation exposure they're receiving—the journey to their relocation staging point is simply taking too long! They need medical attention, not an extended journey crammed in the holds of refurbished cargo ships!"

Picard's annoyance faded away, sharply refocused on these new facts. "What about the medical support teams accompanying them?"

"They're spread too thinly; they don't have the facilities." She shook her head, gave a gesture of helplessness. "I'm by no means criticizing them. They just can't handle the Ntignano needs in transit. And as it is, *transit* is taking entirely too long."

For a moment, he didn't say anything; his frustration swirled around thoughts of Tsoran sensibilities—and insensitivities—and he felt the potential for providing on-site support to Geordi slip through his fingers. "All right, Beverly," he said. "Perhaps I can find a way to prod Atann into action."

"But you won't leave Tsora," she said, searching his face, looking for confirmation. "From what I've seen of Atann, it would take years before he'd even consider speaking to us again."

"I won't break orbit without further discussion," Picard acceded, feeling some inner part of him rail against his failure to rush to the away team's rescue. But the promise satisfied Crusher.

When she left, he immediately called Deanna Troi. She was off-duty—as, technically, were he and Beverly Crusher—but that didn't stop her from arriving in the ready room, in uniform, within fifteen minutes of his request.

"What," he said, with very little preamble, "would

you predict of the Tsoran response if they discovered we had initiated mapping of the space under discussion?" *Or not under discussion, as the case may be.*

"I doubt they'd have anything to do with the Federation for a long, long time," Troi said, tucking her hair behind her ear—the long, unruly curls were the only sign that she'd been caught out of uniform, although her fatigue was evident, and worry rested in her eyes. Worry over Riker, no doubt. The past ties that bound them were strong—stronger, sometimes, than Picard thought either of them realized, regardless of what other entanglements they entered.

But not so strong that she couldn't continue to focus on the question at hand. Quite practically, she added, "I'm not sure how much the Tsoran reaction matters. Is our goal here to rescue the Ntignanos, or to establish sturdy relations with the Tsorans?"

"I'm sure Starfleet would prefer that we do both," Picard said dryly. "And there is certainly some question, according to Geordi's report, whether we could accomplish the mapping in time to do any good. Dr. Crusher has made it clear that for some of the refugees, we're already too late."

She sat quietly for a thoughtful moment. "It's not an easy decision."

That it wasn't. Throw the fate of his first officer into the mix and it bordered on the impossible.

"I'd like to see what we can do to jar Atann into responsiveness," he said, after his own moment of thought, moving away from the conflicts of the mapping issue for the moment.

"As a matter of fact, I've been giving that some thought." She scooted to the edge of the couch, resting her entwined fingers over one knee. "I think, if we made it known to him, perhaps through Nadann, that you had heard of their accomplishments—the way they've thrived in what used to be a difficult and dangerous environment—you might well prompt an invitation to visit their historical sites or kaphoora training facilites. The question is, will Atann merely walk away again when you bring up the subject of the charted space?"

"Quite likely," Picard muttered. "Unless I have some news of his son."

"Have you heard from Geordi recently? Do we know anything more than we did?"

"Not recently." La Forge was, however, in occasional contact with Data, and if there had been any significant development, Picard was quite sure he'd know about it. "And I'm afraid not." He took a deep breath, feeling decisions settling into place. "Counselor, come planet morning"—the same as ship morning, as they'd arranged it—"I'd like you to contact Ambassador Jesson. See if you can convey our needs to her. And until then . . ." He looked at her, seeing again the subtle signs of worry eating around her edges. "Until then, see if you can get some sleep. I, for one, have no intention of disturbing you again."

"It was no disturbance, Captain," she said, and he was certain she'd just stifled a yawn. Certain enough that it passed along to him, and he, too, yawned, discreetly behind the curl of his hand. She smiled at him, genuine and warm. "Maybe you should take your own advice," she offered upon departure.

Perhaps he should.

But first, he'd put in a call to Lieutenants Barclay and Duffy, and tell them to initiate mapping of the corridor.

And to do it quietly.

* * *

"I dunno, Data," La Forge sighed, crouching over a scooterpod and raising his voice slightly so the portable Fandrean comm unit on the floor would catch his words. "I can understand why they installed these tech dampers, but it seems to me that they cause more problems than they solve."

"If that were truly the case, then surely they would have removed the dampers by now."

Data's voice came through with its naiveté intact; in the background, La Forge heard enough murmur and movement to deduce that Data was on watch. No wonder La Forge was tired . . . from the *Enterprise* clock to the Fandrean clock with twelve hours of tight shuttle navigation in between. They'd arrived in the wee hours of the morning, and he'd managed to grab an hour or two of sleep in a museum lounge after the reception when he discovered that his guest quarters had not yet been assigned—only to rise early with the departure of the *Rahjah*.

And now it was late again, and he was staring stupidly at the shield-generating assembly mounted at the back of the scooterpod, trying to imagine how he could adapt it to protect the shuttle engines.

Two of them. It would take two of them, at least.

"Geordi?"

"Sorry, Data." La Forge looked up at the wall speaker, too used to working with viewscreens. "Just trying to tackle some decisions here . . . but no, they might well hang on to the dampers despite the trouble they cause. You've got to look at it from the human point of view. Or maybe the Fandrean point of view, but they're not so very different from us."

"I am afraid I do not follow your line of thought."

La Forge selected a tool, tried it for size, adjusted it. "A project like this, it's a big one. Has lots of people who want it—and people who don't want it. Obviously, the people who wanted it came out on top. And they're not about to admit it has problems."

"But the forcefield and technology damping combination has problems whether they admit it or not." Data's disembodied voice provided La Forge with a clear inner image of his puzzled expression. He smiled.

"That it does . . . but as long as no one admits it, they don't have to do anything about it. And—here's the important thing—if they had to do something about it, they'd be in a very, very embarrassing situation with the people who *didn't* want it in the first place."

"Ah. They have to eat crow. Do they have an available alternative to the forcefield?"

"Only tight orbital patrolling. And someone could still get in. It wouldn't take many men, armed with phasers, to decimate the population of the preserve." La Forge dismounted one shield generator, and started on the second. "Besides, orbital patrolling is aggressive, and the possibility of having to act while on patrol is threatening to the Fandreans. The shield is a passive device. It suits them better."

"I see," Data said, although clearly he did not.

"And to be fair, I suppose it's not causing *them* half as many problems as it's causing *us*."

"Enough so they asked for your help. Passing the buck, so to speak."

La Forge gave the air a brief, puzzled glance while he digested that one, and then nodded. Close enough.

But he still had two problems to solve. Two *big* problems. He clamped an antigrav handler onto one of the generators and moved it to the waiting sled—thank goodness both items were standard equipment for a cargo shuttle, and that he'd chosen to leave them in place on the *Collins* when he'd loaded the extra space with odds and ends that might come in handy on this assignment. And he was lucky, as well, that the natural shape of the scooterpod shield bubbles nearly matched what he needed, even if he did need to figure out a way to enlarge them to encompass the shuttle engines.

"You seem distracted," Data said. "Maybe it would be best if we continued this conversation at another time."

Oops. La Forge scooped up the comm unit—a clumsy thing, as big as his head—and deposited it on the sled. "Sorry, Data. I'm just worried about what I've got to accomplish here. The way that tech-damping field interferes with the transfer of energy within . . ."

"The shuttle shields should have been adequate to protect against that, as long as—"

"Yeah, yeah, as long as Commander Riker restricted himself to basic systems. And it would have been, I'm certain of it, if it hadn't been for that energy surge. It's just that we can't take that chance with the *Collins*."

"Study of the Fandrean forcefields might suggest ways in which you can adequately modify the existing shuttle shields."

"First thing I thought of." La Forge guided the sled out of the scooterpod hangar, and onto the glittering pavement of the Legacy landing pad. The heat that had been pleasant that morning was now oppressively steamy; the heavily clouded sky rumbled at him. "But then I thought it might be a better idea to augment our shields with theirs. Double-layered, so to speak." A heavy drop of rain splatted onto his head as he approached the shuttle; the cargo door opened and lowered on cue, thanks to the security guard waiting there. They all felt a little helpless, the security guards did—La Forge was lucky he wasn't tripping all over them, as eager as they were to help in some way. He shrugged, as much to himself as to the invisible presence of Data. "Double-shielding seems to work for them. We might as well give it a try."

"There is a chance that the two systems will interfere with one another. Too many cooks spoil the broth." Data's disembodied voice seemed odder than ever, away from the building and coming from the sled. The officer—Lieutenant Chueng—coming to meet La Forge from inside the shuttle gave the sled a startled second glance.

Spoil the broth. Right. La Forge shook his head. "Yeah, well . . . we'll just have to wait and see." But it better not happen, because if Riker and the ReynTa had gone down in the carnivore-packed Legacy, they didn't have the time for Geordi to try again.

Chapter Seven

THE KAPHOORA HAD BEEN PLANNED with day hikes—the Tsorans carrying small but adequate packs to get them through the day with plenty to eat and drink, and personal tarps for the late-afternoon rains. That the packs suited Riker's human frame poorly did not bother Akarr in the least; the man should be grateful that there was a pack for him to carry, and should thank dead Pavar for the use of it.

He eyed Riker with annoyance as they followed the crash path past Pavar's memory spot and the human hesitated, eyeing the huge rocks that covered the spot. Impressed, Akarr would have said—and the site indeed deserved such a response. Because the shuttle had dug into rock at this point—throwing it up and aside in a frozen wave of earth—it had been easy to put Pavar to rest, cover the site, and then roll down rocks that ordinarily would have been much too large to handle. Rocks as big as Akarr himself, rocks that would protect the spot as an eternal memory site.

But somehow it raised the hair on his arms to have the human examine it so. "Are you slowing us already?" He kept his voice gruff, knowing Riker had a difficult time understanding him when he did so, and that he had no concept of the significance of different under-purrs . . . or how badly he'd just been insulted.

Or maybe he did. Riker strode away from the memory site, one hand holding the pack to a more comfortable position, a large flashing blade swinging in the other. Akarr stared at it as Riker approached. He hadn't paid any attention to the human as they'd prepared to move out; he, Rakal, and Takan had enough to do, outfitting both themselves and the injured guards with packs. Gavarc and Regen could carry their own packs, but Ketan's shoulder injury prevented him from doing the same. For now, Rakal and Takan would take turns carrying double.

So he'd ignored Riker, noting only that the human was prepared and waiting to go despite his repeated, strongly voiced protests—protests Akarr could quote back at him by now if he'd wished: "Geordi will know we're in trouble. Worf will come looking. And he's not going to be able to *find* us if we're off stumbling through the trees, and he's working on visual in a pared-down shuttlecraft!"

Privately, Akarr thought Riker gave his companions far too much credit. That anyone would interpret a blast of noise as a cry for help was absurd. That a single man in a pared-down shuttlecraft had a chance of finding them in the first place was too remote to contemplate. Yes, privately, Akarr thought Riker—despite his size and bearing—would have done anything to stay with what he perceived as the safety of the shuttle. But Akarr wasn't about to abandon his only chance to wrench daleura out of this misbegotten kaphoora by clinging to a useless shuttlecraft, eating down their rations and bringing himself no closer to the preserve boundary.

Not that he'd explained it to Riker. Not in the least. What Riker thought or didn't think had no relevance. He'd had the choice of sitting there by himself, or tagging along with the Tsorans. And addled Gavare might have been the only one of them to have experience with the Legacy, but all of them had trained for it, had earned their way here. All of them, even the son of the ReynKa. Riker was the one who was unprepared—no tranquilizer gun, since Pavar's had been as broken as its owner. No training. No other weapons besides a puny little knife.

Or so Akarr had thought. Until now, when his mind, busy with thoughts of Riker's inadequacies, had no control over his eyes—which had greedily locked on to the sight of the formidable weapon Riker carried. Two parallel curving blades, connected with bracing sections. The back blade provided leather-wrapped handgrips between sections; the ends, with the front blade significantly shorter than the back, hooked wickedly—as though they'd been designed with Tsora's now extinct, heavily antlered troph-deer in mind.

Riker, to his surprise, seemed perfectly comfortable with this shining, sharpened weapon in hand.

And Akarr didn't know quite what to make of it, or of the way the human strode confidently forward, as alert as any Tsoran to the brief movement in the foliage to their side, knowing to ignore the light fluttering of insignificant lizbirds high above them . . . not intimidated. Not reluctant.

Just damned annoyed.

Akarr did the only thing he could. He turned his back on Riker, pretending he hadn't spoken those last, provocative words—no Tsoran did anything else, when faced with conflicting facts. Ignore the other person, even in midsentence, until things became clearer, that was the way of it. And Akarr fairly dove for the safety of those ways, pushing his pace to fall in ahead of Riker until he nearly trod on Takan's heels.

Above them came the first patter of rain in the upper leaves; soon enough those leaves would be drenched, and dripping their own rain down on the next level, and so on, until the kaphoora party was soaked. Not that it mattered in warmth like this, not with his thick, short fur to keep his skin dry. But come evening, the temperatures would fall, and if he were wet . . .

Not even the bravest Tsoran foolishly left himself open to hypothermia. But Akarr waited until Takan pulled out his rain tarp before donning his own, not hesitating in his steady, marching progress.

A glance behind showed that Riker had done the same, although Pavar's tarp was too small for him; he hadn't come with wet-weather gear—or gear of any sort. The only thing he'd contributed was the medical kit he carried.

And that wicked blade.

Akarr stumbled; he'd let his glance rest behind him too long, lured by the weapon. And they were running out of easy travel, though the crash path had taken them farther than he expected. Now they'd navigate with a primitive compass—standard issue for any kaphoora party—and push their way through an unfriendly jungle.

Think of the daleura. Never mind the discomfort, the effort, the wearying state of vigilance . . . it was only a few days of inconvenience, compared to the daleura he'd earn. Even Tehra would acclaim him now, and quit looking at his younger sibling with such an attentive eye. Yes, he'd trained for his time here on Fandre . . .

trained hard. And he was determined, and strong, as were all his guards—even the injured ones. Against all that, walking out to the portal would surely present no obstacle he could not overcome.

Riker slashed a clinging, thorn-covered vine out of his way and hoped that Worf never learned he'd used the *bat'leth* for such a purpose. The Tsorans had it somewhat easier, ducking obstacles that met Riker at chest level—but even so, their progress remained slow. At least the deluge of rain had eased, although he had the suspicion that he was likely to mold before he managed to dry off. In that, at least, the Tsorans had a disadvantage; their fur, despite use of the simple rain slickers, had turned damply dark, a baptism from the thick foliage at their level. The Tsorans trained and prepared for their time here, he knew . . . but they'd never come this deep into the preserve before.

Apparently it made a difference.

That difference hadn't fazed Akarr, who forged ahead with unflagging determination—aside from his occasional covetous glance at the *bat'leth*. Riker would have preferred to move more slowly, take better stock of their surroundings. He'd already learned to spot the sticky vines at several meters, and the thorny vines had gotten his quick attention as well. There was also a certain broad-leafed bush he'd pegged as responsible for the stinging red welts across the back of his hand; that one was harder to see at a distance.

But it wasn't the plants that worried him, or the insects—which, so far, had all been of such a size that there was no subtlety to them at all, no chance of one landing unnoticed to take a chunk out of him. Even if he was bitten, he specifically remembered reading that none of the local insects were anything more than annoying; for all their size, they left no more sting than a mosquito.

Although he didn't imagine it would take as many of them to drain a man dry.

No, the plants were so far only an annoyance. The insects were an annoyance. But the various hoots, calls, and chattering that he heard in the distance, he took as warning. And the one oft-repeated call—where it came from, he wasn't sure, except that it seemed to bounce among the trees, swelling significantly before it finally faded away—that one, he found alarming. Damned alarming.

It came again—to his ears, closer than ever. More than anything, it reminded him of the sound of a stick running across the boards of a snow fence . . . if amplified many times and imbued with an underlying tone of menace that no fence had ever produced.

He stopped, engulfed in foliage, unconsciously lifting the *bat'leth* closer to a guard position as Ketan stumbled past him, followed by Rakal, their last man. Slowly, he turned a complete circle, searching the layers of green on green—dark greens, shadowed greens, green spreading to reveal glimpses of grayish tree trunks, green splashed with the vibrant color of arboreal flyers and flowers—hunting for the owner of the haunting cry.

If he hadn't viewed the reports, if he hadn't paid close attention in the museum, he'd have been struck by the strong suspicion that the carnivores they sought to avoid were also green.

The carnivores, he corrected himself, that *most* of them sought to avoid.

And then there was Akarr.

Some part of him couldn't blame the Tsoran's resistance to abandoning the kaphoora. He was a kid, after all, a kid trying to impress not only his parents and peers, but his entire society. A kid with too much authority in a dangerous situation, and none of the experience to wield it.

Riker's inspection of the area revealed nothing. If there was anything out there, anything close, he couldn't spot it. And the Tsorans hadn't waited, hadn't even slowed down; there was no point in standing out here alone, exposed. He turned back to the trail—easy to follow, given all the foliage that had been hacked, broken, and otherwise disturbed—and instantly froze in place at the movement directly before his feet.

He couldn't even tell what it was, not at first—only that in the tangle of roots, leaves, and fallen branches at his feet, something moved. A gliding motion, with no beginning to it and no ending. Gray-green patterns meant to distract his eyes did just that, and he stared, baffled, not sure if he was about to die or if he was merely seeing things.

And then the shapes and patterns snapped abruptly into place, and the primordial part of his brain, the part that still lived in caves and walked on all fours, bellowed *snake!*

Damn big snake, bulky and stretching from here to there, neither end visible, its body muscular and lumpy . . . as if the last meal hadn't quite settled down yet. He assessed the thing's girth, looked down at himself . . . it'd be a tight fit.

But it would be a fit.

Had he seen anything on snakes in the museum? Were they poisonous, were they constrictors . . . would this one even care that it had crossed his path? Would it leave him alone if he simply waited for it to pass, or was it circling back? If he moved, would that draw its otherwise uncaring attention? He hadn't seen the tail of it yet; it just seemed to go on forever. He could well believe that this end could be passing him by while the front end came by for a second look.

For another moment, he hesitated, not sure of the best move. Then . . . *what the hell.* If he was going to be eaten by the biggest snake in the universe, he'd do it with flair. He leapt over the cumbrous girth of the creature, landing as far away as he could get—and as lightly as he could manage.

Not far enough, not lightly enough—the snake whipped around, a lightning-fast motion he hadn't begun to suspect it possessed, whacking him across the back of the legs even as he intended to put more distance between them. *Shouldn't have hesitated, shouldn't have taken that one look back*—Riker went down, breaking through the foliage with his face, landing with his arms outspread and his fingers splayed against the ground, the *bat'leth* under his open palm—little good it could do him while he sprawled so thoroughly across the fungus-filled ground. He tried to flip himself around, hindered by the leaves and branches that clung to him, nearly blinded by whatever had gotten into his eyes—and was stopped short by the thick muscular body suddenly clinging to his calves. Not only clinging to them, working its way up with a prickly, gripping oddness, pinning his thighs—

Riker twisted to discover that the snake had legs. Or hands. Small, three-fingered hands that had emerged from a protective groove along its side and now clung happily to his trousers while the tip of the tail—finally visible—curled around to possessively claim an ankle.

And then he heard the rustling glide of the front half, coming back for its share.

The shock of it, the hesitation, left him—and left him cold and grim and *moving.* With a growl, he snatched up the *bat'leth* and heaved himself up to his knees, whipping around to bisect the tail with the sap-sticky blade.

Too thick—it was too thick, and he didn't have the leverage—the blade sunk two-thirds of the way through and stuck there, and Riker clung grimly while the tail flailed against him, battering him, knowing he couldn't afford to lose the weapon and hoping that—

There! Slicked by the creature's own blood, loosened by its own contortions, the *bat'leth* abruptly yanked loose; Riker fell back with the momentum of it and turned it into a roll, his legs free of the creepy, clinging hand fingers and his feet solidly under him—just in time to see the head of the monster shooting toward him, lancing through the air in a deadly swift strike.

He let the *bat'leth* do the thinking for him.

Slashing, striking, ducking, skipping out of reach . . . in the end, he didn't know if the snake-thing was badly wounded or merely annoyed enough to leave. It left enough of its blood in evidence so he felt he'd at least ruined its day; already the insects were swarming. He stood, panting, looking at the evidence of the struggle—but only for a moment. Then he wiped his face against his shoulder, clearing it of sweat and . . . less pleasant things . . . and turned to walk briskly down the trail.

It took him some moments to catch up with the Tsorans, who had made no attempt to wait for him. Even so, Rakal turned to give him a disgruntled look. "Best if you don't slow us down," he said, the Universal Translator faltering and barely comprehensible over the gruffness of his under-purr and his steady panting. Definitely affected by the tech damper, dammit.

"Just taking a look around," he told Rakal, wiping sweat from the side of his face; he merely smiled when Rakal caught a glimpse of the bloodied *bat'leth*, giving it an obvious double take. It distracted him enough, in fact, that when Ketan—whose short, slightly bowed but normally sturdy legs had gone distinctly wobbly in the moments since Riker's arrival—folded neatly to the ground, Rakal almost walked right over him.

"Ketan!" Rakal's exclamation wavered between concern and annoyance. "On your feet, then, Ketan—we need to make more distance this day."

"I think it would be wiser to find a place to camp," Riker said.

"There is still plenty of day left," Rakal said, although beneath the canopy, it was hard to judge the fading light. "We'll move until Akarr says otherwise."

"And is Akarr going to carry your friend? Because maybe you can't see it, but he's gone just about as far as he's going to go." Riker doubted they had much of "this day" left. And if there was one thing he knew, it was that he wanted to have a good, defensible camp set up before twilight settled in.

Most hunting, he recalled, took place in the twilight hours.

"What delay has Riker caused now?" Akarr shouted back at them, already retracing his steps and bringing the others with him.

"Just trying to save your hide," Riker said between his teeth, feeling his remaining patience trickle away through the hole in his temper. More loudly, he said, "Your men are injured, Akarr. They're beat. We need to find a good place to spend the night, and we need to do it while we've still got the energy to fight off whatever comes after us in the next few hours."

Akarr lifted his head slightly, his nostrils flaring as he sipped in a quick series of breaths. Scenting the air. More accurately, Riker knew, than any human could ever do the same—but not nearly with the accuracy of even the most overbred Earth dog. Nonetheless, Akarr spoke with assurance. "There's nothing in the area."

"Is that what you thought a few moments ago, when you walked past *this?*" Riker lifted the *bat'leth,* holding it vertically; obligingly, the last drops of maroon blood slipped down the edge to splat dramatically against the leaves below.

Silence fell over the group. Silence more or less, considering the increasing activity in the trees around them; the creature of the hollow, clacking cry loosed another series of calls.

Well. He'd been hoping that one was gone, but on the other hand it hadn't seemed likely that it was the defeated snake-thing, either.

"It would be best," Akarr said, struggling to maintain his grasp on a command presence, "to make more distance while we're still fresh."

Gavare chose that moment to wander into the middle of them and slowly sink to his knees. As unobtrusively as possible, Rakal tugged him off to the side, next to Ketan.

"Can't get much fresher than that," Riker said. He plucked a giant leaf and used it to wipe the worst of the snake-thing's blood from the *bat'leth.* "Face it, Akarr. They're not going anywhere. I'm going to look around for a better spot to spend the night. Someplace that doesn't look so much like something else's dinner table." He turned away from the group, hoping for something resembling high ground.

"That's my decision to make," Akarr cried out as Riker walked away.

"Then make it!" Riker shouted back without even turning around.

That's when it struck, a huge, long-bodied blur of

motion with big ears and plenty of teeth—the only glimpse Riker got as it bounced toward him, shouldering into his hip and knocking him flat, *again,* only to bound away again.

"Sculper!" Gavare called, apparently not so addled that he couldn't keep track of the things that wanted to eat him.

Riker, already back to his hands and knees and peering suspiciously around, found that the Tsorans had fallen into defensive positions around their injured. "Where'd it go?" he said, wary and disgruntled, and not at all sure he wanted to get back on his feet. But climb up he did, easing back toward the Tsorans to take up a new position, his feet set in a wide and stable base. The jungle was silent; nothing moved.

"Sculpers," Rakal said. "They prefer their prey dead, and if it lives, they play with—"

"There!" Takan shouted, pointing, taking aim; Riker got a better look this time, was able to spot the two happily whisking tails, to see that while the sculper's interest was in the wounded men, it targeted those who protected them. *Would try to intimidate them,* according to what he'd read, disposing of them with hit-and-run.

Easily bigger than the Tsorans, it launched in to bounce off Regen, sent him flying, then bounded away and came from an entirely new direction—at Riker again. Huge, happy, overgrown hyenas with too many tails and too many teeth. And a thing or two to learn about the mettle of Starfleet's officers.

Until now, the attack had been silent—only the rustle of leaves, the short cries of warning, the tension of waiting. Until now. Riker snarled a challenge and lifted the *bat'leth* to meet the creature as it sprang for him, lowering its head, presenting its shoulder—

He had no chance of staying on his feet. But he

slammed the *bat'leth* at the creature anyway, turning the collision into a head-on crash that sent him tumbling across the ground. Disoriented, he staggered back to his feet, trying to find the menace—hell, trying to find *any* of them in this dizzying assortment of greens and grays—and more than a little glad when he backed up against the support of a gnarled ball of tree roots. Something moved behind him and he jerked around, *bat'leth* at the ready—

"Peace!" Rakal stopped short and held out his hands in the reasonably universal gesture of *I mean no harm.* "The beast is gone, Riker."

"Gone?" Riker repeated, looking out over the jungle.

"You drew blood. It is a scavenger, and for all its size prefers to avoid real confrontation. It merely sought to annoy us into leaving, so it could have our wounded."

Riker shook his head, which didn't do anything to clear it—*it never does, when are you going to learn*—and licked the blood from his lip, rubbing the shoulder he'd landed on. On second thought, why bother? Everywhere else felt just as battered. "It did a damn good job."

"Ah?"

"Of being annoying." Riker pushed himself away from the tree, discovered he was only on the other side of it from the Tsorans, and drew himself up to enter the fray again—this time with Akarr.

Except this time, Akarr didn't seem interested. He conferred quickly with his guards—aside from Regen, who only slowly climbed to his feet on the outskirts of the group, hunched over his broken arm, clearly in agony. No one paid him any attention, and Riker's swift anger fortunately turned to understanding before he acted on it; they were giving Regen the space to express his pain without losing face over it. Riker, too, turned away.

And then Regen's sudden scream cut the air—not a scream of his pain, but of mortal terror—and they all whirled, crouching, ready for action—

Not that it did them any good. The guards released dart after dart, none of them close enough to penetrate, as a lumbering sholjagg—heavy-bodied, with huge, clawed front paws and a short, stiff tail riding the spine of the main tail—ambled in with amazing speed. Right up to Regen it went, clamped the scrambling guard in its massive jaws, and ambled away without breaking its rapid stride. Regen's wild struggles ceased almost immediately; his scream gurgled out into a fading gasp.

The kaphoora party stared after him in shock. Any number of trank darts dangled out of the retreating sholjagg's thick fur; plenty of others had disappeared into the foliage. Riker doubted there was much left in the way of ammunition.

No, the Tsorans had never hunted the Legacy this deeply before. And they clearly had no idea what they were up against.

Finally, Akarr spoke, his words quick and decisive. "We will find a place to stop for the night," he said. "We will gather wood, as a group. We will make clubs and spears as we can. No one of us will ever be out of sight of another." And he looked up at Riker, as if defying him to find fault with any of it—to make note of the fact that he was effectively breaking all the rules the Fandreans had set for such expeditions.

Riker straightened, drawing back his sore shoulders; he tilted his head in the slightest sign of acquiescence. He did not say, *I told you so*.

But he thought it very hard.

Chapter Eight

WORF CLOSED THE NEWLY PROVISIONED med kit firmly enough to elicit a protesting *snick* from the container, and La Forge looked up from his last-minute adjustments to the new secondary shields. He knew enough to recognize the glower on Worf's face for the impatience it was. "Just a few more minutes," he said. "It won't do Commander Riker any good if you go down, too."

"It will do him even less good if he is eaten before I arrive," Worf said implacably.

Well, that was true, too. La Forge fine-tuned the frequency interaction between the two shields, and confirmed that both scavenged generators from the scooterpods were precisely aligned. *There.* He stood back and gestured to the shuttle controls. "Remember, keep these engine shields on at all times, even if you leave the shuttle. Other than that . . . it's as ready as it'll ever be," he said, and that was true enough. It didn't have enough seats—some of the returning passengers would have to sit on the floor—but it had Tsoran medical supplies and drugs, extra rations suitable for all the species involved, and a waiting crew of several Fandrean rangers.

"It is about time," Worf said, not quite under his breath.

"Yeah, well, it's about *timing,* too," La Forge said. "Don't forget that it takes tremendous energy to open that portal. It'd be one thing if we could be sure of hearing communication from within the shields, but—"

"I know," Worf said, and then stopped abruptly, wearing the expression he often had when he seemed to be restraining himself. He recited, "The portal can only open three more times, and it will do so in six-hour intervals."

Unfazed by fraying Klingon temper, La Forge added, "After that, you'll have to wait two days before we can begin the cycle again. Recharge time."

"It is a ridiculous system," Worf grumbled.

"Which is why I'll be working to solve the communications problem the whole time you're in there," La Forge pointed out. "We'll be trying to raise you, so keep your ears open. If it works, we'll take the portal off the timer and wait to hear that you're ready to come out." He glanced at the newly mounted shield generators, couldn't think of anything else to adjust, and reluctantly headed for the shuttle door. "Good luck, Worf."

Worf's rumbling reply was low enough that La Forge wasn't sure it was meant to be heard. "A Klingon does not need *luck.*"

No, of course not. But La Forge's smile quickly faded as he stepped aside for the Fandrean rangers. Maybe Worf didn't need luck, but he had the feeling that Commander Riker and the Tsorans could use a goodly dose of it.

Riker crouched to pluck a dart out of a wide, rubbery leaf, dropping it onto his palm. He straightened, and, holding the dart up to eye level, rolled it slightly in his hand, examining it. Takan, on a similar dart- and wood-gathering mission, came by and held out his hand for it. "We'll need that."

"Of course," Riker said, and handed it over. He'd get a better look at another one later. For now, he didn't have the time to waste. He left the rest of the darts to Takan and Gavare, and joined Rakal, Ketan, and Akaar in their search for defensible ground . . . and plenty of firewood.

"Over here!" Rakal called, excitement in his voice. Too far from the others for Riker's taste, but if they had a window of safety within which to operate, it would be now, in the aftermath of the sholjagg's presence. Cautiously, he left Takan and made his way to second group, watching the ground with distinct attention for any tubular threats.

Rakal, he discovered, had ample reason for the triumph in his voice. He and the others were crouched before a steep bank, a cliff that seemed equal parts clay and rock with striations of darkly rich soil layered throughout. The ground directly before the cliff was tangled with foliage, but free of any large-girthed, towering trees; there would be room to build a bonfire or two. Defensively, it looked to be about as good as this area was likely to offer—better, in fact, than Riker had ever expected to find, because for all the challenges of the footing, the actual terrain had been fairly mild. Not only did the spot put a wall at their backs, but it curved around, enhancing the shallow indentation which—if one were *very* generous—might be called a cave formation.

Riker was inclined to be generous.

"You see?" Akarr said, noting his arrival. "We don't need your shuttle."

"Regen might feel differently," Riker said dryly. "If he were still able to feel anything at all."

"And," Akarr said, as though Riker hadn't spoken at all, "we're significantly closer to the portal."

Riker wasn't so sure about that, either. But instead of saying so, he added his armful contribution of wood. Not dry . . . nothing was. But the incendiary tablet would take care of that.

It had better.

"We'll need more wood." Akarr poked the small pile with his foot. "Enough wood to keep the fire high all night. That should keep them away."

If I were a sholjagg, would I be afraid of a little fire? Riker recalled the size of the beast and wasn't entirely convinced. But it was definitely a first step. "I'll get more," he said. He thought again of the tranks, hanging ineffectively in the sholjagg's thick, coarse hair. *Lots more.*

"Now that we've found a defensible spot, we'll all look," Akarr declared. He lifted his head and bellowed, "Gavare! Takan! Join up!"

They set to gathering wood with intensity, combing the woods near the cave while the ambient light slowly dimmed and the bird and insect noise cranked up to the point where it was hard to hear anything else—even the sound of Riker's own movement through the jungle. He found himself on alert, freezing each time the increasingly active insects sounded off nearby. A small, froggy creature that might or might not have had beetle-like wings poinged off his temple, dropped down to his beard, and got its sticky feet tangled there so thoroughly that Riker had formed a distinct image of himself striding through the *Enterprise* corridors with a small winged frog stuck to his face before he finally freed the thing and sent it off into the brush.

But nothing tried to eat him, and he had at least two of the Tsorans in his sight at all times. Very cozy, just a nice roaring bonfire for a pleasant little campout. . . . When he returned to the cave, he could barely see the dark hollow behind the stack of wood piled before it.

Riker began sorting through it, moving the main bulk of the wood—fallen branches ranging from green to punk-wood rotten—to the side so there was room to build the actual fire. He picked out the driest pieces for the fire-starting process, hefting anything that came into his hand that felt like it might serve as a club. Something with a longer reach than a *bat'leth*.

Besides, Akarr's men had not yet thought past the firewood to the extra weapons they would need—even if the tranks worked on the next creature to come after them, they'd already severely depleted their supply of darts—and Riker had a feeling they'd follow suit if they saw him arming himself with crude tools.

Gavare wandered in dragging a branch almost as thick around as he was and dropped it beside the newly sorted wood, immediately sitting down beside it. His mind seemed to have cleared—or, at least, he was no longer apt to wander off on his own—though the actual process of serious thinking remained beyond him. "Wood," he said. "That's good."

"It'll help keep us alive," Riker agreed, selecting a heavy green wood stick as thick as his arm and just as long, and thinking it would be even better if he could lash a stone of some sort to the end. Or a stone with random spikes, each tipped with poison—

Definitely spending too much time in Worf's holodeck calisthenics. Or rather, in the toned-down version for humans. Worf Lite.

In any event, this would do nicely for a club. Riker set it aside, and looked over to see Gavare poking through the sorted wood in a desultory way—though he soon ceased, as though he'd forgotten what he might have been looking for. Unlike the rest of them, he didn't seem tense or worried; he looked content, as Riker would define "content" in a Tsoran, and he hummed to himself, a gentle under-purr.

"Why is it," Riker said, considering that getting knocked on the head might in fact be a good strategy for making it through the next few days, "that all of you are willing to go to such extraordinary lengths to continue this kaphoora?"

"Everything must be just right," Gavare said, answering in distraction as he found a potential spear that delighted him; he took out his small knife and carved away at the tip.

"Just right for the kaphoora? It's too late for that."

"Kaphoora," Gavare said, and made a short snuffly noise, an odd flapping of his lips. "For the Federation. That's what this whole kaphoora is about . . . more than just prime kaphoora to Akarr. He's got Takarr to worry about."

"Takarr?" Riker stopped arranging the fire circle he'd started and gave Gavare a hard look. Idle and wandering words from a concussed Tsoran, and he had the feeling they held the first truly crucial information the Tsorans had revealed.

But the sharp edge to his voice must have cut through Gavare's fog, made way for some sense in the guard's head. He said, "Better get that fire started. This time of day, the sculpers come out in gangs—" He cut himself short, tilting his head, listening.

Riker heard it, too, just as the others drifted to the heart of their camp area, cautious and hunting out the source of the noise.

Overhead.

Not as powerful as usual, but no less the sweet for that. A shuttle, flying low and steady, from the direction of the portal right along the flight path the *Rahjah* had taken.

Worf. The *Collins*. No doubt he was heading for the *Rahjah*'s planned landing site; with any luck the light was not yet so dim that he couldn't see the crash path.

Not that there was anywhere near the *Rahjah* to land *except* in that crash path, and a tricky bit of flying that would be.

It didn't matter. Worf was in the air, come to look for them in response to the broadband cry for help. He'd find the *Rahjah*, all right.

"And we'll be nowhere near it," Riker muttered out loud.

"What?" Akarr switched his attention from the now-fading engine noise to glare at Riker; surely he'd guessed the source of the noise, for he wasn't asking. "What did you say?"

It was a dare, Riker thought. A dare to say *I told you so*. But not a dare he had any intention of taking. Not when he still had to get through the night, and that wouldn't happen if the Tsorans decided to take serious exception to him.

"Come morning," Riker said, his voice carefully neutral, "we'll have a way out of here."

"How long," Gavare said, squinting out into what was definitely growing darkness, "will it take you to light that fire?"

"Depends on just how wet this wood is," Riker told him, slinging his backpack off to pull out the incendiary tablets. "Why do you ask?"

Gavare didn't answer right away; as his companions glanced warily about themselves and Riker shaved a quick pile of curling bark for tinder, the answer became evident—a slinking, long-bodied shape, a double-tailed whisk of movement in the foliage . . . the sculper was back.

"Get that fire started," Akarr said, ignoring the fact that Riker was already assembling the tinder and kindling, had placed the flat button on the ground beneath it, and was prepared to pull its activating tab. "Everyone else—take a point. Use the rocks and spears, and save the tranks!"

Had they found time to make spears and gather rocks? Riker hoped it was so, but didn't look away from his task, flinching as the tablet flared to life with intense heat and light, and wincing at the strong sizzle of the larger kindling. If it was that wet, it might well take two tablets to establish a self-sustaining fire.

One of the Tsorans shouted; Riker didn't bother to check who, though he could tell why, even with ruined night vision. The rush of a sculper, its soft chittering laugh of a retreat—sounds he already knew by heart. He couldn't help the others now; he kept his focus on the fire. Adding small branches to the small tablet-inspired inferno as fast as he could, daring to try a larger branch . . . he hesitated, ready to snatch it away if the fire dimmed, all too aware of the brief skirmish taking place off to the side.

But the tablet fueled the flames, and by the time it died, they had a large, healthy fire blazing before the cave—enough of a fire to spook the naive sculper . . . for now.

And no one else had been hurt.

For now.

"Akarr!" Takan shouted from the other side of the fire. "It returns!"

"No, over here!" Rakal cried, his warning harsh with under-purr.

In front of Riker, something bounded in close to the fire, bouncing back out again before his recovering night vision could quite see what it was. Not that it mattered; he didn't need to see it to know exactly what had happened. The sculper was back . . . and he'd brought his friends. Riker picked up his newly made club in one hand, and adjusted his grip on the *bat'leth* in the other.

It was going to be a long night.

"What is the scuttlebutt?" Data asked over the comm link, his tone just slightly off normal. La Forge stopped his work at the Fandrean communication board for a mental double take on the words, then gave his head a slight shake and returned the greater part of his attention to his work—not that he had much attention to give it. The normal dull ache of the VISOR's interface at his temples had sharpened into a true headache, a nagging discomfort that generated the frequent impulse to remove the device. As tired as he was, one of these times he was going to have the thing off his face before he even realized what he'd done.

"I said—"

"I heard you, Data. It's the middle of the night here, everyone else is asleep, and I keep staring at this communications board, waiting for a solution to pop into my head. Meanwhile, Worf is off in the Legacy somewhere, and we have no idea if he's had any luck finding Commander Riker's shuttle, or even if he's run into trouble himself."

"Groovy," Data said. La Forge's link to the *Enterprise,* his link to anything outside of this museum, and he'd said *groovy.*

This time, La Forge did stop work, carefully replacing the spanning microflux calibrator in its special protective tool case. *"Not* groovy, Data. Not groovy at all."

"I misapplied the word? I meant to indicate support and approval of your work there."

"Well, you didn't." La Forge had no trouble visualizing Data's slightly puzzled response, the tilt of his head as he searched for more information about the subject. "This isn't the first time you've used an unusual phrase. Are you off on another slang kick?"

"Not precisely. I am running an experiment. After so many of the officers in the briefing indicated a familiarity with *The Wizard of Oz,* I thought I would see how many other twentieth-century phrases and allusions people would respond to. I am attempting to use them casually, in the course of a conversation. It is not my intent that the phrases be noticed for themselves, but to see if the participants in the conversation respond to the phrase with an understanding of its meaning."

La Forge, sitting cross-legged on the floor—and why *were* these boards always so close to the ground—felt his mind go numb and foggy.

"For instance, when Captain Picard was leaving for the Tsoran reception, I advised him to paint the town red. He did not seem to have a full understanding of the phrase, but I fear the results of that particular experiment were skewed when it turned out that Atann actually *had* painted the reception room red."

La Forge leaned back on his arms, smiling. "I heard it was curtains and rugs."

"To be precise, although my point stands."

To which La Forge didn't respond, other than to give in to the impulse to remove the VISOR and sit in his pleasant haze, listening to Data's voice—which eventually said, "—my understanding of human physiology leads me to suggest that you will achieve no practical purpose in driving yourself this way."

"Was that your way of telling me to get some sleep?"

"I believe it was."

"Yeah," La Forge said, and sighed. "You're right. I just hate to think of them in there, with no way to communicate to us . . . who knows what kind of trouble they're in. But . . . I can't think straight anymore."

"Then you are hardly doing your best for them," Data said, as blunt as usual. Not to mention correct.

"Thanks, Data. That's just the kind of pep talk I need."

"It was not meant to be a pep talk."

No, never mind. He was too tired to straighten that one out. But before he went to bed . . . "Data, how's it going with the Ntignano evacuation? And with the Tsorans?"

"I would say . . ." Data started, and hesitated, hunting for the best response, his very hesitation a blinking red alert in La Forge's mind.

"Just tell me, Data."

"I am sorry to report that neither situation is progressing in a positive manner. The Ntignanos have much less time than expected, and the extended evacuation journey is creating problems. Dr. Crusher has the details; I can have her—"

"No, no, this is fine," La Forge muttered. Well, he *had* asked. "And the Tsorans?"

"It is hard to ascertain how they feel about the situation, since they have broken off contact. I believe that Captain Picard has something in mind; he has not given up his attempts to acquire the charts."

"Has he—" La Forge stopped, trying to think if Data would know about his request to send out a modified charting probe. He'd made it of Picard, who would work with engineering if he decided to move ahead . . . but would he have brought Data in on the decision-making process? "I'd been hoping we could start in on our own charts, Data. Do you know if Captain Picard is considering it?"

"Officially, no," Data said. "However, I assisted Lieutenant Duffy with the necessary changes to the probes, so I am 'in the know.' "

"He's gone ahead with it then." Relief. It wouldn't give them results as soon as they needed them—but in the end, more lives would be saved than if they waited for the Tsorans and never got the charts they'd been promised.

"The probe was launched several hours ago. They are performing up to expectations. But, Geordi, it will not give us results in time to save—"

"I know, I know," La Forge said through a tired groan. "It won't save them all. We can't build even a rudimentary chart of those eddies in time to do that. Our current charts of this system are so old, and so seldom used . . . the areas with the eddies might as well be labeled like the ancient maps of Earth's oceanic trouble spots. *Here be monsters.*"

A phrase that was pretty darn appropriate for the situation right here on Fandre.

Here be monsters.

Chapter Nine

NIGHT IN THE FANDREAN JUNGLE.

Deep in the tangle of night-blacked foliage, slick fur slid between thickly leafed branches, making no more than a whisper of sound beneath the clamor of myriad insects crying out for the company of their own kind.

A shriek ripped through the chorus, startling it to silence.

Bones crunched.

Tsoran bones.

Here be monsters.

Riker quickly lost track of time; he lost track of the fact that time had any meaning at all. The scavengers came after them in rounds of overlapping activity, always making sure someone in the camp had reason to be shouting, alarmed, scrabbling for a defensive position . . . or screaming. After the first major attack, Riker built a second fire on the other side of the cave entrance, hoping to create a more secure area in between the two, at the mouth of the cave. For a while it worked—until the beasts lost their initial respect for the flames, and learned to shoulder the humanoids away from the clear spots and *into* the fires—or nearly into the fires. Singed Tsoran fur, singed sculper fur, singed Starfleet uniform . . .

The *bat'leth* threw swooping firelight around the cleared zone, whirling with Riker's fierce attacks, his twisting retreats; the club hit the ground early on, wrested from his grip by sculper jaws and then discarded. Around him, the Tsorans wielded their lances and clubs and trank guns, but the sculpers were too quick for the short-range tranks and only momentarily deterred by the hastily made weapons.

Somewhere in the middle of the night, the sculpers took a break—time for a little nap, Riker thought, a break in the entertainment. For that's what this was—entertainment. Nothing about the sculpers, not their lolling tongues or their exuberant body language, led him to think that he and the Tsorans provided anything but amusement, and the moment the scavengers tired of the game, they'd barge past all defenses and take who they wanted.

Or eat them on the spot.

"If we can at least stun one of them," Akarr said to Rakal, possibly unaware that Riker stood on the other side of the currently blazing second fire, feeding in another batch of now-dry logs, "I can take trophy. Trophy from the very animals attacking me!"

"Nothing Takarr does will be enough to elevate him beyond that in our people's eyes," Rakal agreed.

Takarr again. Who was Takarr?

Rakal added, "But I worry about Ketan, ReynTa. He

was honorably injured. Even putting him in the cave with Gavare doesn't seem likely to protect him from these sculpers if they quit playing with us and determine to take food."

No doubt about that; the injured men needed protection.

Riker rounded the fire to join them uninvited, offering them glare for glare—a greeting he'd received so often he now responded in appropriate Tsoran body language without thinking about it. "We should pull in, and not attempt to protect anything but the cave mouth." Not that it was much of a cave, but every little advantage . . .

"If we do that, they can come upon us several at a time, and take us all down," Rakal said, pouching his lower lip in disapproval. "As we are, they might get one of us, but the others will survive."

"But they *aren't* coming in several at a time." Riker cast a pointed glance out at the black and impenetrable foliage surrounding them; something rustled loudly and they all tensed, but nothing came of it, and after a moment he looked back at the Tsorans. "No reason to risk losing anyone else."

"We will continue as we are," Akarr said stiffly, the hair on his arms rising slightly.

Suddenly Riker understood. Akarr wasn't making any attempt to keep the animals away from the cave, not at all. He approached each strafing run as an opportunity to stun or trank one of the sculpers long enough to harvest a trophy. And while defending the cave meant chasing them off in any fashion possible, going for the trophy meant letting them get close enough to take one down. If that meant standing aside while it went for the cave, then that's just exactly what it meant—no matter the cost to Gavare and Ketan.

But nothing in Rakal's attitude suggested that it was

commonplace to leave their wounded to die, or even to fend for themselves.

Who is Takarr?

Why would he inspire such behavior?

Riker looked down at Akarr—bloodied from minor wounds, his fur sticking out in random cowlicks where he'd run into sap, his stiff leather vest scratched and scarred—and knew he looked no better himself. Never mind daleura, never mind the world outside this small, recently made clearing. "You're making a mistake," he said. "And your men will pay."

Akarr lifted his lips, exposing his teeth, his eyes cold in the firelight. "It is you who err, Riker. We would duel this moment if it wouldn't jeopardize the very men that worry you so."

"If there's one thing that *doesn't* worry me, it's the prospect of—"

"Sculper!" cried Takan from the other side of the fires, where he'd remained either ignorant or uncaring of the confrontation within the camp. "More than one!"

Careless movement in the brush came on the heels of his words, and Riker whirled away from the fire, grabbing the opportunity to scoop up his club—and finding himself suddenly eye to eye with the sculper. His breath exploded out in a startled shout of attack as he turned the scooping motion into a swing, right at the sculper's head—

It was gone again, effortlessly bounding back out of reach—and, as Riker staggered ahead with his own momentum, leaping forward once more. Not to shoulder him out of the way, not this time—this time the creature came in all jaws and teeth, its hackles raised, its two short tails standing stiffly at attention, and Riker wrenched himself back into a ragged guard, bringing the *bat'leth* up, arms bent to take the shock of impact as the animal launched itself—one bound, two—and abruptly stopped, its nose in the air, and just as suddenly changed course, no less purposeful.

Riker, no longer between the sculper and the cave, threw himself after it, landing heavily in the damp, trampled ground growth—

Missing the creature entirely.

But the creature didn't miss its intended prey. A harsh Tsoran scream filled the night as Riker scrambled to his feet, heading for the dark pocket of space in the shallow cave, driving himself at the braced hindquarters of the sculper—*braced, like a dog playing tug-of-war*—and then throwing himself to the side when it whirled to turn on him. Even then, he kept his forward movement, aiming the end of the *bat'leth* right down its throat.

It dodged, of course. But the blade dug into its neck at the shoulder, and it screamed just as throatily as its Tsoran victim as it broke away and bolted out of the cave.

Panting, somehow already smeared with sculper blood, Riker climbed to his feet and ran to the cave, where he found Ketan sprawled in a dazed and bloody state, his previously wounded arm now badly bitten as well. Gavare, a club discarded at his feet, knelt not by Ketan's arm, but by his legs. As Riker frowned, trying to make sense of it, Akarr rushed into the cave.

"It's gone?" he demanded, looking around as though it might be lurking nearby.

"It's gone," Riker affirmed, and when Akarr reacted with an angry snort, Riker gave him an incredulous look and said, "That's a *good* thing, Akarr."

Akarr stalked to the entrance of cave, standing by the edge of dirt and rock and staring into the darkness, his nostrils flaring, his pouched lower lip working. "You might have delayed it until I arrived."

So that's what this was about. *Again.* "I *meant* to drive it off." Actually, he'd meant to *kill* it. "If you want to gather a trophy, you're just going to have to be faster."

"Akarr?" Rakal called from beyond the fire, his voice anxious.

"Stay on watch! All is well," Akarr shouted back.

Riker looked down at Ketan. "Not exactly *well.*" He crouched down, joining Gavare, finally able to see that Ketan's leg had swollen to alarming proportions. "What happened?"

"This," Gavare said, holding up a stout quill as long as Riker's hand. "From the creature's tail. When I attacked it . . . when it turned on me, Ketan was behind it. There's just not enough room in here . . ."

Gavare. Clearly still dizzy and finding it hard to navigate, never mind to attack an animal as big as he was. Befuddled enough to answer Riker's questions without posturing, without measuring daleura at every word. Riker eyed the quill, found the dark trickle of blood on Ketan's leg where it had gone in. "Is it lethal?"

"It's not supposed to be," Gavare said, which told Riker more yet. *The Tsorans didn't have any close experience with the sculpers. They should never have been this deep in the Legacy, no matter what they said about being prepared.*

Riker nodded at his backpack. "The med kit is on the top. See what you can do to make him comfortable, and to clean that arm up."

Befuddled, all right. Gavare didn't protest taking orders from the human, but did as he was bid. Riker climbed to his feet and moved up behind Akarr. "This didn't have to happen," he said. "We could be in the shuttle. We could pull your men in and cover the mouth of this cave, dammit!"

"It's not necessary for you to understand the reasons behind my decisions," Akarr said, coldly. Remaining remote, as if Riker weren't even worth challenging. Not turning around.

"Oh, I understand the reasons behind your decisions, all right," Riker said. "I just don't agree with them. No leader—no *good* leader would."

"And what do *you* know of leading?" Akarr said, with the short gurgling sound that passed for Tsoran laughter, although even Riker could tell there was no humor in it.

"Jean-Luc Picard is my captain. He's the best, Akarr. I know it when I see it."

Akarr still did not turn to look at him, although the hair on his neck and shoulders looked distinctly prickled. "You know nothing. You are not a captain; you lead no one."

"That's where you're wrong." Riker put a hand up to lean against the entrance of the cave, his arm just clearing Akarr's head. "I command the *Enterprise* away missions. All of them. This is what I do, Akarr. I know how to do it right—and I know when I'm seeing it done wrong." He leaned closer, speaking into Akarr's cupped, snug-to-his-head ear. "Your men are counting on you—hell, they're so loyal to you that they'll follow you right into the jaws of a sholjagg—and you're *killing them*."

Akarr snorted loudly and left the cave, making a gesture that Riker didn't recognize but that had a distinctly rude air about it.

So much for the diplomatic relations between the Federation and the Tsorans.

"Rakal!" Akarr shouted, as if the entire conversation had never happened. "Keep an eye out for more of them—they'll probably be back."

"Yes, ReynTa," Rakal responded, hidden in the darkness on the other side of the first fire.

This one time, Akarr was right. After the sounds of struggle in the darkness—the wounded sculper, torn to pieces and consumed—the sculpers came back.

Picard tugged at his uniform, waiting while the transporter technician confirmed the beam-down coordinates. He'd barely been through an earlier-than-usual morning tea with Beverly Crusher when Nadann Jesson contacted him, pleased to extend Atann's invitation to visit the kaphoora training facility. It was, she let him know, quite an honor.

Picard thought of Will Riker, stuck on Fandre for the real thing, and once more squelched the impulse to take the *Enterprise* right out of orbit and across the graviton-eddy-laden system to Tsora's sister planet. The probe charting was under way, after all, and Atann and Tehra certainly didn't seem interested in any discussion about the charts.

"*Make* them interested," Crusher had said implacably, and in this case she'd been right. Besides, with any luck, Will and the others were sleeping through an uneventful night in the Legacy preserve, and within a few hours, when daylight arrived, Worf would find them and transport them out.

"They're ready, sir," Lieutenant B. G. Robinson told him from behind the transporter console; Picard had the sudden impression that she'd been shifting uneasily for some moments, trying to find some way to interrupt his thoughts.

"Thank you, Lieutenant," he said, and positioned himself on the transporter pad, preparing himself to step forward and greet Atann—

Except, when the moment of slight disorientation passed, he found himself facing Nadann Jesson. Nadann

Jesson against a backdrop of burnt orange and deep pea green draperies, in a small receiving room that held nothing but a low couch facing a thick wall monitor. He winced at the cacophony of colors. "They must really find our own decor inexplicable."

Nadann—a sturdy woman with short chestnut hair and richly brown eyes as framework for her pleasant expression—smiled. "I've almost gotten used to it." And indeed, her own clothes had a bold red/orange theme. "Welcome to Tsora, Captain Picard. It's nice to meet you in person."

"Likewise, Ambassador. I'm intrigued by anyone who's spent so much time with these people. I understand you were in place here before the current crisis arose?" He took a short turn around the room, discovered the monitor blank and not likely to be anything other, and ended up where he'd started, none the wiser.

"Shortly before. We'd had our eye on this system for some time, wondering if they might be ready to join the Federation. I volunteered to do a preliminary study here. And please, you should feel free to call me Nadann. Most of the Tsorans consider it throwing about unnecessary daleura to use titles constantly. They prefer to save that daleura up for a time when they can really nail you with it."

"Sounds like a society in which no small grudge is ever forgotten."

She shrugged. "Perhaps not, but they use hard feelings in a constructive way, rather than brawling them off in the streets." She frowned, then, looking at the door as though by all rights it should be opening to admit someone. "I don't know where Atann is. I'd understood that he'd be here. Though he won't be, not at this point—arriving late under these circumstances would be an embarrassment. It's just as well. I heard something this morning I gather the Tsorans have been very careful to keep from me; I was hoping for a chance to discuss it."

Picard forgot all about the clashing decor. "Please do."

"You can imagine that a rulership based on daleura—even one as entrenched as the ReynKa's—does not tolerate dissent well. Even the *apparent* lack of support of key staff members has a far-reaching impact." Nadann watched him closely, and when he nodded his understanding, assessed it as if to be sure she'd truly made her point. Then she said, "I don't know who . . . but apparently there are some staff members who resent Atann's interaction with the Federation."

Picard waited a moment. "That's it?"

"Put it within the context of what I just said, Captain. For there to be enough contention that any word of it reached me is of great significance."

He tried, but ended up shaking his head. "I think I would have to spend much more time here to truly understand," he said. "But I'll certainly take it under advisement."

For an instant, he had the feeling he'd disappointed her. But then she smiled, and reached for the door. "We might as well meet Atann at the training center." The heavily carved wooden door slid lightly into the wall at her guidance; an air current from the hallway rippled her garments.

"Sleeves," Picard said.

"Excuse me?"

"You're wearing sleeves. Counselor Troi told me about your experiment."

"Ah, that. It got me nowhere—after a while it became obvious that no one had any intentions of saying anything, no matter how I 'flaunted' myself. I'm trying something new, now . . . it is utterly amazing the lengths to which these people will go to avoid exposing themselves to embarrassment."

"Is that your job here? To embarrass them?"

She gave him a moment's assessment, and might well have responded to his challenging question with irritation. Instead she met him with confidence-backed humor. "My job is to make an unfathomable people . . . fathomable. In order to do that, I need to learn their boundaries, to explore the scope of their reactions. How will we know how hard to push them on an issue unless we know the results? How will we know how to push them at all? Finding ways to embarrass them, to provoke them, to engender reaction other than the arrogant public face of the high daleura and the fawning responsiveness of the low daleura . . . yes, that's all part of my job here." She led him down the hallway—apparently deserted—and through a large events room, also deserted, aside from the few servents scuttling to collect glassware and linens. "It's also the reason I was not suitable to enter into this charting matter as a negotiator."

Ah. That did indeed make sense. She'd never been positioned as a negotiating diplomat; she was more of an explorer. Pity she was still in the beginning stages, and couldn't offer him more guidance. "What is this place?" he asked, as they finished traversing the huge, high-ceilinged room. Stately draperies swooped from column to column—intense purples interwoven with screaming reds—and the columns themselves were as heavily carved as the receiving-room door. Picard caught glimpses of stylized animals that might correspond to those he'd seen in the Fandrean report . . . or to Tsora's extinct indigenous predators.

"The main bestowing hall," she said promptly. "Where training participants are awarded honors. Historically, the kaphooras began and ended here, but no longer."

"No," Picard said. "Considering they've wiped out any animal large enough and dangerous enough to provide daleura on a hunt, I can see why they would end that particular tradition. Has it not occurred to them to seed some of Fandre's creatures here?"

She laughed, a pleasant sound. "What makes you think the Fandreans would allow that? They know well enough that no matter what the Tsorans *say*, sooner or later the animals would be offered up as sacrifice to special kaphoora, and not remain protected under the current—and stringently enforced—Fandrean rules."

Yes. Of course.

Nadann pushed aside another door, a huge and hugely ornate thing, and sunlight flooded in. "The actual training takes place outdoors, in the central area. The young Tsorans learn to use the trank guns and their knives, and build their strength and endurance. There are classrooms for studying the flora and fauna, and mock battles in which crude holograms represent the creatures." They headed across hot, bright sand toward another structure, one whose walls scooped outward in the clamshell shape of an outdoor viewing venue. "It might be worthwhile to add that none of these kaphoora candidates is given much information on the deep Legacy, the area in which your Commander Riker was directed to land. That landing was the ReynSa's idea, a way for her son to earn more daleura than anyone before him. Her second son, Takarr, is already incorporating deep Legacy information into his studies, in case he should acquire the same opportunity."

"Well," Picard said, preparing himself to deal with Tsoran social patterns again, "let us hope that while

Atann explains and displays these aspects of the training, he'll also find himself amenable to discussions of a more serious nature."

"It was a good move, I think, to express such interest in the daleura-laden kaphoora training," Nadann said, optimism on her clear, open features. "He really couldn't pass that up. Now . . . I'm afraid it's up to you to turn the encounter into something more."

"It is, isn't it," Picard muttered to himself, giving Nadann a small, wry smile as they entered the shadow of the training facility and hesitated before another pair of intensely carved doors. Even as they halted, a Tsoran youth walked briskly around the curving exterior, his eyes on the ground and his chin pouch tense with thought.

"Pardon us," Nadann said instantly, stepping out of his path; her hand on Picard's arm indicated that he should do the same.

The youth looked up. By Tsoran standards he was slender, even for an immature male, but his vest was as ornate as any Picard had seen, and he quickly drew himself up into a stiffer, more arrogant posture. With that movement he suddenly looked familiar, although it wasn't until Nadann gave a respectful acknowledgment that he knew why. "Takarr," she said, turning her head ever so slightly to reveal throat.

"Ambassador Nadann," the youth said, his tone still reserved—but already he was relaxing his aggressive stance. More easygoing than Atann or Akarr, on the whole.

"Let me introduce Captain Picard," Nadann said. "I'm delighted to have the opportunity."

Takarr showed his teeth slightly, a startling reversal of his pleasant response to Nadann—albeit quickly squelched. "I'm surprised they allowed it to happen."

From Nadann's sudden poker face, Picard surmised that she was just as surprised—by the fact that Takarr had said as much. Definitely undercurrents here, and ones about which he knew nothing.

He would.

Meanwhile, the less friction, the better. "I'm honored to meet you, Takarr."

"Not," Takarr said, "honored enough to ask for my presence aboard the *Enterprise.*"

Picard didn't bother to hide his puzzlement. "You have a standing welcome aboard the *Enterprise,* I assure you."

Takarr studied him a moment—most likely not familiar enough with humans to measure the sincerity of the offer. Then he said, "I have business elsewhere," and left as abruptly as he'd arrived.

Picard looked at his slender back as Takarr entered the building he and Nadann had just left. "I think I've just been snubbed."

"Don't take it to heart, Captian," Nadann said. "Recent weeks have been a trial for him. Over his mother's protests, the ReynKa chose to leave Takarr out of the shipboard activities. These are Akarr's days of glory."

"Surely having the boy present wouldn't—" Picard started, but stopped himself. "Foolish question. It obviously *would* make a difference."

"Not much of one," Nadann said. "Frankly, I think it's Atann's way of making a point with his ReynSa. But that's speculation on my part."

Speculation. Of course. As Troi had told Picard . . . a complex people. "I only hope I can gain a better understanding of this culture befo—"

The doors before them slid aside, and a young Tsoran barely checked his momentum before crashing into Picard.

"Apologies, apologies," he said, barely glancing at Picard as he quickly flashed his throat to them both. He'd clearly been about to speed onward, but came to a second abrupt halt as he saw Nadann. "Mighty sybyls! Ambassador, I'm supposed to meet an important hu—" and he cut himself off, finally truly seeing Picard for the first time.

Picard was not without sympathy . . . but that sympathy was limited. He wasn't at all slow to add up the pieces. Nor was Nadann; her optimism faded, her expression turned inscrutable. "That is most likely to be me," he said to the youth. "I am Captain Jean-Luc Picard."

"Captain," said the young Tsoran, his lower lip drawn tight in what struck Picard as an appalled expression; the boy's under-purr was tight and high. "I'm sorry I'm late, esteemed sir. I wasn't told—that is, my assignment came la—that is, there is no excuse, Captain. Please accept my apologies for not meeting you at the inroom." This time, he held position with his head twisted to expose his throat . . . waiting.

"Apology accepted," Picard said, although there was a tight edge to his own voice; he understood just what had happened here; the boy had fallen into trouble, but the insult was meant to Picard. "What is your name?"

The boy relaxed a little, if cautiously. "Ekenn."

"And you are to be my guide, am I right?"

"You and the ambassador, I was told. It will be my honor."

Indeed. Nadann had intended to excuse herself, to leave Picard in a better position to discuss the charts with Atann. *If* Atann had been here, as expected. Picard cast through the discourse since the previous night, messages passed and taken, with no direct communication between himself and Atann. "Atann," he said to the boy, "is not coming. Is that right?"

Ekenn shifted uneasily, recognizing the loaded nature of Picard's question, but not the reasons behind it. "No, he isn't," he said. "I will show you the kaphoora training. It was said that such a tour would mean more, coming from a student in training."

"And indeed it will," Picard said, though he exchanged a glance with Nadann and said, quietly wry, "We've been set up."

"That we have," Nadann said. "But there's only one thing for it, and that's to sally forth with delight, as though we could not have arranged things better ourselves. Are you up for that?"

Picard gave her a gentle snort. "Ambassador—Nadann—it is the least of my worries."

"I expect it is," she murmured, and then turned to the boy. "Ekenn, we entrust our experience here to you. Please show us those things you deem most important."

As Ekenn ducked his head in a quick bow and preceded them into the cool interior of the training rim, Picard forced his frustration aside and turned his attention toward learning as much as possible from what Atann had meant only as a daleura ploy. The one interesting thing he'd discovered about children, as ill at ease as he generally found himself when around them—when you put a question to them, they generally answered it.

Chapter Ten

As DAWN FINALLY TRICKLED DOWN to the bottom layers of the canopied forest, Riker dropped the tip of his club to the ground and leaned the handle against his leg while he wiped the sweat and grime from his face—careful not to use the sleeve stiff with dried sculper blood.

They'd survived the night. The sculpers were gone, slunk away after a series of attacks that never reached the intensity of the one during which Ketan was wounded. *No big surprise. Their bellies were full of their buddy.* And Ketan had survived, although his leg looked terrible. He said nothing, but Riker had no doubt he was in agony. *If only the med kits had Tsoran drugs.*

Gavare came up to him, silently offering one of the rations from Riker's pack along with the water bottle; together they stood and regarded their surroundings as the details emerged with daylight. Ragged-looking Tsorans—and human, Riker thought, knowing he looked no better—moving around a battered little area of trampled foliage, dying fires, depleted firewood . . .

They'd given their all to survive, each of them. But Gavare—Riker gave him a second look. Gavare actually looked *better* than he had. More alert, more deliberate in his movements. "Your head feeling better?"

Gavare gave a short gesture, one Riker took as affirmative. He didn't look at Riker as he spoke, but he did take a quick glance over his shoulder to see if the others were paying any attention. "I heard what you said last night. To Akarr."

"I was out of line," Riker said. Out of line, but not sorry; it came through in his voice.

"Akarr," Gavare started, and hesitated, chewing on his own sticky ration bar—a smelly concoction Riker was glad not to share—and taking his time to swallow. "Akarr is young. He does not understand. He has been pushed to this before his time. He will be a great leader, if we can keep him alive through this. A great leader."

Pushed? But Riker didn't ask, and he wouldn't have had the chance, for Gavare turned away, leaving him the outcast that he was.

He finished up his own ration bar and could have done with five more, but knew better than that. They'd heard the *Collins* arrive . . . and if he knew Worf, the tactical officer would strike out on their trail as soon as it was light enough to do so. The smart thing to do would be to turn around and head back, but he had the feeling he wouldn't get that concession from Akarr.

The second best thing . . . stall. Keep them here long enough to allow Worf to find them. Once they had a working shuttle on their hands, Akarr might well insist on trying to complete his kaphoora, but that was something they could settle later. Later, when that shuttle sat snugly around them, sheltering the wounded from the Legacy's creatures and putting some of the decisions back into Starfleet hands.

Not, however, a moment he would take for granted until it actually occurred. So for now, a single ration bar would do it. He tossed the biodegradable wrapper into the glowing ashes of the fire pit and began the job of searching out recoverable trank darts.

Riker wasn't sure how many tranks the Tsorans had used; he *was* sure that he'd never stake his own life on the effectiveness of the things. Of course, they were short-range—very short-range—and it had been dark and confusing during the night's attacks . . . but he didn't know of a single animal that had gone down from a trank, or even been deterred by it. He was beginning to wonder if the little guns might not make better hand clubs than anything else.

A glint of bright metal—the short body of one of the tranks—caught his eye, and he winnowed it out from the torn and crushed leaves that half covered it. Almost, he didn't take a second look. But something compelled him, and he held it up before his eyes, examining the shiny barrel, the short, primitive needle delivery system.

The blood-tipped needle delivery system.

This dart hadn't missed; it hadn't hit thick fur and failed to penetrate. This dart had found its mark and been dislodged . . . but none of the sculpers had fallen here last night. None of them had fallen anywhere within the bounds of the firelight, and as far as Riker knew, the sculper he'd injured had been the only one to go down at all.

Dart in hand, he returned to the cave, and found the Tsorans in the middle of an intense conversation, with which the Universal Translator struggled.

"Morning . . . part of the day to travel," Rakal said, looking at Gavare for confirmation, which he received in the form of a short gesture. "We can't afford to waste it."

"Travel in which direction?" Riker said from the cave entrance, not bothering to ease into the issue. "Worf will be looking for us."

Akarr snuffled rudely at him. "So you say. What if the shuttle we heard last night also crashed? What if your *Worf* is dead? We could be killing ourselves, too, if we backtrack now."

"There was nothing wrong with that shuttle's engines." Riker jammed his water bottle back into his pack, made sure the rain jacket was on top, where he'd need it this afternoon—and stuck the dart into a side pocket as an afterthought. "If we move on, we'll be moving away from safety."

"If we go back, we'll be moving away from safety," Akarr countered, with just as much certainty.

"What is it?" Riker asked. "Do you get more *points* if you get out of this in the hardest possible manner?"

"Do not presume to mock our ways," Akarr snarled, and this time all the Tsorans turned their challenge-gazes on him—all but Ketan, who was simply too miserable. Even Gavare, the only Tsoran who had offered Riker any small degree of respect—in fact, Gavare most of all, his gaze not only hard but his lip lifted in a gesture of snarl.

Riker took a deep breath. "My intent is not to mock your ways." *Well, maybe it was, but at least it got your attention.* "Just because you don't push your courage to the obvious limit doesn't mean you don't have it, Akarr. Courage can mean facing that of which you're most afraid. It looks to me like you're *afraid* of returning to the museum in a manner in which it looks like you've been rescued."

"He doesn't *need* to be rescued," Gavare snapped. "None of us do."

"Rescuing you is not why Worf is here," Riker said. Word games. How he hated them. "He's here to replace the faulty transportation."

Word games . . . but it got their attention.

"You've already done more than any before you— even those on their tenth kaphoora," Takan said thoughtfully to Akarr. "It should be enough."

Enough for what?

"Not without a trophy," Akarr responded. But he looked over at Ketan.

"There's still time for that," Rakal said, giving Riker a hard look, one that said *stay out of this.*

Riker was glad to, although he couldn't help an inner observation that there was bound to be plenty of opportunity for further contact with trophy beasts on a walk back to the shuttle, given their experience so far. As if to reinforce the thought, the clattering cry from the day before echoed above them, starting out in one place, ending in another entirely. They'd never identified that cry, Riker recalled uneasily.

Gavare gestured at Ketan. "Ketan needs a litter; he cannot walk on that leg. Once we have made that, we can act on the decision you make."

"Attend to it." Akarr's echoing gesture seemed casual, but he caught each of his guards in a hard stare, holding them that way until each twisted his head to bare a flash of throat.

The Tsorans dispersed, leaving Riker to watch Ketan against any morning activity. Gavare left last, giving Riker a parting look that would have been hard to interpret had it been coming from a familiar human face; Riker couldn't make much of it from a Tsoran.

Until he realized that Gavare had accomplished just exactly what Riker had hoped for—a delay. And Akarr's dignity, still intact. Gavare hadn't abandoned him, hadn't turned on him. He'd gone at the problem from a Tsoran direction.

Fine by Riker. Whatever it took to get the job done. If he had to play the role of the bad guy . . . why, he'd find some way to relish it.

With this bunch, that wouldn't be hard.

"Jean-Luc, what are you and your people up to?" The admiral's tone was slightly suspicious, her face impatient, even in miniature on the screen in Picard's ready room. "We don't have time for shuttle malfunctions, we don't have time for diplomatic tap-dancing with the Tsorans. Haven't you read your own chief medical officer's report on the projected Ntignano fatalities? This is a serious situation!"

"And I can assure you, Admiral Gromek, I'm taking it quite seriously. I have personnel down and missing in an intensely dangerous environment, and I take that seriously, as well." No real news from La Forge at last contact, either—Worf was still gone, and the communications problem still unresolved. "I'm acquainted with Dr. Crusher's report, and I receive constant updates on the status of the Ntignano sun. But the Tsorans are . . . difficult. We're doing our best to draw them out, but frankly . . ."

"Don't mince words—you're only wasting my time."

Picard shrugged. So be it. "They don't want to come out and play, Admiral."

Admiral Gromek stared at him, her face gone stiff with disbelief. "Did I hear you correctly, Captain? *They don't want to come out and play?*"

"That's the gist of it," Picard confirmed. "They're stonewalling our attempts even to open conversation about the charts. Their excuse is the situation on Fandre, but frankly, I think that's all it is—an excuse. They like being in the position of having something we want. They'd like to prolong that situation as long as possible."

"We don't have time to stroke their egos over this," Gromek said. "Figure out how to get their attention, Captain Picard, and then *get those charts.*"

"Understood," Picard said, and nodded, holding position until the screen blanked out. Then he pivoted away from the desk to go look at the rippling stars. *Understood, by damn.* Better than either the admiral or Atann would be pleased with, no doubt—thanks to Ekenn and the tour, and the chance to absorb a great deal of daleura in action.

But first . . . the web-probe project. He'd expected a report from Barclay and Duffy before this. And since he hadn't gotten one . . . this was one project he wanted to check out in person.

Picard found Barclay hunched over a schematic on deck nine, occupying a cartography work alcove, frowning deeply and utterly unaware of his entrance. As he hesitated, searching for the right moment to speak without sending the skittish diagnostics engineer across the room, Duffy came charging in from the direction of the torpedo launch bays.

"The launch log shows everything went—" he said, and faltered to a stop. "Captain!"

Barclay jolted upright. "Captain!"

"Lieutenant Duffy, Lieutenant Barclay," Picard said evenly. "You were saying?"

Duffy completed his entrance in a much more restrained manner. "I was just checking the launch logs. Didn't want to check them through the system, because that would be traceable, and we're trying to keep a low profile."

"I appreciate that. Is there some problem?"

Duffy looked at Barclay, and Barclay looked at Duffy, and finally Barclay said, "Well, you see, Captain, we're trying to—that is, we need to . . . well, yes."

"Yes, there's a problem," Picard confirmed in question, never quite sure when Barclay started to ramble.

"I'm sure we can handle it," Duffy said. "Lieutenant Commander La Forge's new program is a work of art, Captain. It's just that—"

"I'm sure," Barclay interrupted firmly—and then stopped short, as though he'd startled himself, "I'm *fairly* certain, I mean, that, uh, given time—"

"Time," Picard said, "is the one thing we don't have. If I didn't make that plain enough before, let me do so now. Whatever the problem, gentlemen, I suggest you address it."

"Just a minor adjustment in the probe synch tracking," Duffy said. "I still think it happened in the launch. We'll take care of it, Captain. Right away."

"See that you do," Picard said, giving them each a hard look. And, turning to stride out of engineering, reminding himself that Geordi La Forge had placed his trust in these two men. He would have to do the same.

And move on to other problems. "Picard to Data."

"Yes, Captain?"

"Mr. Data, please contact Atann's estate. Don't waste time trying to raise Atann himself, but see if you can determine if he's within earshot."

Moments after Data's acknowledgment, Picard sat at his desk to face one of Atann's many social secretaries.

"Captain," the Tsoran started, before Picard was even

fully seated. "It is always a pleasure to speak with you. The ReynKa, however, is unavailable—"

"It doesn't matter," Picard said, interrupting with startling rudeness. Startling to a Tsoran of this one's daleura, in any event, which got just the results Picard wanted—a moment of stunned silence, which he wasted no time filling. "We need to talk to the ReynKa. The ReynKa has made himself unavailable to us despite a stated commitment to the negotiations that brought us here, and our own good-faith efforts to fulfill the favors we offered to his son. Our patience is at an end. Therefore, we will make the ReynKa available to us in our own way."

"I—I don't understand—"

"No, you wouldn't. Let me explain. Each time we beam someone up with our transporters, as we have done with your ReynKa, our transporter system makes a record of that individual's molecular pattern. With that molecular pattern, we can search for, find, and beam up anyone who's been aboard the *Enterprise.*" Picard didn't elaborate on the time involved in carrying out such a procedure with a population the size of Aksanna's. *Need to know* information, and the Tsorans definitely didn't. "We have every intention of prevailing upon the ReynKa in just this manner. However . . ." and he let the word trail off most thoughtfully.

"However . . . ?" the secretary obligingly repeated, a bit of a squeak in his under-purr.

"We are not unmindful of the undignified position in which this would place your ReynKa. The purpose of this communication is to offer him the choice to make the beam-up arrangements himself."

Silence. The Tsoran simply stared at him, his under-purr filling the silence as its squeaky quality intensified, until his gaze darted off to the side and he said, suddenly and so quickly his words spilled out over one another, "Pleasestandby."

The viewscreen filled with the official Tsoran seal of orange, red, and purple, a complex thing full of glyphs and images. Picard blinked and looked away, but a smile lurked around the corners of his mouth, and he didn't expect to wait long.

He didn't.

The Tsoran returned, cleared his throat, glanced off-screen once, and said, "As it happens, ReynKa Atann has just contacted me with a request to arrange boarding. He considers it convenient that this seems to be a good time for you."

"It is indeed convenient," Picard said, keeping his expression neutral. "I have great expectations for our next conversation."

If only the ReynKa knew.

"Tk-tk-tk-tk-tk-tk-tk!"

Now, there was a sound to brighten anyone's day. Whatever it was.

Whatever it *was,* Riker didn't like it. And it was getting closer.

"Doesn't anything ever *sleep* in this place?" he muttered.

Akarr heard him, and offered a grim smile—his teeth covered, but a mocking look in his eye. "If it were easy, it wouldn't earn so much daleura," he said. "The harder it is, the better for me."

Riker eyed him a moment. "And just why *is* that?"

Startled out of his posturing, Akarr fumbled around like any teenager caught off his guard. "It's just the way it is," he managed, after a moment of looking for words.

A simple enough answer, if it had been simple for

Akarr to come up with. But that he'd had to search so hard to find those words that said so little . . .

"I don't think so," Riker said. "The prime kaphoora is meant to be hard . . . not impossible. It's meant to challenge you, *not* kill you."

"As if you'd know anything about it." Akarr watched as Rakal and Takan returned to the clearing, moving warily and dragging two long and reasonably straight lengths of flexible vine.

Not, Riker noted, vine with thorns or sticky sap, though he had to wonder what this particular plant might have in store for them. "I know enough." He tried to keep his voice neutral, to dampen his naturally assertive manner—a manner this environment had done nothing but reinforce. "I can read. Do you really think I'd be a party to this expedition, even just as pilot, without knowing some details? I've seen enough data to know that fatalities are unheard of, and serious injuries are rare—your minimal med kit speaks to those facts. It seems everyone else has had better luck using the tranks than we have."

"There is always one," Akarr said in a low voice, words which didn't quite make sense on their own.

Riker didn't try to clarify them. He waited.

"One person that historians remember, one person whose deeds can't be surpassed. We had one such on Tsora, before we hunted out our kaphoora species there. An ancestor of mine. My father, Atann, is named for him. There are others—those who excelled in dueling before it was outlawed, those in the past who led their warriors to victory against the face of great odds. They made their names stand out against all the others . . . they secured their places in society. And in history."

"I've got news for you," Riker said, still of the feeling

that something had gone unsaid. "Plenty of times, the historians write history how it suits them."

Akarr looked away from his men to give Riker a hard stare. "You mock us again."

"No." Riker drew his tired frame up, an emphasis for his words as he looked into the cave; Takan shifted restlessly, the dark purple of his blood seeping to the surface of the bandages around the sculper bites. "I think you hunt for impossible honors, and your men are paying the price. In my world's history, we do not honor leaders who earn their . . ."—well, why not use the word—"*daleura* this way."

"Words that might matter to me if you had any true concept of what daleura *is*." Akarr gave a dismissive sniff. Through talking to the outcast, apparently.

Didn't matter. Riker walked away from the cave with more information than he'd had a moment earlier. He knew that something drove Akarr beyond normal expectations for a kaphoora, and he knew it probably had something to do with a Tsoran named Takarr, whoever that was. He knew—Akarr's *own* men knew—that it was affecting Akarr's judgment, and that it would continue to do so.

And that they had no true recourse. They wanted to survive—but they had to do so in a way that allowed them to live afterward, as well, and Tsoran discipline for mutiny and insurgence was harsher than any Federation penalty.

"*Tk-tk-tk-tk-tk-tk-tk!*"

So close that Riker instinctivly ducked this time, though he saw nothing. It was overhead . . . that meant not a sholjagg, not a sculper . . . presumably not the snake-thing he'd run into earlier. And fast-moving, too fast—looking up, he snapped his head around to follow the sound. Still seeing nothing.

And then there they were. Black, darting between the

trees, coming down for a quick strafing run on the newly created miniature clearing. Akarr stood in the cave mouth, staring . . . squinting up at them with no sign of recognition on his face. Riker took a step forward and then stopped, having no idea what to do in response to the flock. It moved like a school of fish, changing direction as one entity, swift and agile and hard to follow as it flashed behind high leaves at one altitude and reappeared only a short distance later at a totally different altitude. "What . . . ?" Riker said, confusion finding its way out of his mouth, and his grip tightened on the *bat'leth*—almost a part of his hand at this point—but he didn't know what it could do against anything so small and quick as the members of this flock. Reptilian? Avian? They reminded him of streamlined miniature pterodactyls.

And then the flock was upon them, in a rush of air over leathery wings, no longer *tk-tk-tk*'ing, but making horrible hacking sounds that immediately brought Spot's unfortunate hairball incident to Riker's mind. And just as quickly, Rakal and Takan were down, writhing in the depleted woodpiles; Takan screamed and babbled, clearly more seriously affected as they both batted and clawed at themselves, as if trying to brush off—

Spitting. The things were *spitting*.

Spitting something as nasty as it gets, and the trailing members of the flock drew up short and reversed course in what might have made a perfect hammerhead stall in an aircraft.

Coming back for another run. Riker started a run of his own, dashing for the giant rubbery leaves still intact at the edge of their clearing; the *bat'leth* sliced a handful of them in one stroke, and he grabbed them as they fell, sprinting for the men Gavare was now trying to haul to the safety of the cave. "Here!" he bellowed, throwing the leaves—leaves almost as big as the average Tsoran torso, and thick enough—

Maybe they'd work. Maybe not.

"Tk-tk-tk-tk-tk-tk-tk!"

Gavare had to drop Takan in order to snatch the leaves, so Riker went for the fallen Tsoran, shoving the flexible shelter over him, trying to shield himself with another, crouched protectively over the writhing being— and here they came, shooting over the clearing in a flattening dive—

That noise again, the hairball noise; a gooey substance splashed to the earth beside him, and Riker grunted with surprise and shock as some landed on the back of his exposed arm. In an instant it turned to liquid fire, soaking through his uniform, eating at his skin; he jerked in reaction as a splatter worked into his shoulder blade. Beneath him, Takan's struggles slackened; above him, the flock sounded off again, coming around for another run.

Riker grabbed the trank gun from its holster within Takan's stiff hunting vest, and, digging his fingers into the leaf midvein to wield it before himself like a literal shield, he twisted around to meet them, firing the tranks point blank and close enough to see one of the creatures jerk back from the blow; several of them wheeled away from the flock.

And then the trank-gun chamber was empty and Riker was down to the *bat'leth* and a scored, floppy leaf, his arm burning so hot he thought he'd feel it forever— burning right through his skin and into his brain, scattering any useful thoughts far and wide. That the attack would return meant nothing to him—that was a concept, and agony was the only concept for which he had room.

He threw himself against the nearest tree like a bear

with an itch, mindlessly trying to rub the pain away; when two Fandreans grabbed him, one on either side, he didn't know or care who they were or how they got there, he just fought them. When a Klingon roar filled the air, he didn't care who'd made it; he'd already flung one Fandrean into a bush and was close to dislodging the other, all so he could throw himself back against that tree and rub the fire off, and keep rubbing even if he had to go all the way to the bone.

They shouted back and forth at one another, the first Fandrean charging back in to rejoin the second, and this time they pushed his back up against the massively wide trunk of the very tree he so savagely sought, trying to hold him there—*why?* wondered the still rational corner of mind, *why* and *who* and *how had they gotten here*—but it was a tiny spot indeed, and quickly chased away by the agony of the burning.

Still, for that moment, for that single instant, they kept him shoved tightly against the tree and in relative safety, even as the flock—no longer moving as one, but fractured and crisscrossing the clearing in random patterns—continued the attack. As several swooped past at Riker's head level, dark blurs of leathery movement, the Klingon roar sounded again, followed instantly by the *thunk* of heavy metal sinking into wood.

The impaled flyer drooped around a Klingon knife next to his head—close enough to brush his cheek—was finally enough to get Riker's attention, to create a break in his struggle. Enough of a break that the clever Fandreans somehow levered him around so his face pressed into smooth, lichen-covered wood as they took his very own shield, broke the leaf at the mid-rib, and glopped the sap all over his back.

Relief.

Instant relief.

And what an incredible . . . smell.

Riker closed his eyes and slowly unclenched his fingers from the tree, becoming aware of the wood jammed under his fingertips, sorting out the tingling pain of the burns from the actual process of the burning—now that that process had ceased. In the background, he heard the discharge of several trank guns, and then . . . quiet.

When he opened his eyes, it was to see Worf's face, much closer than he was accustomed to viewing those dark, craggily sculptured features. Worf jerked his knife from the tree and let the flyer slide to the ground as if it were inconsequential—as if just anyone could have pinned the thing in midflight, and had the confidence to do it centimeters from his ranking officer's face. "Are you all right, Commander?"

"All right," Riker said slowly, "is a relative thing." Slowly, he straightened, pushing himself away from the tree. "Compared to a few moments ago, I'm outstanding." Compared to the day before he'd first spoken to Akarr . . .

Carefully, he settled his shoulders back, rotating the injured arm. Perfectly functional, even if it didn't want to be, even if his body wanted to stagger away somewhere in shock. Then he eyed the scene around him— the discarded leaf, milked of all its pungent juices, and the two Fandreans, still straightening themselves out, wiping their hands off against the ground. Takan lay just exactly where Riker had left him, while Gavare and Akarr worked over Rakal at the mouth of the cave, a pile of flaccid, milked leaves beside them.

Of the flyers, there was little sign. The dead one at the base of this tree . . . the two flopped limply on either side of Takan. Tranked, Riker saw. He straightened his uniform and cleared his throat. "I wasn't expecting to see you quite this soon, Mr. Worf."

"We hurried," Worf said.

Riker took the statement in, mulled it over, and nodded. "I commend you for your hurry, Mr. Worf. In fact, I will downright worship your hurry if you still have a functioning shuttle to go along with it."

"The *Collins* is running low-tech and heavily shielded, sir, but it *is* running."

One of the Fandreans plucked the tranks from the two downed flyers and gently tossed the creatures into the woods.

"Giving them a chance to come back for another try?" Riker asked, easing over to join them at Takan's body— for there had been no mistake, not even as Riker fought the flyers away over the Tsoran, that Takan had died during the battle. Riker winced now to see him—his fur was patchy and matted, and the exposed skin beneath peeled back to muscle. Did his arm look like—? He brought it around, trying to see, and couldn't.

"We stopped the digestion in your arm, but it will need treatment," the Fandrean said. "And yes, we will give the skiks every chance to live. They have done nothing wrong here; this is their home, and they only hunt it as is their nature."

"This is Zefan," Worf said, somewhat belatedly. "He commands the Legacy rangers. He and Shefen volunteered to assist us."

"You have my gratitude," Riker said. "We can use the help—in case that's not obvious."

"What I don't understand," Worf said, "is why you left the *Rahjah* at all. It was perfectly good shelter—"

"I was outvoted, Mr. Worf. Let's leave it at that."

"Yes, sir," Worf said in the neutral tone he'd cultivated for those times when he really had quite a bit he might like to say after all. Riker recognized it well enough, and let it pass.

"Skiks, you called them." Riker looked back at the one by the base of the tree, and found it gone; sometime during their grim inspection of Takan, Akarr had taken it, and was quietly trimming its claws off. Riker, although admittedly fuzzy on the fine points of being Tsoran, had the feeling that it didn't quite count as an appropriate trophy.

On the other hand, if it made Akarr happy and expedited their return trip out of here, he didn't give a damn how badly the kid cheated.

"Yes," Shefen said, eyeing Akarr with distaste and then turning away. "The substance that wounded you and killed this Tsoran was a digestive poison. Most skik prey is half-digested before the flocks alight to feed."

"No need to worry about this particular flock," added Zefan. "It'll take several days before it re-forms. They're quite nervous creatures, really, and very social. This encounter, along with the loss of their flockmate, will slow them down for a while."

"Ah," Riker said, not quite trusting himself to say anything else at this point.

Gavare exited the cave to join them, warily eyeing the upper canopy—for while they'd created this small clearing at ground level, the trees closed in high above them to prevent any direct glimpse of the sky.

"They're gone," Riker told him. "For now. How are the others?"

"Rakal has serious wounds," Gavare said. "But he will live, thanks to you. We say thank you, also, for your efforts to save Takan."

"I'm sorry I couldn't," Riker said, glancing quickly at the body and away. *A horrible death.* He'd had just a taste of it, just enough to imagine what it might have been like. His own injuries now burned with a deep, strange heat, as though his body didn't even know how to process what had been done to it.

"He had already been fatally wounded before you reached him," Gavare said. "His family will honor this death, as will we."

"Better to worry about your survivor, now," Zefan said, blowing out his cheeks in a way that made Riker think there was real concern behind the words. "We must cover the wounds before the zetflies find him." He looked at Riker. "Yours, too, Commander. Unless you'd like to be eaten from the inside out."

"It wasn't one of my goals for the day, no."

Shefen gathered up several of the limp leaves and headed out of the clearing. "I'll be back with some isnat sap," he said. "It will be sufficient until we return to the shuttle."

Zefan nodded. "Excellent thinking." To Riker, he said, "We were lucky he returned from patrol in time to join us. Aside from myself, he is our most experienced ranger—and it's been too many seasons since I spent extended time in the Legacy."

"Believe me," Riker said, "I'm most grateful for *all* your help." Especially if it kept Akarr alive and zetflies from eating Riker himself from the inside out. He glanced back at the cave and said to Gavare, "Looks like we'll need two litters—unless Rakal can walk?"

"He says he can," Gavare said. "It would not be appropriate to make a litter until he says otherwise."

Delay now, delay later . . . it didn't make much difference. Riker turned to Worf, who stood off to the side slightly, his gaze roving over the clearing as if daring it to offer any more challenges. "I'm assuming Geordi reported our signal to the *Enterprise*," he said. "Has it affected negotiations?"

"It has put a stop to them," Worf said. He looked at Zefan, and cast a glance toward the cave to which Gavare had returned—but from which Akarr, skikless, approached—and hesitated. "I believe the engineering department has started a new project."

The high-speed drone charting Geordi had proposed. *Good.* Riker, too, eyed Akarr, as the Tsoran joined their small gathering. Even if they got Akarr out of this mess, the Tsorans were not likely to be pleased with the way things had gone, or impressed by the way Riker had spoken to Akarr.

Does it ever really get any easier? Guinan had asked him, after he'd said so confidently, *Nothing I can't handle.*

Define handle. Or, more important, define the priorities. Keep Akarr—and his ReynKa father—happy, or keep Akarr *alive* against odds made more impossible each time the young ReynTa made a decision? There was no way he'd do both, if keeping Akarr happy meant playing *follow the leader.*

You knew that the first time you argued with him. Quit second-guessing.

On the other hand, he'd have to explain himself, sooner or later.

"Commander Riker," Worf said, loudly—the kind of loud one would use when trying a second or third time to catch the attention of someone feebleminded.

"What *is* it?" Riker snapped, not pleased to be caught wandering. Not pleased to feel the pain of the burns intensify. He had a feeling he'd had what grace period there was to have, in those few moments of relief that Zefan and Shefen had provided with their leaf milk.

The stench, however, remained.

"Nothing," Worf said. "I was . . . momentarily concerned."

"No need," Riker said. He glanced at Akarr—who had so far remained silent, assessing the mood of the Fandreans, sizing up Worf—and decided to ask anyway, the question he'd been headed for before he distracted himself with inner dialogue. "How's the Ntignano situation?"

"Not good."

Details. That's what Riker loved about Worf . . . he never failed to cut through to the heart of a matter.

Shefen returned with the sap he'd collected, apologizing when Riker hissed with pain as he applied it. "Just do it," Riker muttered at him, as Zefan took the remainder of the sap to the cave.

Soon enough, they were back on the trail home, with Akarr strangely quiet about trophies, Ketan in a travois litter and Rakal limping along behind, and both Fandreans keeping a careful rear guard. Riker and Worf led the way out of default as opposed to plan, while Riker struggled to keep a sharp watch out for day predators— as for some reason, the image of tranked skiks falling out of the sky kept intruding on his thoughts. Finally the image faded, leaving him only with questions. He and Worf readily swapped point position again, *bat'leths* at the ready, retracing their trail out from the shuttle. "Watch the ground," Riker warned him at one point, and succinctly described the snake-thing, rueful that Takan's trank gun rode emptied in someone's pack, corroded by skik poison. The next time he came across one of those snake-things, he wanted more than a *bat'leth* in his hand.

"If we don't make faster progress, we'll miss the portal opening," Worf commented some time later. And then, later yet, when they were farther ahead of the rest of the party, "Captain Picard is most displeased at the deadlocked status of the negotiations. I believe he is attempting to reopen discussion, but Atann is—"

"Stubborn," Riker grunted, trying to summon energy he didn't have to maintain the pace, and intensely annoyed to feel his body fail him. Behind them, Shefen had picked up the end of the litter Gavare dragged, trying to speed the injured Tsoran's progress. "Like son, like father."

"Unless we return Akarr before the portal closes for its two-day recharge cycle, I don't see how the captain can accomplish negotiations with the ReynKa," Worf said, pausing momentarily to check movement to the side and catching up to Riker with several long strides. "At least, not in any time frame that will prove useful to the Ntignanos."

"Frankly, Mr. Worf," Riker said, too light-headed with exhaustion and pain to make any attempt at keeping up morale, "I don't see any way the captain can accomplish negotiations with these people if we *do* bring Akarr back. In any time frame."

Worf looked at him, seemed to consider and assess. "Things have not gone well."

"You don't know the half of it."

"I know enough," Worf said.

Chapter Eleven

Akarr thought again of the skik claws in his vest pocket. Thought unhappily of them.

They'd come from an animal he hadn't personally downed. In fact, despite the many opportunities, he hadn't tranked any of the various creatures the Legacy had thrown at them. Riker was the only one who'd been truly blooded on this kaphoora. Riker and the Klingon, who'd killed the skik.

They had weapons. Real weapons. The knives . . . the bat'leths . . .

Akarr wasn't allowed weapons, not by the rules. And neither should these humans have them . . . except some part of him wasn't altogether too sure he wasn't glad of it. They, then, bore the real responsibility for his safety.

Nothing had prepared him for the deep Legacy. No kaphoora training came near it.

Still, he'd survive. He might not have drawn blood,

but he'd kept the sculpers off, and unlike Riker, he'd stayed out of the way of the skiks.

Riker had been helping Akarr's own men.

Now, Akarr was glad that between the remnants of his uniform in the affected area and the gloppy sap, Riker's wounds were barely visible. Unlike Rakal's. Rakal's fur stuck out in gooey clumps—where there was any fur left at all—and the raw skin and exposed muscle showed plainly in color if not in detail, despite their sap coating. It was Rakal who slowed them now, prevented them from keeping pace with the two Federation officers; it was Rakal's grunts of effort filling Akarr's ears—though with never a complaint. In truth, Rakal needed a litter, but he'd refused it; he didn't want to waste time assembling it. Bad enough they had to carry Ketan.

But Akarr glanced ahead at Riker—barely visible ahead of them—and wondered if a truly good leader would have insisted on a litter for Rakal, anyway.

Too late to worry about that now. And the daleura of this kaphoora was so tangled, between the pitched battles they'd fought, the injuries they'd suffered, the sustained contact with the very creatures that most kaphoora participants had to track with care . . . He doubted that those who reckoned such intangibles would ever be able to straighten it out.

In which case, his brother Takarr still had the chance to establish a daleura dominance over Akarr when he went on his own prime kaphoora, despite all the unique factors their father had arranged for Akarr. Not that Takarr had the driving nature to excel so emphatically . . . but as this expedition itself proved, stranger things had happened. Of course Akarr had overridden his own shame to harvest the skik claws . . . he *must* have trophy.

But now, in a more objective moment, he knew those

skik claws represented as much hazard as victory, for there were those alive who knew exactly from where they'd come.

He'd take another trophy. Something more appropriate. Surely there'd be a chance before they returned to the shuttle, despite the waxing heat and the increasing midday somnolence of the predators. If only his own aim with the tranks—aim he'd been proud of at the training center—hadn't failed him here. Something about the strange light, or all the foliage—reaching leaves, grabby branches, drooping fronds—must be interfering with his aim.

Yes, that was it.

Ahead of him, Riker—on point—slowed. Worf moved close, but not so close that Akarr couldn't see Riker waver, reaching out for the nearest vine for support—a thorn vine; Akarr could see it from where he stood. Worf quickly pulled another vine within Riker's reach. Akarr waved the others to a stop and eased into earshot, surprised by a momentary pang of concern for Riker. Akarr generally thought of him as a profound annoyance and a blot on the kaphoora—for piloting them to a crash, for challenging Akarr's authority and daleura every chance he got—mighty sybyls, for simply not being the captain in the first place—but he'd somehow begun to think of him as a *stable* annoyance. One on which he could count to *be* annoying . . . and to swing that *bat'leth* around with vigor.

"We are close, now," Worf was telling Riker. "There are medicines aboard that will improve your situation. We have a med kit suitable for the Tsorans, as well; we can ease their pain. We simply chose to travel . . . light . . . in our pursuit of you."

"A wise decision," Riker said, sounding distracted.

Akarr suddenly realized Riker was simply trying to

stay on his feet. "We cannot carry *you*," he said, imagining the size of such a litter with some horror.

Worf turned an unreadable stare on him. "I could," he said, bluntly. Pointedly.

"It could affect your own survival," Akarr said, challenging not out of any great need, but to observe the reaction. To understand this humanoid culture, and why it would consider Riker fit for his rank after all the various weaknesses he'd shown Akarr. He was not at all bothered by the fact that Riker was within earshot. "Riker has earned no great daleura here. Why would you imperil yourself for him?"

Worf's expression changed. His reply was even and low-key, although Akarr discerned that this took much effort. He had the instant revelation that Worf had pegged him as an idiot, and that there was therefore no point in displaying anger.

"A leader must do more than put himself in a position to . . . earn daleura. He must make the difficult decisions that no one else wants to make. He must think always of his crew, and not just of his glory." Worf looked down from his considerable height and added, "He would do the same for me."

His words struck no resonance in Akarr. "You make as little sense as he does. He has done nothing since our arrival but interfere with me. How does this suit your image of a leader who inspires such risk?"

A flicker of humanoid annoyance crossed the Klingon's face, all the more noticeable for his formidable brow. "I am not in the habit of repeating myself. And your questions are irrelevant. As I said, we are close."

"I don't understand." Akarr looked around them. It seemed obvious to him that they'd simply followed the same path in return as they'd used on their way out—

they'd even passed the area where Riker's snake-thing had torn up the jungle in its angry, wounded thrashing. "We haven't even reached the crash path yet."

Worf looked up at the trees, where shadowed movement caught Akarr's eye as well. "When we first found the downed shuttle, I landed there. The *Rahjah* was too damaged to fly again, so I determined which direction you'd taken and relocated to the end of the crash path. That is the only distance we must go."

"Worf, I like the way you think," Riker said with a crooked grin; it annoyed Akarr simply because he couldn't properly interpret it. He'd come to understand the varying intensities of the human smile, but was this one of them? Or was it something else entirely? Riker lacked the arrogant-looking posture he often assumed with such a partial grin . . . but then, Akarr had never quite interpreted *that,* either.

"After I found the opened grave, I had reason to believe it was imperative to catch up with you as soon as possible." Worf's gaze flicked from one tree to another; Akarr couldn't see just why, but he warily aligned himself to have the same field of view. The others, who had gladly stopped at his command to rest, moved a little closer to them; one of the Fandreans came up to join them. Then Worf's words caught up with him.

"Open grave?" he said. "We left no open grave."

"I believe that is the point," Worf said.

"It probably took a sholjagg to move the rocks we saw," Zefan said, inviting himself into the conversation and ignoring Akarr's glare. "From the looks of the shuttle interior, the crash is what killed him?"

"I'm afraid so," Riker said.

"It is amazing that anyone was able to walk away

from an engine-failure crash in this terrain," Worf said, giving Akarr another one of those . . . looks.

Akarr began to realize that the Klingon did little of his most essential communicating with words. "If you want to hear words of praise for your Commander Riker, you won't. Am I supposed to be pleased that he managed to land an inferior piece of equipment, stranding us here in the Legacy and injuring my men? I am not."

"I take it then that you will not find it necessary to join us aboard the *Collins* when we leave?" Worf returned his attention to the trees, apparently not concerned with Akarr.

This cool adeptness with Tsoran insults surprised Akarr, and the hair on his arms rose no matter how he willed it down—just as he couldn't squelch the trickle of anxiety the Klingon had created. They wouldn't leave him here in the Legacy. They *couldn't*.

Another glance at Worf's expression made Akarr think that maybe the Klingon *could*.

But Riker wouldn't do it. Riker had already demonstrated how he felt about leaving men behind, about doing less than his best for those in his hunting party. Or away team, as he generally called it.

Still. Safest not to answer that one. To just let it fade away.

"Commander," Worf said, glancing at Riker, and then at the wounded Tsorans ranging behind Akarr, "if you are ready, I think we should move on."

"Yes," Riker said. "I saw it."

Saw what? Akarr almost asked, but stopped himself just in time. It wouldn't do to admit that he hadn't yet seen whatever the two Federation officers were worried about. Then a startling little inner voice said, *Which is more important, saving daleura or being prepared for danger?* So startling, in fact, that he failed to respond when Riker stood away from the vine and straightened his shoulders, drawing them back in the *ready for anything* stance Akarr had come to expect from him.

"Akarr?" Riker said. "Are your people ready to move? We've got an arborata on our tails—"

Akarr shook off the internal conflict, deciding that it was merely the unwelcome influence of Riker himself, and the man's unceasing hubris—so certain he knew how things should be handled, especially when it came to the welfare of Akarr's men. "We're ready," he said, without looking back. At least now he knew what to watch for—as if anyone ever really saw an arborata before it was ready to be seen.

At least, from what trophied kaphoora hunters had told him. Although now he suddenly wondered if those trophied hunters had ever actually seen an arborata. None of them had ever been in this deep. Where they merely repeating the same Legacy wisdom back and forth at one another?

It occurred to him that were he one of them, he would do the same without thinking. In that moment, his world perspective gave a sudden, unwelcome lurch.

"Akarr!" Riker shouted, grabbing at his side as if he expected to find some weapon there, his gaze riveted above and behind Akarr as Worf came crashing back through the undergrowth. *Arborata!* Akarr whirled, drawing his trank gun—and found the arborata swooping down so closely that he squeaked—*squeaked!*—and fell on his bottom. But he didn't lose the trank gun or his aim, and when the creature whooshed close overhead in the nadir of its dive, he squeezed the release—and for once, he saw the dart thunk home.

The arborata flapped its scaled, triangular wings and disappeared into the trees.

He couldn't have been any closer. He couldn't have been any more on-target. He *hadn't* missed, not this time—

"Here it comes again," Riker said, his voice rising into a warning shout as the thing increased speed, its barbed and prehensile tail lashing, preparing to strike— looking like a giant skik as it skimmed the air, tilting to maneuver with ease between the trees. It set itself at the group of wounded, and Gavare threw himself over Ketan's litter as the Fandrean rangers both went to their knees, trank guns braced and aimed. Two almost inaudible *phuts* of noise, and the arborata veered off. Moments later, it folded into a limp black arrangement of long-scaled wings, floppy scooped ears, and drooping tails, crashing down through the undergrowth until it hit the ground with an audible thump.

Riker started after it.

"Commander!" Worf said, but hesitated at the look Riker gave him. Even humans, it seemed, had their daleura ranking. "With respect, sir, our priority is to return to the shuttle."

"Humor me," Riker said shortly, intent enough on the arborata to draw new energy from . . . somewhere. "It's more important than you think. Get the others moving— I'll catch up."

And Akarr, though he wasn't sure why, followed along behind Riker, Zefan in his wake. On the run and panting-hot, Akarr located Riker more by sound than by sight, batting giant leaves away from his face and ducking—at the very last moment—a huge sticky mess of an insect nest that seemed to materialize at eye level. Even as he straightened, he came upon Riker, crouching over the limp body of the arborata.

He hadn't realized it was quite that *big*.

But its size didn't seem to be what had Riker's attention. There, buried in its plump breast, was Akarr's dart—quite distinguishable from the Fandrean dart lodged in the muscle of one leathery gliding wing. Riker glanced up at him. "You might as well take trophy from this one before it comes around. It should have been yours."

"I don't understand," Akarr said stiffly, though he was suddenly very much afraid that he did. "The creature didn't go down with my dart. It's not any more my trophy than—"

Than the skik claws he'd already taken.

"No?" Riker raised an eyebrow at him, a purely human gesture that Akarr associated with the wry Tsoran response of perking tightly cupped, streamlined ears. And then as Zefan joined them—without so much as a gesture of intent or request—Riker appropriated the trank gun from Akarr and shot himself in the thigh.

"Damn," he said, hissing at the pain he'd brought himself—but still looking like he'd done exactly what he meant to do.

"Commander Riker!" Zefan snapped, his under-purr as harsh and angry as Akarr had ever heard in a Fandrean. "If you think we have the luxury of *carrying* one who could otherwise walk—"

And then he stopped, for by then it was evident enough that Riker wouldn't need to be carried anywhere. "I don't understand."

"Neither did I, at first," Riker said. "I thought that the sholjagg's fur was too thick . . . and after that, that the Tsorans had simply missed the sculpers, in the dark. But Akarr's people are well trained, and clear-thinking in a fight. And I nailed one of those skiks myself. I saw it jerk when the trank hit. So if we weren't missing the targets—"

"Then the tranks were no good," Zefan finished. "You couldn't have found another way to test your theory?"

Riker pulled the dart out with a grimace. "Nothing came to mind. Nothing we could be sure of. I already had *that*." He nodded at the arborata.

"None of the tranks," Akarr said slowly, "are any good." Not just one of them, or a small percentage of them. None of them.

"You might as well take trophy," Riker said, standing and nudging the black-scaled arborata with one foot. "You've earned it. You've probably earned it many times over—you *and* your men." He was angry, as deeply angry as Akarr had ever seen him despite Akarr's own knack for clashing fangs with him—and it took Akarr an instant to realize that this time, the anger was on his own behalf.

"Someone," Riker said, "wanted you dead."

Treachery? Akarr rejected the thought in an instant, too aware of what would happen to his father were such a thing to be known. Only an ineffective ReynKa allowed such treachery to develop. Only a weak ReynKa allowed it within his walls. Akarr mustered a glare. "You will say nothing of this."

And then his mind's eye flashed back to the night before his departure, the kaphoora fete he'd had. How pleased he'd been that Takarr, younger by several years, had not displayed any of the poor humor so common to his presence at Akarr's daleura events. Takarr? He'd always wanted more than his life allotted, in a sullen way, even though the second son of the ReynKa lacked for nothing. Nothing but a few final points of daleura, and the chance to earn a place in history.

But the system held choice. The ReynKa would pick one of them over the other. Although the traditional choice raised the older up over the younger, Atann himself was by no means tied to tradition. If Takarr wanted to rule, he had had—and still had—many legitimate opportunities to prove his worth over Akarr.

Riker made an impatient gesture, indicating the out-of-sight men who waited for them at the shuttle. "What do you mean, say nothing of it? And leave your men thinking their own tranks are of any use whatsoever?"

"Shefen and I can replenish your tranks with our own," Zefan said. "They are interchangeable. But we must have a reason for doing so."

"The truth would work nicely," Riker said shortly. He gave the useless dart a look of disdain, and Zefan took it from him, tucking it away in the section of his pack meant for carrying out disposables.

"It is *not* the truth," Akarr said, his fur rising. He glared up at Riker. "It is not the *whole* truth. Who has done this and why . . . these things, we don't know. Until we *do* know, partial truths could hurt those who have no part in it." His mother, if Takarr was implicated. She would take any treachery on her younger son's part badly, and Akarr would not have her thinking it until he knew it was true.

"Fine," Riker said, exasperated and cranky. "Zefan, tell them that you suspect the animals have adapted to the Tsoran trank chemicals, and until the Fandreans can perform tests to confirm or negate this, it's best to use Fandrean darts. Tell them you meant to offer the darts as soon as you caught up with us in the first place, but that the skik attack distracted you."

Zefan stared, caught in surprise at the change in tactics. Then he moved his hand in Fandrean agreement. With a hint of admiration, he said, "That's good." He smiled, teeth covered. "That's very good."

As one, they turned to Akarr, waiting for his reaction.

"Akarr?" Riker prompted. "You have to tell them *something*—"

Akarr found himself caught up in fear of the implications of the useless tranks, envy at the way even the Fandreans responded to Riker—he hadn't failed to see how even some of his own men admired the human, oh no!—and pure turmoil over how to proceed. His hair stood on end, his lips drew back from his teeth—

And Riker did the one thing Akarr never expected. The one thing that got his attention and got it fast. He dropped to one knee, lower than Akarr, and twisted his head to the side and back, exposing his throat.

Akarr's flaring temper deserted him, a response to the submission display all but hardwired into the Tsoran system. Confused, he could only stare—not a daleura stare, just a blank look.

"We'll handle it your way," Riker said, his voice strained by the angle of his neck, "as long as your men are protected." Slowly, while Akarr recovered his composure, Riker got to his feet.

"Your idea is acceptable," Akarr said, finally recovering his composure, and finding himself acutely aware that Riker had not submitted out of fear . . . not out of lack of courage. Out of wisdom. "Although they are probably to the shuttle by now."

"There's something to that," Riker said. "Take your trophy before it wakes up, and let's join them."

But Akarr turned his back on the arborata. He would not take trophy from that which had brought him awareness of betrayal.

"I don't like the looks of *this*." La Forge frowned at the Fandrean version of a padd, on which was displayed the most recent series of yet-unexplained Legacy shield surges. "I've got confidence in the modified shields the *Collins* is carrying, but I sure didn't want to put them to *this* sort of test."

Yenan reclaimed the display and stared mournfully at it. "Since you're working on the communications problem, I've released my best engineers to apply themselves to the shield surges. I regret to say they have not yet suggested any solutions."

La Forge nodded at the displayed chart. "They've got plenty of data to work with after *that*. When did you say it happened?"

"Early this morning."

"And no way to know if it affected the *Collins,* because I don't have *my* part solved yet, either," La Forge said. He raised his voice slightly, glad for his connection to the *Enterprise,* and for Data's unfailing pattern of check-ins. "You getting this, Data?"

"Everything but the padd display, although I can infer its contents." Data paused, then added in a practiced tone, "It is just peachy."

"How's that?"

"Another twentieth-century colloquialism. I am drawing from a wide range of years. The point is not to see how familiar people are with any single time period, but to get a general sense of how much of the language lingers from generation to generation—despite the usual loss of the origin of each phrase."

"Ah," La Forge said, for the moment distracted—and willing to be distracted—by Data's latest foray into the nature of being human. "Okay, but have you considered—"

"For instance, do you know the origin of the word *okay?*"

La Forge hesitated. "Well, no," he said finally. "I never thought about it."

"In 1839, it became common to facetiously spell 'all correct' as *o-l-l k-o-r-r-e-c-t.* Later this was shortened to the initials *O.K.,* which eventually became the word *okay.*"

"Which brings me back to my original point. I was *going* to say—okay, but have you considered that your previous, um . . . explorations into language have exposed the crew to an unusual amount of this sort of variety in phrase and language usage?"

There was momentary silence from the other end—Data, in his quarters, most likely sitting at his complex computer science station with Spot in his lap and a puzzled look on his face. "You are suggesting that I have skewed my sample population. In essence, created my own red herring. A phrase, by the way, which originated in the late seventeenth century, and which refers to the practice of using smoked herring as a method to draw hounds off a trail."

"No kidding," La Forge said, smiling a quirky one-sided smile. Yenan looked at him in utter incomprehension, but La Forge didn't make any effort to explain, and the Fandrean moved off to present the surge figures to his engineers. Up until now, things had been altogether too intense in the Legacy's underground warren of communications panels. "That's what I'm suggesting, all right."

"I shall have to consider it," Data allowed. "Not that I have much time to devote to this project, at the moment. Things are about to come to a head here."

"Why? What's going on?" La Forge asked. Once again sitting on the floor rather than trying to adjust to Fandrean chair ergonomics, he leaned forward and prodded idly at the open communications panel before him, waiting for an idea to strike—as they so often did when he let one part of his mind talk with Data while the other considered the matter at hand. Then he stopped short and said, "Wait. You did it again, didn't you? That was a good one—I'll bet most people wouldn't even notice it."

"You are the first to do so, and I suspect your awareness is heightened by this very conversation. The phrase dates all the way back to the 1340s, and references boils, and the way they—"

"That's all I need to know about *that* one," La Forge said hastily. "What is going on?"

"I am not sure." Data hesitated. "I would have to say . . . I think Captain Picard is up to something."

La Forge thought that if he asked, he could probably get the history behind *up to something,* but decided against it. "Up to what?"

"Unknown," Data said. "The ReynKa is apparently coming back on board; it is a sudden development. And Captain Picard looks . . . I would have to define his expression as *determined.*"

"That's good news, then," La Forge said, by way of a prompt. "Is the probe web still functioning?"

There was enough hesitation that La Forge knew the answer before Data finally offered it. "There have been some data positioning synchronization problems," he said. In the background, Spot's short, querying *mrrrp?* came through. "Lieutenant Barclay appears to have pinpointed the problem and solved it, but the delay was unfortunate. By the time we have a rudimentary chart from the results, many Ntignanos will have died. Still, I believe it is our current fallback."

"Well, then, *determined* is good. With any luck, Captain Picard *is* up to something." He looked again at the open panel before him. "I wish *I* were up to something. You know, when I went to sleep late last night, I really expected to wake up with the solution to this mess waiting for me. Like a side dish at breakfast."

"It is possible that you have a hole in your head." Data sounded pleased with that one, though Geordi heard him only in distraction, thinking about the probes and his own problems here on planet.

"I've considered meshing frequencies," he said, "and fine-point broadbanding transmissions—similar to what Commander Riker did—and I've explored pulling the interwoven shields apart separately—putting a little air between the layers, so to speak—to allow a transmission to weave its way through. But none of those have any real promi—Data, what did you say?"

"It was an attempt at humor, Geordi. I was implying that you had actually thought of the solutions, but that you had lost them again."

"Yeah, yeah," La Forge said impatiently, his inner eye searching frantically for the elusive image that had flashed by at Data's words. "But what did you *say?*"

After a short hesitation, Data told him, *"It is possible that you have a hole in your head.* The origin of the phrase is somewhat murky—"

"No, no, don't you see? That's it!" The image settled before his mind's eye, the opaque forcefield, the opening portal . . . the huge whine of the shield generators, choking down power, limiting the portal to so few moments of existence, to so few openings at all. They'd already gone past one of the timed openings for Worf's return; he had only two, and then everyone on the *Collins* would have to wait through the recharge cycle.

"What is *it?*" Data asked. He must have stood, because Spot made an aggrieved noise and padded away; almost immediately, La Forge heard the crunching of feline supplement. Number 221, if he remembered correctly.

"My idea *is* the hole in my head," Geordi said, up on

his knees and disappearing into the comm panel, going to set everything back to rights, to the way it was before he started poking around. "Gotta go, Data—I'll let you know if this works!"

"Good-bye, Geordi. If I see Captain Picard, I will inform him that you are up to something."

La Forge grinned into the dark recesses of the comm panel innards. *Up to something.* That he was, and he hoped it was something big.

Picard stood outside a deck eleven turbolift, down the corridor and around the corner from the holodeck where Atann waited for him, putting on a display of impatience and disgust at this new interruption. Picard himself was not eager to delay the impending confrontation, but when requested in stellar cartography—only two decks and a few corridor turns away—he'd deemed it worth the trouble.

"Be quick about it," he said shortly, sweeping into the same work alcove where he'd earlier found Duffy and Barclay at work. Startled, they looked up from the console as one—and their expressions put him right on alert. Triumph. Even on Barclay's face, totally overwhelming his usual hesitation. "Good news?"

"We figured it out, sir," Duffy said. "We were right about the launch problems—these Class Five probes have a history of minor physical damage at launch, it's just usually not an issue."

"But with this job, we had to be so precise, so perfect—" Barclay brought his thumb and index finger together to indicate an infinitesimal amount of leeway, and in doing so caught a glimpse of Picard's impatient expression; abruptly, he dropped his hand. "Well, that is, it made a difference. Once we found the sensor displacement and compensated for it—"

Picard felt a surge of hope; how much easier it would be if the Ntignanos' fate didn't rest in his next hour with Atann. He searched their faces. "The probes are functioning?"

Neither of them showed any reticence; Barclay nodded emphatically—overemphatically—and Duffy said, "Yes, sir!"

"And will we have the results in time to resolve the evacuation problems?"

Duffy looked momentarily confused; he exchanged a glance with Barclay and said, "Well, sir, we'll certainly have the results before that sun goes nova."

Engineers. Buried in their projects with blinders on. Sooner or later they'd realize that *before that sun goes nova* would almost certainly be too late, but for now they might as well ride their success. "Very good, gentlemen," he said, feeling the weight of responsibility settle back down on his shoulders. "Keep things moving along as quickly as possible, and keep me apprised of the results. Written report will do."

"Yes, sir," they chorused, already talking to his back as he used swift strides to reach and reclaim the turbolift he'd commanded to wait—there were, after all, perks to being a captain—and returned to deck eleven.

And Atann, who might do well to be edgy, after facing Picard's threat to snatch him from his own home by the very people who had been plying aught but diplomatic wiles up until this point.

Diplomacy. Picard made a disgusted noise in the privacy of his own mind. It had its uses, of course, and in its purest sense, it was the Federation's strongest tool.

But so often diplomacy got the diplomats so tangled up in the very process of *being* diplomatic that they—

Well. They forgot about the holodeck.

"I don't understand why we're here," Atann said, somewhat warily, not even giving Picard time to reach him by the holodeck door. Behind him were arranged three personal guards, whom Picard had ignored since they'd arrived. He'd also ignored the fact that he himself was alone despite the fact that their negotiations had gone distinctly bad, and that the most recent sally—his own—had been downright aggressive.

"What is there to understand?" he replied. "We're having difficulty coming to terms over the issue of the charts. In fact, to be fair, ReynKa, I'd say we're having difficulty even coming to terms with the conditions under which you're willing to discuss the charts."

"You humans use a great number of words to say simple things."

"Exactly!" Picard smiled broadly at him, letting some tooth show—but not so much that Atann could discern between human error and deliberate insult. "We're having trouble communicating. Therefore, I thought we should allow our eyes, our experiences, to help us understand one another better. That's why I wanted to see your training center this morning. And now, here, I want to reciprocate."

Atann glanced at the holodeck's exterior computer interface; Picard already had a program up and running. "You still don't make yourself understood."

"Then perhaps it's time for actions to speak louder than words. On this holodeck, we can re-create many things—a favorite planet, a scene from a play or book . . . or we can create something entirely new. This particular program is more or less analogous to your kaphoora training center. It's an exercise program for the crew. When you step inside, it will be as if you stepped onto another world."

"More Federation technology."

"Some of it, yes."

"Federation technology lost my son in the Fandrean Legacy."

Glitchy Fandrean technology *lost your son in the Fandrean Legacy.* But Picard shrugged. "If you're concerned, of course, I can understand why you'd rather not—"

Atann's arm hair fluffed slightly. "I did not say that."

Of course not. "Then shall we?" Picard said. "To start with, I've programmed it to present you with a brief demonstration of the actual training exercise."

Atann looked at the holodeck doors, and then at his men. "Wait out here," he said, and gestured stiffly for Picard to precede him.

Picard did so.

Right into Worf's calisthenics program.

Despite Picard's comments, Atann was startled by the sudden new environment; he stood stock-still, his low-set nostrils flaring with the scents of the place—the mist-carried odor of a nearby swamp, the old wood from the decaying structures around them, the musky smell of the brushy foliage and sparsely graceful trees. The sunlight held a cast different from both Sol and the brighter Tsoran sun, though Picard had never quite put his finger on what that difference was. Something that reflected strangely off the rugged, jutting rock features around the old buildings, and seemed to energize the shifting mist. Haunting cries—some bird, some animal—punctuated the mist with syncopated regularity.

Then a hologram sparkled into place, an average human woman wearing generic gray workout clothing—formfitting but unrestrictive. "The exercises start unarmed," Picard said, his voice low even though the hologram wouldn't care; it wasn't programmed to. Besides, it had plenty to deal with—for Picard *had* programmed the demonstration to start with three opponents at once. Three hulking humanoid creatures with the kind of breath that could knock you down all on its own, two of them with spiky long feathers as collars, all of them with skull-like features vacant of any expression . . . it only served to make their ferocity of attack more startling.

Atann watched with intent interest, practically quivering, as the beings rushed in on the crewwoman—and as, one by one, she put them on the ground, grunting with realistic effort and taking on a few quickly coloring bruises. "This is not a real human?" he said, watching intently as the creatures got up and went after the woman again.

"No. She is basically an image with substance, programmed to behave as a real woman—and to respond with appropriate injuries when she is hit."

"If she were real?" Atann said, as the woman rolled from a throw, miscalculated, and took several hard kicks before tangling the creature's feet and bringing it down. "This exercise program would wound your crew members? Your females?"

"There are fail-safes in place to prevent mortal injury," Picard said. There were additional fail-safes available to prevent serious contact as well, but he didn't mention them; they'd been created after the program drew the attention of the crew, and several had been hurt playing to Worf's standards. "The computer chooses opponents well matched to the participant's size. My people, men and women, find this program a useful tool; it keeps them sharp." Those few who actually chose to use it, that was. Not a fact Picard would mention.

The woman put one creature down for good; another had taken all the abuse it was programmed to tolerate, and ran off. As she faced the third, the program phased into the next level, providing her with protective padding, and giving both she and the creature a set of wicked short swords.

"Swords?" said Atann. "Your people still fight with *swords?* When you have phasers in your arsenal?"

"As you noted, ReynKa, we do not always have working technology at our disposal. We have other venues for phaser practice; this is where people let off steam. It is something they do by choice, not as mandatory training."

She fought two of them at once now, her blades whirling and blocking and thrusting; each time she disposed of one of the creatures, it lay as dead for only a moment, and then jumped up to reengage her.

"They don't stay dead," Atann observed. "How does she win?"

"It's not a game. She accomplishes her goal by avoiding computer-declared fatal injuries for the duration of the exercise time period. Of course, some of the crew do establish contests among themselves over who can stay 'alive' the longest." He stepped forward, commanding, "Computer, end demonstration."

The woman faded away in mid-sword; the creatures, a moment behind her.

Picard looked at Atann. "Would you like to try it?"

As if Atann could have said no.

Chapter Twelve

THE SHUTTLE *COLLINS* SAT neatly at the very beginning of the crash path, not quite level but placed well in the available terrain; there was already a vine drooping over it, and stains indicating it had served as a resting spot for bird and beast. Katan's litter lay just outside the shuttle; Rakal sat beside it, and Gavare, a Tsoran med kit by his side and Shefen assisting, tended them both.

To Riker, it looked like home sweet home.

Worf stood beside the shuttle, alert, his hand on his *bat'leth* and his gaze moving constantly around the surrounding vegetation. Riker had no doubt Worf had spotted them long ago, although he'd given no indication of it. Too busy watching the area—and the only guard, since the Tsorans were deeply involved with their wounded.

He stumbled, then; Zefan came up beside him, trying not to be obvious about it. "I'm fine," Riker grunted at him.

"Of course," Zefan responded, without moving off.

Akarr broke ahead of them both, running the remaining distance to the shuttle despite the heat; he knelt down by his men, pointing at Ketan's leg, examining the dressings draped over Rakal's arm, side, and leg.

"Ah," Zefan said with an under-purr-filled sigh, drawing Riker's gaze. "I'm not sure I was ever that young."

Riker grinned at him, a wry expression. "I can't remember it myself." Or maybe it was just hard to recall a youth based in snowy Alaska while the sweat trickled down between his shoulder blades. Nice shuttle . . . nice, climate-controlled shuttle . . . and finally, he was here. He stood before the *Collins* and wondered if he should sit, or if he should simply stay on his feet until he could sit for good.

Worf looked directly at him for the first time. "We have a problem."

Riker felt his eyes narrowing. "And that is . . . ?"

"I cannot get the shuttle energy levels to stablize."

Akarr stood up. "*More* shuttle trouble?"

Riker turned on him. "Don't. Even. Start."

To perhaps everyone's astonishment, Akarr, though stiff and aggressive in posture, held his tongue on any response, giving Riker the chance to turn back to Worf, rub his hand over his eyes, make an internal note that the neutralizing sap on his back *still* stunk most stupendously, and say, "Will it take us out of here?"

Worf bared his teeth. "Do you want guarantees?"

"No, no," Riker said. "Heaven forbid there should be guarantees."

"Then, yes, it will take us out of here." Worf hesitated, tracking something through the upper trees before returning his attention to the conversation. "Lieutenant Commander La Forge speculated that the surge problem the Fandreans have been experiencing with the interlocking shields and technology damper is to blame for problems with the *Rahjah*. He modified the *Collins* shields with this in mind. It does not appear to have been completely successful."

"Define success," Riker said. "I define it as getting us out of here."

"We'll be ready to move Ketan in a moment," Shefen said, looking up from his ministrations.

"Let us know if there's anything we can do to help," Riker told him.

"Sir, I respectfully suggest that you go inside," Worf said. "There is a med kit inside. Your wounds should be tended."

Riker said, "I was kind of getting used to the smell of the sap. What do you think? Not too bad, is it?"

Worf merely looked at him. Wordless, expressionless . . . saying it all.

Riker put on the appearance of great deliberation. "I suppose it might get a little overpowering in a closed shuttlecraft. Especially if we're light on environmentals."

"We are," Worf said distinctly, "going to be light on environmentals."

"Let me help," Zefan offered. "I'm not familiar with specific human needs, but I know these injuries."

Riker nodded. "Thank you. Mr. Worf, keep an eye on things out here."

"Sir," Worf said, meaning *as if you had to ask.*

Zefan worked quickly but with a light and careful touch. Cleaned up reasonably well, filled with broad-spectrum antibiotics, antimycotics and antivirals, his arm and back sprayed with a light topical anesthetic and his system responding to a mild hypospray restorative, Riker had to admit the time taken was well spent. The Tsorans were aboard and strapped in, the Fandreans had conferred about some issue they hadn't cared to share, and Worf had closed the shuttle door, only then securing his own and Riker's *bat'leths* in the weapons locker. Everything snug and cozy. Riker contemplated the large, hard-shelled and slow-paced insect inspecting the juncture of the shuttle floor and wall, and decided to leave it alone. It could get off at the next stop.

He slid into the copilot's seat as Worf fiddled with the communications control. "I have sent a message telling them we're on our way," he said, not looking up at Riker. "I do not expect them to get it."

"Neither do I," Riker said. "We'll have to stick to the portal schedule. How are we doing for time?"

"We should make the next scheduled opening," Worf said, and this time he did glance over at Riker. "If the shuttle stays in the air."

"If," Riker agreed. "And if we miss it for some reason . . . ?"

"We will have another opportunity, six hours later."

"And then two days after that," Riker said absently, eyeing the shuttle engine status monitors as Worf brought the engines up to full standby power and spotting the same sort of fluctuations—albeit more subtle ones—that had taken the *Rahjah* down.

"No offense, Commander," Worf said, "but I have no intention of staying in this shuttle's current atmospheric conditions for two days. We *will* make the first opening."

Riker grinned. "No offense taken, Mr. Worf."

Akarr, his voice full of some of the regal imperative it had lost over the last hours, inquired, "Do some of us need to get out and push this vehicle to start, Riker?"

"It is *Commander* Riker to you," Worf said. "And that will not be necessary." He made a few quick adjustments and Riker's eyes widened slightly; he had just enough time to sit firmly in his seat before the shuttle leapt into the air, climbing a nearly vertical path to clear the trees. Oblivious of the cries of protest, Worf immediately leveled their flight path. Then he turned to say casually to Riker, "Unfortunate power surge."

"Most unfortunate," Riker agreed sternly. "Do you have things under control now, Mr. Worf?"

"Entirely."

"Keep it that way."

And though the grumbling from the back of the shuttle ceased, Worf was unable to comply. He ran the shuttle slow and nap of the ground—a cautious approach despite his beginning maneuver—but while the power fluctuations remained more subtle than those the *Rahjah* had experienced . . . they remained.

"We're not going to make it," Riker observed as the *Collins* slowly lost power; the landscape beneath the shuttle changed from thick, towering rain forest to shorter, less dense trees. They crossed a low ridge that ran endlessly in both directions, and the flat valley on the other side changed dramatically in nature. Too full of surface rock to support trees, it instead sported a patchwork of dark ground vegetation and sandy brown rock layers. Along the ridge ran a wide, flat, lazy river, and Riker got the distinct impression he was looking at a giant floodplain.

"No," Worf said, "we are not. But the power loss is steady and manageable."

"Take us as far as you can, then, and still provide a controlled landing." At least they had that much. And if Riker wasn't mistaken, he saw the faint glimmer of the Legacy forcefield in the distance.

He left the copilot's seat and helped himself to an empty seat in the back. "We'll be landing soon," he said, hoping for the chance to say more but only just barely getting his mouth open again before Akarr took over.

"We're going down," he said, a marked tilt to his ears and eyebrows that Riker hadn't seen in him before and couldn't interpret. Amazed disbelief? "Is it not possible for you people to build a shuttle that can travel across the surface of a continent without failing?"

It doesn't look that way. "Your engineers assured us, over our concerns, that our shields would not only operate within this environment, but would protect our shuttle engine integrity," Riker said. "The Fandreans backed your assessment"—and at this, Zefan sat bolt upright—"and we trusted your skills. So if you want to assign blame, let's spread it around a little. Or else keep it to yourself, and work with the rest of us toward overcoming the problems!"

Quietly, Zefan said, "We were not consulted."

Silence. Akarr's mouth worked, but his gaze shifted from man to man, and ended up resting to Riker's left. He looked like a young man caught in a lie . . . with the spotlight on . . . and trying to work up enough gall to bluff through it.

The silence stretched out into moments, during which Akarr looked as shocked as Riker felt, if nowhere near as angry. But the shuttle increased its descent, and he took it as a warning. Now was not the time, no matter what he felt building inside him. If nothing else, it gave him a kick of energy he had a feeling he'd need. He turned a hard look on Akarr. "When we get through this," he said, *"if* we get through this . . . we're going to have a talk. My people to your people. Until then—"

"We *did* consult the Fandreans," Akarr said, making an effort to pull himself into a rigid posture. "Zefan simply has no knowledge of it—"

"—*Until* then," Riker repeated, biting the words off hard, not even bothering to stand, to use his height to emphasize the command status he was wrenching from Akarr, "we'll have to work together. Do you think you can do that? Because if you can't, tell me now, so I can find some other way to deal with the situation." He briefly entertained the image of Akarr, thrown over Worf's shoulder with a gag over his mouth, being carted from the landing to the portal.

Because *this* time, they really were going to have to walk out.

"We will do our part," Akarr said. "As always."

"I am about to land," Worf said over his shoulder. "It will not be smooth. Be prepared."

It struck Riker as a good way to end the conversation.

The descent speed increased even more; Riker watched as Worf tried to compensate, achieved partial success, and managed to bring the nose up just in time to jar heavily to the ground in a level—if somewhat abrupt—fashion.

"That's it?" Akarr said, clearly braced for another outright crash.

"For which," Zefan said pointedly, as he rose from his seat, "I am grateful. Your chief engineer's double-shielding has clearly made a significant difference."

"We are fifteen kilometers from the portal," Worf announced, triggering the shuttle door and powering down what was left of the engines. "Take what you will need in that time."

Med kits—especially the Tsoran med kit. Ketan looked much better since Gavare's ministrations before takeoff, but he'd no doubt need painkillers before the end of the walk—not that he'd be doing much actual walking. They'd left the litter behind, but Ketan wouldn't be going anywhere without some serious support from his fellow Tsorans. And they'd need food, and definitely water. Riker hoped for a breeze, now that they were out of the trees, but the heat would no doubt remain oppressive.

Unless it rained here as it had rained in the jungle. In which case they might have the floodplain to worry about.

Riker joined Worf at the door, looking out across the rough, undulating landscape, beyond the kilometers they had yet to traverse and onward to the sparkle of the forcefield, barely visible from this side of the barrier. There, starting at the horizon and extending up in a square, was a dark blot. "What . . . ?" he said, as it slowly shrunk into nothingness—and then, realizing, stood suddenly straighter, lifting his chin a little at the challenge before them. "The portal. We just missed the second opening. And now we've got six hours to make those fifteen kilometers." Over rough terrain, with most of their party filling the role of walking wounded—or barely walking wounded.

"Then there is no time to waste." Worf disappeared back into the shuttle, no doubt to reclaim his *bat'leth*.

Riker followed.

On the *Enterprise,* Atann straightened from his final "kill," panting like a dog. His stiff leather vest—clawed, dented, gore-stained and in other ways much the worse for wear—spoke as much of his effort here as the blood—not his—splashed on his fur and the similar blood—his—trickling from his nose.

Picard wore creaking leather-plate armor and bore his own bruises—and took his cue from Atann's changed posture. No longer ready for the next opponent. "Computer, remove holocharacters."

In silent compliance, the computer cleaned the area

of temporary bodies, abruptly stopping the approach of the creature—a stouter, Tsoran-sized version of the original beings Worf had programmed—that had been slinking up on Atann.

They stood in silence for a moment, assessing one another, Atann somewhat more warily than he had earlier. "You were right, Captain Picard. Seeing this aspect of your people does help me to gain a better understanding of you."

"I hope it does, ReynKa," Picard said, quite sincerely. *Because otherwise, you're in for a really big surprise.*

"I am now ready to take this knowledge back to Tsora with me and consider it as regards the other matter we need to attend together."

Picard gave him a quiet smile. "Oh, I think not, ReynKa."

Atann stilled his panting with visible effort and focused his entire self on Picard—stiff, but a little too tired to call up his most daleura-filled expression. "Again, you are not making yourself understood."

"I expect that you understand me perfectly well, and you simply don't like it." Picard tossed his Klingon sword away, letting it clatter against the partial structure of the ruins behind him. "We came with polite words, making every attempt to respect your daleura in our interactions both formal and informal. That doesn't seem to have done us very much good. Now, we'll deal with this situation as we choose."

"And *I* choose to return home." Atann raised his voice as if preparing to call for his men, even glancing over his shoulder out of the habit of having them there.

"They can't hear you," Picard said. "This deck is, out of necessity, perfectly soundproofed." He walked around Atann, circling him, playing the part of the hunter. "ReynKa, we came here for a very specific reason. It was not to ferry your son to Fandre, and it was not to play waiting games with you and your ReynSa. We came to discuss the navigational charts we need in order to save the Ntignano people. When we approached you about this goal, you indicated you were amenable to discussion about it. Based on that response, we not only came to your system, we allowed you the use of our shuttles, the expertise of my chief engineer, and the escort of my first officer." Picard lifted an eyebrow. "Did you think we wouldn't notice if you made no attempt to follow up on your end of the discussions?"

"Things changed. My son—"

"Is not relevant to this conversation." Picard lifted a hand to cut short Atann's instant protest. "As crucial as his fate is to all of us, it is a separate issue. It is not a reason to discontinue discussions that we never even started!"

"It is reason enough to me!" Atann snarled. "We make our own decisions in this regard!"

"Look around, Atann!" Picard raised his own voice, meeting Atann's escalating body language, and gestured widely at the fight ground. "Why did you come here today? Because I was about to snatch you up and bring you here. Have you learned *nothing* from this exercise? We are not a people who give up easily. We are not a people who give up at *all*. We're not simply going to walk away without having even *discussed* the terms under which you're willing to give us temporary use of the charts for that crucial space corridor." He rounded on the ReynKa, and pushed his voice back down low. "Unless you're going to tell me here and now that you brought the flagship of the United Federation of Planets out here on a *pretense* to run errands for you?"

"No, no, of course not—"

"Then you'd better find some way to convince me of that, and fast. Because we're not leaving here until you do."

Atann shifted his gaze from object to object until it rested off to Picard's left, very much like a man caught in a lie . . . with the spotlight on . . . and surrounded by evidence of why he shouldn't even try to work up the gall to bluff it through.

Akarr seethed with resentment. Here they were, walking again, and Riker had somehow made it seem like Akarr's fault. Not only were they walking, they were a straggling, limping group, interfering with his final chance to collect a trophy—as if there was anything around here from which it was worth collecting anything, now that he had tranks that worked. The vegetation continued to trip them, the rocks twisted under their feet, and small scaled creatures ran away from their approach . . . but there was nothing here big enough to threaten them. And if it couldn't threaten them, it wasn't worth collecting. Yes, Akarr seethed.

It was so much easier than thinking about the things he'd learned on this trip.

Things like the fact that his people could betray him. Not only by outright treachery, but with ingrained patterns of daleura that deluded him—that deluded them *all*—into thinking he was prepared for this deep jungle kaphoora. Such thinking had created an attitude that left him unprepared—for the aggressiveness of the predators, for their sheer size and number, for the effectiveness of their attack methods. He'd come without an adequate med kit . . . and armed with a false assurance that had led him to march his men out into the Legacy, away from the safe shelter of the Federation shuttle. All because he'd never thought to question that daleura might drive his elders to assume and pass on a knowledge of things they hadn't actually experienced, simply because they could never admit it was so.

He had never even considered these things before. Hadn't even been capable of formulating the concept. And he hated the thought that they occurred to him now. Their existence took his neat world of daleura, posturing, and self-assurance and turned it into something else—a place where the wrong decisions were made not honestly, but because no one could afford to open their eyes. A place where he himself could no longer act instinctively on his skills for preserving daleura, but would have to stop and consider the true ramifications of his actions.

That's what this trip had done to him.

He wondered if Atann had ever struggled with such concepts. But Atann had not dealt extensively with offworlders before now—at least, not offworlders other than the Fandreans, who were used to Tsoran ways and had found their own passive countermeasures—with rules and regulations. These new offworlders had a lack of understanding, a tendency to challenge behaviors and decisions that had stood Akarr's people in good stead for generation after generation.

At least, as long as his people were only dealing with themselves.

Gah. His head hurt. Too many hours under this infernal sun. Akarr kicked a rock from his path, and watched with satisfaction as it took flight in a long, shallow arc and dropped out of sight beyond the next patch of vegetation. The others turned to look at him, and he pretended not to notice.

Were they even any closer to the portal? Too sybling hard to judge the distance of a shimmer in the sky.

And still he didn't think about the thing that truly bothered him. That someone hadn't wanted him to seize his trophy. Had sabotaged his dart supply so he couldn't. Because surely, that had been the intent behind the tampered darts. Denying him the daleura of this hunt, daleura no one else would ever have the chance to obtain. *Federation flagship. Transport deep into the jungle.*

Transport deep into the jungle . . . When the leap of thought first hit him, Akarr stumbled over a root, barely catching his balance in time to save himself from a nasty fall. What if Zefan had been right? What if the Fandreans *hadn't* ever seen the report? If the coordinating engineer had falsified Fandrean approval? *Both events led to the same potential outcome.* What if it hadn't really been about his daleura at all, but something . . . more? *He could have died in that crash.* The tampered darts. *He could have died in the jaws of the Legacy's predators.*

Maybe . . . someone *hadn't* wanted him to come back.

Akarr tried to compose his face, to keep his thoughts from it. No one must know where those thoughts had led him, past conjecture and on to such complete treachery. It was a Tsoran thing, a private thing, and no one outside his family could *ever* know. It would damage them beyond repair, and ruin the dynasty that had followed his father's line for years almost beyond counting.

"Akarr?" Riker said, stopping to look back at him.

Akarr realized that he was standing alone, some distance behind the rest of them. And of course Riker had noticed. He glared at the man. It was all Riker's fault, this confusion of his—it was Riker who had been pounding at him since the very beginning of this trip. Presenting him with conflicting input—how could he not respect a man who fought with such determination

as this one? How could he not despise a man who so fla-
grantly disrespected Tsoran ways? Always Akarr had
found it easy to assign beings into one category or the
other. Always until now.

"Are you all right?" Riker persisted, not wise enough
to back off at Akarr's clearly meaningful expression.
Human with a *bat'leth*, standing there, waiting stupidly
for trouble—

With movement off to his side. Not small and skittery,
not something blown about by the breeze. Akarr, his
every fiber focused on glaring at Riker, gave the movement a startled look, a change that Riker did *not* ignore.
But though Akarr examined the area carefully, he saw
nothing. Riker's frown would seem to indicate a similar
experience.

"Commander?" Worf called, hesitating at the front of
the group

"Coming," Riker said, giving the spot one last glance,
and then looking back to Akarr.

Akarr bit back a snarl and moved to join the rest of
the group, not wanting to do it but wanting less to be the
one who kept them from reaching the portal in time.

Within moments, Worf had stopped them again, performing his own narrow-eyed scan of the area. And then
it was Gavare who pointed, and then Rakal—which surprised Akarr, since the ravaged guard was on enough
painkiller to keep him seeing everything *but* reality.

"Cartiga," Zefan finally said, and Shefen nodded unhappily.

"Cartiga," Worf repeated. "The creature from the museum."

The one between whose paws La Forge had stood
while Akarr had so successfully baited Riker in the museum. Huge. Endowed with astonishing camouflage.

Akarr remembered them well from kaphoora training . . . they stalked in pairs, day or night. They lurked on the edges of the Legacy, the barren areas east of the Eccedama ridgeline. There weren't many of them. No one had ever returned with a cartiga trophy, and the trainees were frankly advised against trying it their first time out. And second.

They were bigger than sholjaggs. Faster.

Akarr glanced back over his shoulder at the ridge the shuttle had managed to clear before going down. The Eccedama.

Cartiga trophy. It might well make up for all the frustration he'd endured.

"They travel in pairs," Zefan said, and at the surprised response of all the Tsorans, added, "Something we've only just discovered. It's difficult to track them when we work only with visuals."

"Then we'll all have to keep a watch for them," Riker said, looking surprisingly bolstered by the injection he'd received. Darkly, Akarr wondered how long it would last. "But we'd better do it on the move. We don't have any time to waste."

Worf looked at the sun—their only time device, in the absence of tricorders and chronometers—and shook his head. "We have less than that. We must pick up the pace."

Which they did, without complaint. Akarr took his turn at Ketan's side, supporting the weight of the guard's wounded leg; Worf led the way, while Riker held back to pick up the drag position, one hand always on the trank gun he now carried. Ketan's gun, appropriated and loaded with viable tranks.

It wasn't long before Akarr got his first good look at a cartiga. A startlingly close look, with the animal not there and suddenly *there*, coming from nowhere to bound along aside the group for a few strides, then fade back and crouch against the rock, its randomly patterned coat—sand and taupe variations with edges of brown—allowing it to almost literally disappear from sight when Akarr blinked and lost his visual hold on it.

"Damn," Riker said under his breath, probably not expecting Akarr's sharp Tsoran ears to pick it up. They locked gazes and he knew he'd been heard, though he didn't seem to care, didn't seem to feel it had decreased whatever humans were wont to call daleura. Instead he took the connection as an excuse to say, "Take it down, if you can. Maybe we can get far enough away before the trank wears off to discourage it from following." Then he gave a strange smile—showing his teeth as the humans did, but in an asymmetrical way, and with something extra in his eye. Something . . . acknowledging. "Besides," he said, "something from a cartiga would make one helluva impression on the folks back home, don't you think?"

Akarr had no idea how to reply. How was he supposed to interpret this expression within the ever present structure of daleura? It was in no way formal, but it seemed to hold some respect, regardless. Then Ketan gave a shout and pointed, nearly losing his balance despite the arm he had flung over Akarr's shoulder. Akarr clutched at him, turning at the same time, trying to follow Ketan's gesture—

Two of them, one on either side. Making a strafing run and veering off again.

"They're checking us out," Zefan said. "They might see a ranger in a scooterpod occasionally, but they've probably never seen such a large party on foot. We generally put down the kaphoora parties just on the other side of the ridge."

"And when they're through checking us out?" Riker asked, still squinting at the last spot he'd seen the cartigas and literally walking backward in the process as he kept pace.

"They'll quit playing with us and do their best to eat us," said Shefen.

Worf said, "It won't be good enough." He, too, held a trank gun at the ready. They all did, aside from Rakal and Ketan. Even Gavare, though his aim looked less than steady.

"There!" Riker said, using the two-handed aim of his trank gun to point, following the target smoothly as the creature came at them.

"Here, also," Worf said without raising his voice, focused in the opposite direction.

But Akarr was watching Riker, trying to spot the cartiga Riker had targeted—there, he had it; he raised his gun, lining up the sights of the short barrel, still supporting Ketan with his other arm. The cartiga was close enough, veering in at them, a massive thing of ponderous fluidity within the gun's range—but Riker hadn't acted. Akarr hesitated, following the rules of the kaphoora—the first hunter to acquire sights on a creature had priority—

"Take the shot, Akarr," Riker said evenly, still targeting the creature, sounding distracted and intent at the same time. "Take the shot, dammit—*before I have to.*"

Because this time the thing was coming in for a kill.

Akarr's hair stood on end with the sudden thrill of it, but his training held firm, and even as the cartiga loped in at them with lazily deceptive speed—at his side, Ketan flinched—he checked his sights and gently squeezed the release.

The dart lodged in the thin skin at the base of one

huge, broad-based ear, and the cartiga squalled in surprise, breaking stride to bat at its face and snarl—movement which quickly became a lurching parody of the creature's normal grace.

"The second one is running," Worf announced as the tranked cartiga folded into a pile of fur.

"I doubt it's ever seen one of its own kind go down," Zefan said.

"And just how long will a trank *keep* one of these things down?"

"Not long," Zefan admitted. "We have little practical experience with the cartiga. But two of the darts might damage it, and we cannot risk that."

Akarr quit listening as he ran to the creature; its half-closed eyes glittered dully at him, and it twitched, as though it knew he was there and badly wanted to sink its teeth into him.

He'd done it. Despite the crash, despite the sabotage, despite his time in the deep Legacy, over night and fighting for their lives the whole time. And now he had his first trophy choice before him.

Akarr circled the animal; his men were silent, as was proper. On this animal, there were a number of legal trophies. Akarr retrieved his trophy knife, touching the lush fur, touching a semiretractable claw—which could only be trimmed, not removed—running his fingers over the full brush of the creature's whiskers. Those were fair trophy. If it had had spines on the ends of its tails like so many creatures here, those would have been fair, also.

Akarr sunk both hands into the depth of plush, patterned fur. He could take only a tuft. A tuft that in no way would ever convey the size and immense strength of this creature. If only—

"We don't have much time," Riker said, having come

up on him while Akarr admired the trophy, admiring what he himself had done. Riker's trank gun was tucked away; the *bat'leth* hung from his grip like a thing that had worn a place for itself, and no longer needed a tight hold simply because it fit so well. "We've still got to get to the portal before it closes for the last time. We miss that, and we'll be out here for two more—"

"Days, yes, I *know,*" Akarr said, remembering then that Riker was to blame for so many of his problems, his new way of seeing the world, and promptly forgetting who'd given him this chance at trophy—for Tsoran thinking was much too black-and-white to allow for both blame and gratitude at the same time.

He turned his back on the man and decided on the whisker. The cartiga had a profusion of them bristling around its long jaws; he found just the right one and plucked it out.

The cartiga made a noise from deep within, unable to do more. Or almost unable to do more—one of its tails twitched.

"*Akarr* . . ." Riker said—such an annoyance—while Zefan, still keeping watch with the group, cried something to Worf, and Worf apparently concurred.

"We have sighted the second one again," Worf called. "It is not moving in. Yet."

"We must keep moving," Shefen said. "We must get away from this one, and make up this lost time, if we're going to make it—"

"Almost done," Akarr said, implacably cheerful. Nothing could go wrong now—at least, nothing wrong enough to ruin this kaphoora. He carefully rolled the whisker and inserted it into a secure, lined pocket along the inside of his hunting vest, patting the scarred vest back into place as he straightened. It had started this journey new and impeccably appointed. Now it bore honorable signs of his kaphoora. His blood, the blood of others . . . stained with sap, deeply scratched by sculper claws, even burned by skik poison. He wasn't sure if he should retire it after this hunt, or allow it to continue gathering such signs of experience.

"If I'd known shooting this thing would evacuate your brains from your head, I'd have done it myself," Riker snapped, eyeing the terrain around them as if yet another cartiga would come down upon them. "We could be half a kilometer closer to the portal by now."

Akarr sneered at him without responding, although he did holster his trank gun and replace his trophy knife. "I'm ready," he said, but he had to walk one final circuit around his "kill," run his hand across that plush flank one more time—something no one else had ever done, he was sure of it. Savoring the feel of it against his sensitive palm and finger pads, he turned away. So this is what it felt like—the daleura of such a kill. No wonder there were so many repeat kaphooras. He knew *he'd* be—

"Akarr!" Riker's voice had changed, and suddenly everyone was shouting, the Tsorans and Fandreans and even Worf—except that Worf went one further, and was pounding directly toward Akarr, trank gun out and aimed . . . at Akarr? Abruptly, Akarr dropped out of the intoxication of his new daleura, and understood.

Not *at* him . . . *behind* him.

Akarr whirled around to see the cartiga directly behind him, lurching drunkenly, its long legs making startling progress. And then Akarr tripped and went down, and the cartiga was on top of him. A smashingly heavy furry bulk, too drugged to attack with swift claws and teeth, not too drugged to try.

"Commander, get out of the way!" Worf bellowed.

Riker blocking his shot, it had to be—Riker had been right there, right next to the cartiga—

And then Akarr couldn't tell what was happening. He rolled between the cartiga's paws, trying to protect himself; an unfamiliar—Klingon?—roar of attack filled the air, only to be cut short by a quick, awkward blow from the logy cartiga—and then the mighty sybyls broke loose, buffeting him, smothering him in heavy fur. His vision sparked from a blow to the head, his breath abandoned him as he slammed into the ground, and then suddenly he was awash in a hot, wet sensation.

And finally, everything stopped moving. Finally, he could open his eyes and see more than flashing shadows of moving fur. Nothing roared or bellowed at him. Just Riker, looking down at him.

"Are you hurt?"

"He *ought* to be," Worf grumbled, picking himself up from the ground nearby and brushing broken bits of crawling basevine from his shoulder.

Akarr looked at himself; his legs were covered in blood, but he felt no pain, and didn't remember being hurt. The cartiga? He pushed himself away from it, traveling on his backside. The cartiga's blood pooled across the ground. He looked at Riker in disbelief. "You killed it?"

By hand? Riker had killed a cartiga—even a *drugged* cartiga—with a *bat'leth* and lived to tell about it? Mighty sybyls, no one would even *remember* that Akarr had been the one to take it down in the first place.

Riker looked down at the animal with clear regret on his face. Not even his oddly patterned facial fur could hide that. "I wish I hadn't." He glanced at the violet, bloody *bat'leth*, and back to the cartiga. "I didn't have any choice."

Zefan approached, picked something up from the ground, and handed it to Riker. He'd lost it then, been unable to simply trank the creature. And everyone else had been afraid of hitting Riker . . . except the Klingon, who'd thrown himself right at the creature in an attempt to free Akarr, and then been thrown across the landscape for his trouble. "No, you had no choice. Akarr left you no choice. Had he but *listened* when we urged him onward . . ." He looked at Akarr. "The cartiga are rare. The death of one in its prime will upset this entire ecosystem, since there are none from beyond the Legacy to move into its territory."

It was dead, and Riker had killed it. Everyone would know that. Akarr looked at the animal and said, "I didn't break the rules to kill it . . . but it is dead. I want the skin for my trophy."

"You *what?*" Zefan's arm hair rose—longer, silkier hair than the Tsorans, and not with quite the same result. Akarr had never seen a Fandrean trigger that threat before. "You cannot possibly consider taking a pelt off-planet! Do you know how it will inflame the poachers? And at a time when our forcefield seems to be unstable!"

"It is unstable in ways that are to your favor," Akarr said. "And the pelt is the only trophy that will offset the things that have happened to me here."

"We don't have time to skin it," Worf growled.

"Akarr," Riker said, "don't make me sorrier than I already am that I gave you this chance. You're the Tsoran ReynTa. Your people take their cue from you. Is this what you want to show them? That you glory in the death of an animal that was fighting drugged? That you bend the rules for the sake of your own daleura, instead of reveling in the daleura you've gained under the same rules as everyone else?"

Akarr thought of the scientist who had reported on the safety of the shuttles, who had presented a fictitious Fandrean report. For the sake of his family daleura, no doubt—whether he'd been told to, or done it on his own. Akarr himself had lived the consequences of that deceit. Then, unable to truly face or acknowledge such fault, he retreated deeply to Tsoran pride. He touched his vest packet—the whisker was secure enough, although the vest itself was more battered yet. "You know nothing, Riker," he spat. "You know nothing of us or our ways or our rules."

"Maybe not. But I know a wrong when I see it."

"I don't need the pelt," Akarr said, rigidly stiff in his posture, speaking to the others as though Riker had said nothing. "I will overcome the unfortunate events of this kaphoora on my own." And he stalked back to the group to reclaim his turn at Ketan's side.

Behind him, Riker said to Zefan, "I'm truly sorry. If I'd seen another way—"

"With the Tsoran ReynTa between its paws and the trank wearing off faster every second?" Zefan said. "We all mourn the outcome. But I cannot say I have ever seen anything more bravely done."

Just what Akarr was afraid of.

Chapter Thirteen

"WELL," TROI SAID, stopping short as she entered the conference room, her expression changing abruptly from preoccupied worry to startlement. "You two look somewhat the worse for wear."

Picard knew what Atann looked like; he could imagine, from the various stinging and swollen spots on his person, what his own appearance must be. Left to his own devices, he was not inclined to use Worf's calisthenic programs with tampered safety protocols. Left to his own devices, he preferred the opinionated but basically obedient gray Arabian from his own holodeck program. All the same, there were appearances to keep up. Daleura, as it were. "Just a short workout," he said, as if it were a typical occurrence. "Looking for common ground, so to speak." But he aimed a short, hard look at Atann, who turned his gaze away in acknowledgment.

The holodeck diversion had been much more than

that—as had his threat to beam the ReynKa aboard. Not just about Picard and Atann and the byplay between them. Not personal daleura, which was the mistake he'd made from the start, although they did indeed each personify their individual allegiances.

No, it had been about the Federation's daleura.

And the Federation had plenty of daleura, regardless of their disinclination to use it as a bargaining tool. More than enough to outrank one lone planet full of Tsorans. All he'd had to do was make that clear in no uncertain terms, and then step back to give Akarr room to respond.

Up until today, he was quite certain the Tsorans had indeed played the Federation for fools. That they indeed had no intention of following up on their promised discussions, and would consider it honorably done, if the Federation could not find the daleura to force them to it.

Unfortunately for the Tsorans, Atann had taken their daleura-driven behavior too far—far enough so that, finally caught out, he was all but obliged to offer up the charts. He looked at Atann again, a more casual glance; the ReynKa had assumed his normal stiff posture, just short of a maximum effect. Wise move on his part. If he puffed himself up past that point, Picard would take him down in front of everyone. *Pride goeth* and all that.

"I take it you found what you were looking for," Troi said, looking at him with enough humor behind her eyes that Picard knew she'd been able to assess the situation.

"Emphatically so." Picard gestured at the conference table. "Atann and I are about to commence discussion about the charts. I'd like you to sit in. Atann has declined an invitation to have his own second; he understands that your function here is to facilitate understanding."

"Fine," said Troi, picking up just the right no-non-

sense cuc. She took a seat between the two of them.
"Let's get started."

"Agreed. There's already been enough delay to jeopardize our purpose." Despite their attempts to create
their own timely charts . . . Picard sat, and noted that
Atann had no trouble picking out the chair that had only
moments ago been replaced with a modified Tsoran design. Atann's feet might not reach the floor, but his head
was no longer significantly lower than anyone else's.
"ReynKa, there is no need to discuss why we need your
charts. It is an established fact that in order to navigate
that section of space, detailed charts are necessary, and
you are the only one to possess them."

"We don't want anyone else to have that ability,"
Atann said shortly. "The graviton eddies keep our system secure from encroachment."

"And we do not want permanent use of that space.
Our proposal is that we provide the charts to a limited
number of guide ships, which will be responsible for
guiding the convoys through the graviton eddies. When
the evacuation is over, we will purge the information
from our ships' computers."

Atann's gaze shifted between them; he pursed his
pouchy lower lip. "How can we be certain all your people will do this?"

*Because none of us will want anything to do with your
system after this.* But Picard only gave him an even stare.
"We do as we say we will do, without convenient manipulation of our obligations. Do you need a demonstration?"

Atann stiffened in his seat, his lips tight over his teeth.

"Captain," Troi said carefully, "that question might be
interpreted as a threat. Is that how you meant it?"

"Yes," said Picard.

There was a brief silence.

"I see," Troi said. She glanced at Atann. "As long as we're clear on that."

Atann sat stiff and silent, staring at the food replicator; there was a slight but noticeable quiver in his ears.

"However," Picard added, "I find it more convenient to simply suggest that we upload the information with a dated self-delete code attached, as approved by Tsoran experts."

"You are so certain when you will be completed with your . . . evacuation?" Atann asked, his under-purr sounding muted and cautious . . . and hopeful.

"We can easily establish the maximum time it will take for the Ntignano sun to go nova." Not as long as they'd hoped. Not near as long as they'd hoped. "Once that happens, I assure you, we will have no pressing need to traverse the area of space in question."

Atann seemed to have relaxed considerably. "What about my son?"

"That's a separate matter," Troi advised him, echoing Picard's words to Atann in the holodeck with a satisfying synchronicity. "Let's conclude this discussion first."

Atann didn't like it. All the signs were there. But after a moment, he offered an awkward human nod. "I find your terms . . . acceptable," he said. "As long as my own people are involved in the process to establish the automatic delete."

"Agreed," Picard said. "Please contact whomever is necessary. We'll begin that process immediately."

"You don't trust—"

"Don't even say it, ReynKa. Just contact your people. You're welcome to use our communications board."

"That won't be necessary," Atann said, his under-purr sharp and tight. He removed a small round device from his vest and issued a few curt instructions to his assistant, and then they sat, silently, waiting—Troi relaxed, Picard satisfied, and Atann impatient—until the transporter room reported the arrival of the Fandrean computer techs.

Picard assigned Data to handle the work—knowing the program would likely be completed by the time Data even reached the transporter room to escort their guest techs to a work area—and settled back to wait. "They should be finished shortly," he said. "At that time, we'll expect to receive the navigational charts."

"Yes, yes," Atann said. "Now what about my son?"

"ReynKa, are you under the impression that we've withheld information about your son's status?" Troi glanced at Picard, who gave an infinitesimal shake of his head. "We honestly know no more than we've told you. We've relayed all the information we've received."

"This is true?" Atann asked, deflating somewhat. "You know nothing? Not even whether he is dead or alive?"

"We hope to hear from Fandre soon," Picard said, taking the edge out of his voice. "If you cannot trust that we will make every effort to see your son to safety, ReynKa, then at least trust that we care enough about our own crew members to do the same for them. And that we are still trying to understand exactly what went wrong."

"I myself have close ties to the officers involved," Troi said, a grim fierceness intruding on her professional calm. "I can assure you that if there were information to be had, I'd have it."

Picard could only hope he'd never be in a position to be between her and any such information.

Atann looked away from them both. "I see."

"I'm sorry," Troi said. "I *can* tell you that the officers involved are our best. If anyone can get your son through this safely . . ."

Atann's under-purr was especially garbling. "I understand."

"While we're waiting for Mr. Data and your own technicians to assemble acceptable code for the automatic delete, would you like some refreshments? The food replicator has recently been programmed to offer Tsoran delicacies." And anything was better than sitting here staring at one another.

"That would be satisfactory," Atann said, not sounding particularly enthused. But as Troi rose to assist him in the replicator's use, his communicating device—still on the conference table—gave a strange warble.

The ReynSa. "Is it true?" she said. "You've arranged to give the Federation our star charts?"

Atann glanced at Picard, who offered no reaction; he and Troi withdrew to the far side of the room, as though it would truly offer Atann any privacy. But he didn't ask for any more than that—and it wasn't far enough away for them to mistake her next words.

"You must stop all progress toward this gift at once," she said. "They have played you for a fool, Atann. They have only pretended to respect you."

Atann gave his device a puzzled look, as though it were the ReynSa herself. "In what way? I am satisfied with the situation."

"How can you say such a thing, with our son still missing?" She paused, and seemed to gather herself with an audible intake of air. "You'll change your mind soon. Takarr and I will board their ship immediately; we must speak in person. Until I get there, Atann, mark this—*they are not to be trusted.*"

"Look at it this way," La Forge said, leaning over the short console to get Yenan's attention. "The problem isn't on the communications end. All things considered, communications aren't that hard to handle within the Legacy. The energy change from one form to another is subtle compared to the energy transfer going on within a shuttle's engines—that's why the Universal Translator is reasonably reliable in there, too." Of course, they'd all expected the shields to be reliable, as well, given the Tsoran and Fandrean assurances. "So the question is— why are we working so hard on the communications end of this problem?"

Yenan looked away from his padd to give Geordi pouch-mouthed uncertainty. "Because it is the communications we cannot get to function?"

"That's what I'm saying. The communications are fine. It's the forcefield we need to work on." And fast. Worf had already missed two portal openings. There was something going on inside the Legacy, and until La Forge knew what it was, no one else could help.

"The shields are a delicate balance of interweaving frequencies," Yenan said, putting down his padd to look straight at La Forge, speaking slowly and deliberately— as if to a child. "We are already having trouble with them. We should fix *that* problem before trying to change anything else."

"That's the beauty of this idea," La Forge said. "We don't really have to *change* anything. Just use it as it's meant to be used . . . on a much, much smaller scale."

Yenan squinted at him, a Fandrean expression of a profound struggle to understand. A plea for more information.

"Look at the portal," La Forge said, gesturing not to the portal area, since they were underground, but to the area of the museum that housed its generator. "Your ability to use it is limited, because of the energy it draws. But how much energy would it use to establish a pinhole portal? Not even that—practically a microscopic opening. Just enough for the signal to get through." *A hole in his head,* Data had said, and he'd just about gotten it right. "You see?"

Yenan's eyes widened again. "We'd need to create new portal settings . . . we might not be able to maintain the opening all the time, even at a microscopic level—"

"Yeah, but you could put it on a schedule, just like the portal openings. You'd end up opening the portal less often, and have more power to spare for the communications."

"Yes!" Yenan stood, fumbled with the padd that had been on his lap, and ignored it as it clattered to the floor. "It is a good answer, Geordi La Forge! Let us descend upon the portal controls and solve the problem!"

La Forge grinned. This was the Fandrean version of being excited? "Good, I'm glad you agree. I know just the people to try to reach as a test. I imagine they'd welcome a friendly voice right now."

For a moment there, Riker thought the kid had learned something. Just for a moment. There'd been a look on his face . . . an uncertainty, and a hesitation.

He'd apparently decided to come down on the side of the familiar and comfortable, to judge by his performance over the cartiga. At least in the end he'd decided not to skin the thing.

Riker wondered if he even knew how much an untanned skin of that size might weigh. Who had he thought would carry it? One of his wounded men?

They'd come quite a distance from that site, and with no further harassment by cartiga or anything else. The evanescent shimmer of the forcefield had been close the last time Riker had spotted it, although Worf and Zefan seemed certain they needed to travel north along its perimeter in order to reach the portal—which, he said, was plainly marked from the interior.

Riker left the navigation up to them. Right now his entire being was centered simply on walking, on placing one foot in front of the other—not stumbling, tripping, or having the footing roll out from beneath his boot— and walking. Sweat trickling, face burning, arm fiercely aching . . . walking.

"Commander," Worf said. Sometime in the last few moments he'd fallen back from point to speak with Riker, though it had escaped Riker's notice at the time. "Are you—"

"No, Worf, I am not all right. Yes, the arm hurts like hell." Whatever analgesic properties the med-kit spray held had worn off long ago. About the time he'd started wrestling cartigas. And the restorative stimulant . . . used up long before its next dose time. "But give me a hot shower—with real water—and a place to put my feet up, and I'll be fine. Eventually."

"How did you know what I was about to—" Worf started, and then broke off. "Ah. I have become predictable."

"I'm afraid so." Riker spared a glance from the terrain directly in front of his feet to assess the Klingon, and found very little sign of this day's forced march—either of them—in evidence. "You're still looking chipper. That's bad form, Mr. Worf. Making a superior officer appear—"

"Weak?" Worf suggested. "Unfit?"

Riker gave him a superior officer's scowl. "Not the words I was hunting for."

"Of course not," Worf said, a little too hastily. "If you

prefer, I will stay out in the jungle an additional day and night, fighting off sculpers, sholjaggs, and skiks. I would then assume your appearance would compare, if not favorably, at least equitably."

Riker almost stopped walking altogether. He did manage to draw himself up, "Worf, you're patronizing me."

"Yes, sir."

"Well, stop it. You're bad at it."

"Yes, sir."

On point, Zefan gave a delighted shout and gestured at a quick shimmy of sparkles ahead of them.

"Mighty sybyls," breathed one of the Tsorans—an expression of relief, as far as Riker could tell. Zefan altered their course northward so it ran along one of what Riker had considered floodplain paths, indications of faster current where the vegetation was sparse or nonexistent.

The going immediately became a little easier, although he quickly realized it was a trade-off—he wasn't tripping over roots, but here, the gritty sand shifted beneath his feet, making each step unpredictable. Rakal stumbled a number of times in quick succession, and Worf moved as if to help—and then stopped himself even as Riker put out a hand to do the same. Not only was there the question of the size mismatch—hard to throw a shoulder under someone who only came up to your chest—but the Tsorans had made it clear that they did not want assistance from anyone outside their group. Worf shrugged and fell back in next to Riker.

"We're making good time. It is perhaps a kilometer away," he said. "Maybe this is a good spot for a rest."

Riker shook his head. "I'd rather be next to the portal, waiting for it to open. We don't have *that* much buffer."

"We have very little buffer," Worf told him.

Shefen drifted back through the group; he picked up a

reasonably straight length of thick, dried vine, and shoved it into Rakal's hand on the way by. Rakal, clearly startled, made as if to return it, but Shefen had moved on, and Rakal wasted no more time in employing his new walking staff.

"Good thinking," Riker said, blowing a drop of sweat from the end of his nose. "I'll have to keep my eye out for one of those."

"I'm not sure you'll find one in your size," Shefen said, ducking his head in Fandrean apology.

Riker shrugged. "It's not that far. Though I'd thought it would be easier walking in these flood paths—"

"These what?" Shefen said, looking around them.

Riker and Worf exchanged a glance; Worf seemed to have made the same assumption. "These paths for the floodwaters," Worf said. "This *is* a floodplain for the river we saw, is it not?"

Shefen flicked his lightly tufted ears. "The river is already nearing flood stage. It does not get much wider than what you saw. The rains have been heavy of late."

Riker felt a subtle rumbling in his diaphragm—or was it in his legs?—as if the rain in question had grumbled in far-off thunder. "If this area isn't kept down by floods, what makes these paths?"

Shefen smiled, his teeth and their remarkable overbite completely covered. "I take it you didn't make it into the secondary museum displays. Most of our visitors do concentrate on the predators."

"No," said Worf, looking around the lightly clouded sky as another, more apparent rumble reached audible levels. Not thunder. "We did not make it into the secondary displays. What might we have seen in those areas?"

Shefen, too, seemed to have felt the rumbles—but his

reaction was entirely different. Instead of answering Worf, he dropped to the ground, holding his hand lightly above it, then lowering his ear to listen to the sand. After a moment, he called "Zefan!" but didn't move from his unexpected position.

Zefan turned, and upon seeing his fellow ranger, instantly emulated his behavior. Riker traded another glance with Worf, a longer and more concerned exchange; Worf frowned. Riker crouched beside Shefen, winced—*that* was a mistake, now he'd only have to get up again—and said, "What's the problem?"

Shefen lifted his head. "Those secondary displays describe the considerable number of prey animals available to the predators. As you might imagine, creatures as big as the cartiga require a significant food source." He gestured at the terrain around them. "Ictaya made these paths—grazing paths. They keep the vegetation down. We've been lucky we haven't seen any—they're stupid animals, who panic at nothing and stampede with frequency. What one of them does, the next does as well—if one of them trips or jumps over nothing, every ictaya behind it will do the same. They regularly run into the Legacy forcefield. And they will mow down anything in their path."

The rumble came more distinctly now—Riker felt it in the balls of his feet, his flexed knees, his chest. It no longer sounded like thunder. Now it came through as an ominous, continuous grumble of earth. "Let me guess," he said, oh-so-dryly. "You think we're in their path."

Shefen gave a short affirmative gesture.

"Then how do we get out of their path?" There had to be some way . . . some pattern the animals usually followed that they could counter.

"Run."

Riker felt like laughing . . . perhaps hysterically. Instead he said dryly, "In any particular direction?"

"There's no predicting what they'll do or where or when they'll turn. They're coming this way—they might stop short a kilometer from here, they might follow in our path simply because something else has recently gone that way." Shefen stood. "Our best chance is to reach the portal." He looked at them as they hesitated. *"Now."*

"Even if we reach the portal, it will not open until the scheduled time," Worf said, as Shefen explained the situation to the Tsorans and got them started, jogging off toward Zefan.

"You have a fine gift for stating the obvious, Mr. Worf," Riker said, slowly climbing to his feet and brushing the sand from his sweat-damp uniform. "Let's go."

And they commenced to run. A run best described as a straggling jog, until they were widely spread out—one of the rangers on point and leading the way, and Worf and Riker taking up the rear. Worf jogged easily, holding himself back to maintain position, the modified Tsoran pack looking like a child's accessory as it bounced lightly against his shoulders. Riker . . . Riker didn't kid himself. He promised himself that hot shower, and then he promised himself more hours of conditioning, but mostly he just promised his lungs he'd keep dragging in that all-important next breath. Breathing, the jar from heel to knee to hip that meant he'd made the next step, and an occasional swipe to take care of the sweat gathering to run into his eyes . . . nothing so complex as a thought to be had.

And still some part of him noticed that the rumbling grew. That it grew significantly. On the heels of Riker's dawning realization, Worf turned for a quick glance behind them—and his eyes widened.

Riker turned to look, chancing his footing to dead-tired legs.

He wished he hadn't.

The ictaya were on their trail, all right, running blindly along in the scent of those to pass most recently before them. Elephant-huge, all of them the same dirty brown, faded-at-the-edges color, with short necks that came off their bodies even with their shoulders and large heads that nodded with their short-legged loping pace, they came on relentlessly, a tumble of moving bodies plowing through anything in their path.

He hadn't thought he'd be able to move any faster. He couldn't believe there was any adrenaline left in his body.

He'd been wrong on both counts.

"Run!" he shouted ahead, picking up speed and coming up on the heels of the lagging, injured Tsorans.

"Run!" Worf bellowed, surging ahead to where Rakal, flagging and at the end of his endurance, stumbled and started to go down. Worf scooped him up, ignoring the being's screams of pain, and tossed him over his shoulder. Riker wanted to do the same for Ketan but knew better; he settled for grabbing Ketan's vest belt and hauling him along, while Gavare supported him from the other side.

They ran. Riker fixed his gaze on Worf's back, on Rakal's bouncing head, and ran. His own harsh and ragged breath overflowed his ears, but his body could hear the immense creatures on its own, and it told him the ictaya closed on them. But it couldn't be much further, it *couldn't*—even running, even with his vision blurred and jarring, he could see the scintillation of the perimeter ahead of them—even spot the widely set, square stone pillars on either side of the portal.

One of the ictaya loped by on his left, outflanking them . . . then another, and another, and the main body of the herd snorted on their heels. A deep, surprised grunt of surprise heralded the first of them to run into the perimeter; the impact staggered one and all. Lurching, Riker lost his grip on Ketan's belt; Rakal flailed in Worf's grip, suddenly slipping down along the backpack. Worf hauled him back into place and ran on, but the dust of the stampede had filled the air and none of them were quite sure of the portal's location—

Riker's combadge beeped; he barely heard it. He couldn't begin to hear the words that came through, but he caught the timbre of Geordi's voice. *Geordi!*

"Geordi! Open the portal! Open the portal *now!*" he bellowed in response, not at all certain Geordi would be able to pick his words out of the din, or even through the distortion of his own harsh breathing. Given time he'd filter out the words but none of them *had* time—

An ictaya ran by, close enough to brush against Riker and leave him sprawling; the startled beast leapt to the side, and all those in its wake blindly followed suit. Riker clawed his way upward, lifting his head in time to see the dark, spreading breach of the portal before them, clogged with vegetation at ground level but as sweet a sight as he had ever seen. The Fandreans entered it; Akarr threw himself after them. Worf heaved Rakal through and dove to the side as an ictaya, screaming its fear but unable to turn aside, blundered into civilization, trampling what remained of the foliage. Behind came the body of the herd, ready to follow—and Ketan tripped and fell beside Riker.

Riker stopped short as Gavare reversed course and came back for his friend; they yanked the injured Tsoran to his feet and propelled him through the portal. Something musky hit Riker in the back, knocking what precious little breath he had out of his lungs and lifting him off his feet. When he landed and stumbled forward, he found himself knee-deep in crumpled vines just outside the museum scooterpod hangar.

The portal snapped shut behind him.

"Wait—Gavare—!"

But the portal had become an opaque gray forcefield. The ground still shook beneath them, recoiling against the impact of the icataya against the forcefield, and against the ground itself, but the sound was gone, replaced by silence.

Or what seemed like silence in comparison, as his assaulted ears adjusted to the relative calm of Tsoran groans, the efficient orders of arriving medical personnel, the security officers surrounding Worf with questions, and his own harsh breathing. He stood there a moment, taking in the scene—the ictaya, down on its side only meters from the museum; Zefan, issuing orders and accepting a rehydrating drink bottle even as he directed the attending Fandrean ranger to the rest of the group with more of the same; the Legacy dust settling around him . . . and La Forge, standing with a phaser, watching him.

Riker's knees gave out. He looked back at La Forge from there.

La Forge glanced from Riker to the giant beast stretched out beside the hangar, shook his head. "Lions and tigers and bears, all right."

Riker gave a sloppy, exhausted grin and said in a most heartfelt voice, "There's no place like home."

Chapter Fourteen

THEY ARE NOT TO BE TRUSTED.

The ReynSa's words echoed in Picard's thoughts as Troi shot him a questioning glance—wondering what he'd decided about the probe charting, no doubt, since he'd told no one outside of the project engineers and Data. Picard, too, suspected that they'd been found out, and that the Tsoran reaction would be just as Troi had predicted. They'd withdraw in a huff, leaving the *Enterprise* with her probes to finish the job on their own. And they *could* . . . but the Tsoran charts would save more lives.

Damn. The Ntignanos had been so close to safety. After days of delay and posturing and rudeness, he'd found the key to dealing with Atann. He'd all but had those charts in his posession.

Data entered the conference room, but—not entirely deaf to the strained nuances of the room—hesitated by the door. "Incoming call from Lieutenant Commander

La Forge, sir," he said. "I thought you'd want to take it, since this will interest the ReynTa as well. There is news of the away team."

Good news, or bad? Data was utterly inscrutable when it came to such things—although Picard couldn't be sure if that was because of his desire to be so, or his inability to be anything else.

Picard glanced at Atann, who'd gone stiff and silent—and, as far as Picard could tell, baffled—since his ReynSa's final words. But not now—now, he came to unfettered attention. Whatever else was going on, it wasn't anywhere near as important as the fate of his son. Picard gestured at the screen at the head of the conference table. "By all means, put it on screen."

La Forge appeared, grinning widely—Data's complement in that regard. "I've got good news for you, Captain. We've got them back!"

"Everyone?" demanded Atann, not waiting for an invitation. "My son? My people?"

"Your son," La Forge confirmed, nodding in a short, decisive gesture. "And—"

"Captain," Riker said, moving into the comm-screen range.

Alive! "Will," Picard said, rather more warmly than he'd intended with the Tsorans present. He caught himself, put a more formal face back in place. "Nice to have you back."

Even more so than La Forge, Riker looked down at the comm screen, which was set for Fandrean use. He also looked like someone had been using him as a kaphoora target—battered and bruised, his uniform torn and covered with blood and a glazed sticky substance, one arm bandaged along its whole length and seeping pinkish ooze . . . but he had that look on his face. The cocky, triumphant look that spoke not of the hurts, but of the victory.

And well he should feel that victory, having gotten out of this one alive, and with the difficult ReynTa in one piece. "Commander," Picard said, "report, if you would."

"The *Rahjah* suffered engine failure shortly after entering the preserve," Riker said. "For the most part, we walked away from the landing, but the shuttle is a complete loss. We spent the night in the jungle," and here, his shoulder went up a notch, an unspoken commentary about the event, as well as his disinclination to discuss it in detail just now. Picard let it go. "And in the morning Mr. Worf found us. The *Collins* also malfunctioned, but Geordi's modified shields made the difference—Worf put us down in a clean landing. We can retrieve the shuttle with the assistance of the rangers, if we can get her running again."

"And then?" Atann said, insistent and pushing up behind Picard, although Picard doubted that Atann realized his rudeness—at least, not this time.

Riker said, "Then we walked out."

"What of my son's kaphoora? What of his men?"

Akarr moved in front of the comm screen, quite comfortably at the correct height to use it. "Our men were honorable and earned much daleura protecting me and each other. But . . . several of them were lost. Pavar, in the crash. Regen, to a sholjagg before the first night. Takan to a flock of skik. And Gavare, who saved Ketan from a stampede of ictaya and was trampled himself, less than a meter from safety."

The Tsoran youth had a different quality about him, Picard realized, than when he'd been stalking around the *Enterprise* stirring up resentments. Still all-Tsoran—that stiff and aggressive way of looking at the world—he nonetheless seemed to have more thought behind his words, and even behind the way he framed them.

"Ketan and Rakal are both injured but survive," Akarr continued. "Commander Riker, too, is injured—it was done in his efforts to save Takan from the skik. He has never hesitated to do what he thought correct to insure the safety of myself and my men."

Picard could easily read behind the lines on that one. Riker and the young ReynTa had clashed, and often. The surprising thing was that Akarr had reported it as he had, and not as insubordination.

"And your kaphoora?" Atann asked, his body language turning a little more formal.

Atann held up a thin circle of what appeared to be filament. "Cartiga whisker."

All the starch went out of Atann in his relief, but he quickly caught himself and returned to public mode. "I'm much relieved," he said. "I was . . . concerned on many levels."

"With reason," Akarr said, and then stopped short; Picard knew enough to recognize the distress in the quiver of Akarr's ears, although he was tempted to put it down to fatigue. Except . . . he glanced at Riker and saw anger there. Restricted to his eyes, but Riker could do quite a lot with anger when it came to his eyes.

Akarr finally finished, "It will be worth much discussion when I return. Discussion I would like to have before leaving the *Enterprise*."

"We'd be glad to provide you with a place for private discussion," Picard said. "Meanwhile, Commander, you'll be glad to know that we have come to an agreement regarding the charts. And ReynTa, your ReynSa is on her way up—we expect her at any moment—and I'm sure she'll be glad to see that you're not only alive, but unhurt."

"And with cartiga trophy," Atann said, and there was no mistaking the pride in his voice. "No one of us has ever returned with cartiga trophy, not even the seasoned pros."

"There's a reason for that," Riker muttered, but he didn't seem inclined to take the comment any further; Picard noted it but let it pass. There were stories within stories, here; the challenge was to find the most important story first.

The ReynSa burst in, trailing both a younger Tsoran and a hapless ensign behind her. Picard waved the young woman away with an understanding nod, and she hesitated, handed him a padd, made good her escape. But the ReynSa's bearing—confrontational, righteously triumphant—lost all momentum the instant she understood what, until her arrival, had captured everyone's attention. "Akarr!" she cried in surprise. "Akarr, you are well, and returned to us!"

Picard took advantage of the noisy reunion—as Atann proudly chimed in with news of Akarr's cartiga trophy and Tehra made delighted noises in response—to glance at the padd. The universe had apparently not stopped so he could take Atann into the holodeck. The padd held notations from Data regarding the current fluctuation and reaction rate of the Ntignano sun . . . a summary from Beverly Crusher, detailing how many Ntignanos had died in the last several hours and at what rate they were continuing to die, as well as how many would still be left on the planet's surface when the sun went nova on its accelerated schedule, and a report on the probe charting process, now that it was up to speed. And of course, a message from Starfleet, demanding an update.

"Takarr," Akarr said in the background, and offered the comm screen a little bow. "I see you made it to the *Enterprise* after all."

"I see that he did," Picard said, tearing himself away from the padd. With any luck, within moments—now that the ReynSa had her son back—he'd have an answer about the charts. An answer for Starfleet, for Dr. Crusher . . . for the Ntignanos. For now, he needed to keep his attention within this room. He handed the padd to Troi and looked over at the ReynSa and her charge. When his expectant expression didn't prompt introductions to the young Tsoran, he said, "I am Captain Jean-Luc Picard, commanding the Federation starship *Enterprise*. This is Commander Deanna Troi, our ship's counselor." Troi looked up from the padd, distracted and unhappy at its contents, and smiled a greeting anyway, her teeth neatly covered. "And this is Takarr. We met briefly while I was on the planet."

"My son," the ReynSa said, all but drawing the boy to her—but then, at a glance from Atann, actually stepping slightly apart from him. "Takarr is the reason we're here today. It is he who discovered your Federation treachery!"

"Our *treachery?*" Picard said, somewhat taken aback by the hyperbole.

She made an affirmative gesture, a quick, annoyed flick of her hand. "Exactly. Explain to the ReynKa, Takarr, what you've found."

The boy wasn't quite ready for this. Not old enough, not inclined enough . . . Picard could see him talk himself up into a properly stiff posture and attitude. "I spend much of my time with off-planet concerns, Captain Picard. It is my area of . . . expertise."

From a youth of this rough-and-tumble society? An interest, yes, but an expertise? Nadann had certainly not mentioned it.

"I have found your charting probes."

Someone had found them, that was for certain.

"I see," said Picard, and there was silence, although Troi stirred and probably wanted to say something—something more conciliatory, most likely, something to make the news on the padd go away. Glancing at Picard, she held her tongue.

"That's all you have to say?" the ReynSa demanded.

"Tehra," Atann said, staring intently at her with as much of a challenge gaze-hold as he seemed to think he could get away with under the circumstances, "the captain and I have come to some common understandings—"

"Did they include sending out probes in our own space, without consulting us?"

"No," Picard said. "They included the nature of the Federation and its peoples, and how we respond when we think we're being toyed with." He came around the table to stand before her, addressing her directly—far more directly, in fact, than Admiral Gromek would ever prefer.

But Picard was the one who'd been doing the daleura two-step, not Admiral Gromek.

"They included a certain number of demonstrations," he told her, "the gist of which is this, ReynSa—we *will* find a way to get what we want. If that means sending charting probes out as backup when it becomes evident you have contrived ways to take advantage of our good nature without any intention of making good on your own promises even to negotiate." He looked at her, let his words sink in, and his understanding of the Tsoran's manipulative intent, and then said, simply but with his gaze locked on hers, "Then that's what we do. Those probes would never have been launched had your own intransigence not made it necessary."

"That does not change the fact that it is treachery," the

ReynSa said, showing her teeth and ignoring Atann's loud under-purrs of protest. "You will never have our charts after this! Let your precious Ntignanos wait for you to complete your work. I cannot imagine it will be in time."

No. It wouldn't be. He didn't need Troi's stricken expression to drive the point home. The padd report made it quite clear enough—the probe charting was proceeding at its fastest pace, and it wasn't fast enough. But Picard just stared back at her, a step closer than he had been—uncertain of the way to handle cross-gender daleura interaction, but going for the bluff.

"Captain," Riker said, his voice harsh with fatigue but still holding a note of intensity that immediately captured Picard's attention.

"What is it, Number One?" he said, despite the fact that the ReynSa was even less pleased to have him turn away from her than she was to have him stepping up to challenge her.

"There's more to this situation than there would seem—information you should have. May we speak privately?"

"I object," the ReynSa said. "You have already done enough behind our backs!"

"Riker—Commander Riker—" On the viewscreen, Akarr had pivoted to look at Riker, his expression conflicted, his underpurr coming in stops and starts. "There is—that is, we need to talk—"

Riker looked at him a moment—what seemed to Picard to be a meaningful exchange, almost a warning—and then returned his attention to the comm screen. "I think it would be best, Captain."

"So be it," Picard said; he did not fail to note that Troi gave the slightest of nods. "We'll be waiting. But," and he caught Riker's gaze on the viewscreen, a silent communication across an entire solar system, "don't be long."

Riker gave a short nod, and the screen went not blank, but filled with the Fandrean flag emblem—one only slightly less remarkably colorful than the Tsoran screen filler.

"Whatever your Commander Riker has to say, Captain Picard, it will not change how we feel about the charts," Tehra said. "You must command your people to cease working on the transfer protocol."

Picard looked at the young Tsoran standing beside her, doing his best to radiate the same belligerent stiffness as his mother, and at Atann, who eyed Picard with a certain amount of suspicion displayed in his tightly pursed chin and lower lip. "Let's just see what the commander has to say," he told them all. "In the meanwhile, it does no harm to complete the transfer protocol. They cannot upload the chart data without your command."

"Which we will never give."

"Then you have nothing to worry about." Picard went to the food replicator and said, "Tea. Earl Grey, hot." And then, as his tea materialized, "Would you like anything, Counselor? ReynTa?"

Tehra made a snorting noise and turned away.

Troi gave him a grim little smile. "Hot chocolate," she said.

She was going for the chocolate. Maybe things were indeed as bad as they looked.

"What's this about, Akarr?" Riker lifted one shoulder out of pure habit, hurt himself doing it, and consciously relaxed.

Akarr looked around the crowded communications

console. Worf, La Forge, Zefan, the Fandrean museum and city managers, and Kugen, the resident Tsoran representative . . . all of them crowded into this small room on the museum's main floor. It held only the comm unit—a pedestal-like affair with the screen set too low for Riker's use and a short standing work table beside it—and it was clearly not meant for all these people.

Just as clearly, Akarr did not want them there.

"Gentlemen," Riker said, a hint that La Forge and Worf took immediately.

"We will be right outside," Worf said, as if anything could happen to them here. Once he and La Forge were gone, it finally occurred to the others that Riker had been asking for privacy, and with some embarrassment, they left.

Aside from Kugen, who didn't move. When the room had emptied, he said to Akarr, "Are you sure you want to be alone here?"

Akarr snorted. "You think too much of yourself. Do you second-guess your ReynTa?"

"No," Kugen said, clearly startled; he gave a hasty bow and left the room.

Akarr wrinkled his lip, a quick gesture that Riker would have missed had he not come to know the Tsoran. "He's been here too long, with too much authority. I'll have to mention it to my father."

"Do that," Riker said. "But that's not why you asked to speak to me. You stopped me from telling Captain Picard about the . . . shall we call it a *miscommunication* . . . over the shuttle shields."

"Yes," Akarr said, and hesitated. "There is more. I think it is pertinent . . ." he started, and then stopped. After a moment he took a breath and started again, holding Riker's eye in the most neutral gaze-hold he'd ever shown Riker. Standing his ground without any challenge at all. "I think it is possible that certain people in my government never intended to see those charts in Federation hands. I suspect that my ReynSa has been . . . in discussion with them, and that they have exchanged . . . commitments of support."

Riker stared at him. "That fits with your notions of dalcura? Implying an honest interest in negotiations when no such interest exists, in order to pry favors from the other party?"

Akarr filled his considerable chin pouch with air and released it all at once with a sharp sound. "It does not fit my understanding of daleura. I am . . . beginning to understand that some of my people twist daleura for their own desires."

Riker let out his own pent-up breath. "So do some of mine, Akarr. And while I appreciate your consideration of the matter, I'm not sure I understand its immediate relevance."

"Because," Akarr said sharply, "there is more to it than that. Information *you* can use."

Against his own people, or against some faction of his own people. Riker began to understand Akarr's agitation. "I'm listening."

"You believe that the Fandreans weren't consulted about the shuttle shields, and not simply that Zefan knew not of it as I said earlier, am I correct?"

Riker nodded, frowning.

"And you know that someone tampered with the tranquilizer darts in an attempt to make my kaphoora less than successful."

"Yes," Riker said, struggling to follow Akarr's line of thought and deciding he was just too tired. "But I don't see the connection between those two things."

"That is because you do not know that I did not know we didn't consult the Fandreans. My father did not know. Our coordinating engineer reported that the Fandreans had inspected and approved of the Federation shuttle shield specifications. At the time Zefan spoke of this, I truly believed him to be mistaken. That is no longer the case." Now Akarr's expression held unmistakeable misery, from his drooping ears to his sagging chin pouch. But he held Riker's gaze.

"Well, I'll be . . ." Riker muttered. Someone really *hadn't* wanted Akarr to have an easy trip. In fact, someone probably hadn't wanted him to come back alive.

Akarr shifted uneasily, and settled into a moderately assertive stance. "Whoever planned this had no idea the two . . . difficulties would combine as they did."

"You can't know that," Riker objected.

"I have said it," Akarr responded instantly, and there was no mistaking it, he was headed for the Akarr Riker knew best, the stiff and difficult young Tsoran in daleura posture.

He'd get nowhere with Akarr if that happened. Riker backed off, started at the whole thing from another direction. That which was more pertinent. "So both events were likely an attempt to keep you from gathering kaphoora trophy." What else had he said? That the ReynSa had exchanged favors with the people who didn't want the charts to go out, and was now therefore obliged to champion their cause? *Favors.*

. . . Like sabotage?

Startled beyond diplomacy, he said, "And you think your *mother*—that the ReynSa was behind the sabotage?"

Stiffly, Akarr nodded—a human gesture that clearly remained awkward to him. "On occasion, the inherited position of ReynKa goes to the second child; it is the

ReynKa's choice, always. It is simply tradition to choose firstborn." He gestured at the blank screen. "Takarr is the ReynSa's favored child. Her . . . natural child."

Ah. Akarr, the firstborn, hale and hearty and well-versed in terms of daleura, the kaphoora, and all other things a budding Tsoran politician would need. Takarr, a slightly built young man clearly trying to live up to his mother's expectations . . . but who apparently had already become the scientist of the family.

In short, the kid didn't have a chance as long as Akarr was around and doing well. The ReynSa must have been beside herself when Atann arranged the Federation escort for Akarr's kaphoora.

"I understand," he said. And he did. But what he didn't know was how to handle it. How to tell Picard the one bit of information that, if badly handled, could severely embarrass the ReynKa past wanting to give them the charts. He could insist on privacy, but that, too, could cause more trouble . . . ."ReynTa," he said, most carefully, "I'd like to offer you the chance to handle this in the way you think would most benefit your family and your people."

Akarr just stared at him.

Riker gestured at the comm screen, currently plastered with an astonishingly garish Fandrean seal. "Be my guest."

Akarr gave him a look that said the colloquialism hadn't translated well, but Riker paid it no heed. Instead he moved away from the comm system, and allowed Akarr to reinitiate the connection.

"Glad to have you back," Picard said, in that exquisitely dry way he had—and which told Riker that things weren't going well at all. One glance at Troi's face confirmed it; she was wearing her "determinedly unaffected" expression . . . which actually worked quite well until you got to know it.

Akarr said, "We have been discussing information that has become available to us during our time in the Legacy."

"I'm hard put to imagine any pertinent information you might have obtained while behind the Legacy force-field," Picard said, but it was to Riker he looked. Behind Akarr's back, Riker gave the slightest of nods. "However, I certainly welcome any information which might help us get past our current difficulty."

"He has nothing," Takarr muttered, probably not aware that the *Enterprise*'s translating equipment would pick up such subtleties. "He's all bluster."

In front of him, Akarr bristled; Riker got a good close-up as the short fur on the back of Akarr's neck rose in a slight ridge. And he groaned inwardly, knowing that daleura would demand a response.

Except that Akarr glanced back at Riker, and offered none. Instead he said, "We have information regarding the shuttle shield failures, and why the Federation *seemingly* sent us out in faulty equipment. I'm sure you've been worried about that, my ReynSa."

"We've all been worried about it," Troi said, the first to catch on to and puzzle over the undercurrents in the communication.

"But no one more than the ReynTa's own mother," Riker said.

Akarr said steadily, "If you'd also known of the problems with the tranquilizer darts, my ReynSa, I imagine you would have been too overwhelmed with worry to concern yourself over Takarr's information about the probes."

She didn't ask him of which problems he spoke; she didn't comment about the importance of Takarr's discovery. She ignored Atann's questioning look and said,

"And yet you still somehow took a kaphoora trophy. Such achievement! How did you manage?"

"That," Akarr said, turning a daleura posture on his own mother, "is a story for another time. But how that story is told depends on what happens here."

Silence followed, in which the ReynSa took a physical step backward and quickly checked Atann's reaction. Atann didn't note it; he was too busy puzzling over the strange nature of his son's words. As were Troi and Picard. While Troi glanced from one to the other of them, hunting for clues, Picard looked to Riker. A captain's demand. *Make this make sense.*

Riker heard it loud and clear. He lifted his chin in the smallest possible increment, an acknowledgment and promise. *Later,* it said, and he hoped it would be enough.

Atann would have spoken to his son then, but Akarr got there just before him, still addressing his mother. "My ReynSa, I was pleased to hear that the ReynKa received acceptable terms for the use of the charts. Nothing that happened here should affect that situation . . . don't you agree?"

"Akarr," she said, "you are not making yourself entirely clear. The ordeal of your kaphoora—"

In another bold move, Akarr cut her off. "There are some things that should remain private, and further discussion of my kaphoora at this time would make that impossible."

"Unfortunately," Riker said, inserting himself back into the conversation, "I suspect that such discussion would be inevitable, if the ReynSa insists on delaying the transfer of the star-chart data."

"That sounds like a threat," Atann said, although he clearly couldn't tell just why it would be.

"Yes," Picard said with a gentle smile—and byplay

that Riker knew he'd missed. He and Akarr weren't the only ones here communicating with implications and innuendos. "I believe it is."

Tehra cleared her throat, a strangled noise involving plenty of under-purr. "I understand," she said briskly. "And after thinking about it, I must conclude that our data concerning the probes is incomplete—and that further investigation would require unnacceptable delay. Atann, I withdraw my objections to the chart transfer. I trust your impeccable judgment in this matter."

"That's wonderful!" Troi said, infusing a little unfettered enthusiasm into the mix, playing straight man for them all.

"Indeed it is," Picard said, and Riker could see the genuine relief in his face. "In fact, I would suspect that Mr. Data is just about ready to proceed. Why don't you and I check on that, ReynKa . . . Counselor, perhaps Takarr would like to tour the ship? There's plenty here to interest a young man of science." And Takarr, who'd gone from studied belligerence to astonishment at his mother's proclamation about his probe observations, now alerted in unmistakable eagerness.

Troi smiled. "I'd be glad to show him around."

Picard looked back up at the viewscreen. "Commander Riker, I imagine you'd like a chance to clean up and have your wounds tended. Do you have any estimate for your return?"

"Worf is already making arrangements to retrieve the *Collins* with the help of the rangers—Geordi thinks he can nurse the shuttle back through the portal, and there shouldn't be any real damage to her systems. I'll call in when we know for sure." He gave Picard a raised eyebrow and added with the last of his asperity, "The sooner, the better," to which Picard gave only a wryly amused smile.

Once signed off, Riker sought and found the only chair in the room, sinking into it without regard for its size, ignoring the fact that his knees jutted up into the air. Rational thought abandoned him, leaving him with vague impressions of a need for cleanup and rest. After a moment he realized that Akarr stood before him, waiting for his attention.

"Commander," he said, when Riker finally focused on him, and that was all. But he held out his hand in an awkward initiation of a human handshake.

After a moment, Riker took it, finding a way to fit his thumb between Akarr's own two thumbs. And then Akarr withdrew his hand and left Riker sitting alone in the small room, staring at the garish Fandrean seal and considering that maybe he, too, had come back from this kaphoora with a trophy of sorts.

Chapter Fifteen

RIKER STROLLED INTO TEN-FORWARD with Deanna on his arm. Hunting grounds of a sort . . . and the kind he'd stick to for a while. He spotted an empty table beside La Forge and Data at the same time as Deanna, and they headed for it, attracted as much by Data's animated conversation as the seating.

"Bodacious," Data was saying. "Catbird seat, gild the lily, eating crow—"

"Data," Troi said, mystified, "what *are* you doing?"

"Recounting some of the expressions I used in my recent experiment to determine how well the meanings of colloquial phrases from previous centuries have carried over to this one."

Riker broke into a slow smile as Troi did an entirely evident mental *hmm!* and asked, "Did you come to any conclusions?"

"I decided against it."

Even for Data, that didn't quite make sense. "Say that again?"

La Forge looked up at them. "I suggested that he's done enough of this sort of thing with the crew that his sample was skewed."

"My wildly varying results would seem to indicate the wisdom of the observation," Data said. "However, I did become aware of some interesting etymologies. *Engineer,* for instance, comes from the Old English word *engynour*—builder of military machines—which the English took from the French *engignear* . . . which can be traced all the way back to the Latin *ingenium,* meaning 'inborn qualities or talent.' "

"Ingenium," La Forge said, with exaggerated thoughtfulness. "I like it."

"Chief Ingenium," Troi said, her doubt apparent. "I suppose it has a certain . . . *ring* to it."

La Forge glanced at Data. "Well, when you say it that way . . . it sounds more like a warp propulsion fuel. I think I'll stick to what I've got."

"That might be best," Riker said in amusement and moved to the empty table, leaving Data to try out a few final phrases on Geordi.

"Commander Riker!" Guinan said, looking up from the dolorous ensign she served. "Welcome back!"

"Definitely good to be back." Riker pulled out a chair and Troi disengaged her arm and took a seat on the other side.

Guinan joined them there, nodding at her gloomy previous customer. "Just lost his sweetheart to the last starbase we visited."

"That's a shame," Troi said, immediately empathetic and glancing back as inconspicuously as possible. When she saw Riker's raised eyebrow, she said archly, "Professional interest only, Commander."

"Of course," he said, not bothering to sound terribly convinced, and took an immediate if light token smack on the arm.

"Ow," he complained. "Don't you think the Legacy did enough of a job on me?" Of course, it had been the other arm, which was indeed still sore enough. Dr. Crusher's magical sickbay tricks did not, she informed him sternly, work on older wounds—nor wounds that had been soaked in a neutralizing sap sealant. Of course, in the next breath, she was wondering if he hadn't been able to bring some of that sap back with him . . . ?

He had to admit that he'd been too busy to think about it.

Troi, not fooled for a moment, said with no sympathy whatsoever, "It was the other arm."

Guinan just smiled, as if all was right with her world. "What can I get you folks?"

"Mareuvian tea," Riker said, and, when they both turned to look at him, said, "What? A fellow can't go light?" He frowned at them, but when it didn't work, gave up. "Dr. Crusher suggested it."

"It does have mild restorative powers," Guinan agreed, as sage as ever. "Counselor?"

"I'll have the same," she said, and gave Riker the kind of mischievious smile that was more likely to alarm him than draw him into the fun. "In the spirit of . . . I don't know, in the spirit of something."

"Two Mareuvian teas, in the spirit of something," Guinan said. "Coming right up."

"Where's Worf, anyway?" Riker asked. "I know he had off time. I half-expected to find him in here raising a drink to the cartiga."

"He's on the holodeck," Troi said, still smiling—although at least this time it was aimed at Worf. "He's trying to figure out a way to integrate those very cartigas into his calisthenics programs. *After* he cleans out all the Tsoran-sized opponents the captain added."

Riker thought about it a moment, then nodded. Yes, that seemed just about right, too. That's all there was left at this point—cleanup. The probes had been withdrawn, the Ntignano evacuation was speeding along—and, an interesting note: just as the *Enterprise* was leaving orbit, one of the more ... dedicated communications lieutenants picked up the planetary news that the ReynSa had abruptly gone on an extended trip to be with her ailing parents, while Takarr remained behind under the tutelage of his older brother. *Indeed*, Picard had said, which just about said it all.

Guinan arrived with two tall, frosted glasses of tea, each topped by a stalk of green. "Mareuvian tea," she said. "With mint."

Riker plucked his out and deposited it into Deanna's drink. "I've seen enough towering greenery for a while, thank you."

Guinan just smiled. But as she turned away, she hesitated, looking at him from under raised, nonexistent eyebrows. "Well?" she asked. "Does it?"

Ever get any easier. Of course she remembered her question to him, the last time he was here.

"Not to judge by this experience," Riker said. Not only stuck in an annoying diplomatic baby-sitting job, but stuck with it in a carnivore-filled jungle. No, make that a carnivore-*overflowing* jungle.

All the same ... his time with Akarr had changed the kid. Neither of them had really wanted to admit it, but it had. A coming of age that the kid hadn't expected when he'd gone looking for tooth and claw . . . a coming of age Riker hadn't thought him capable of.

So maybe they both learned something.

But it was going to be just as damn annoying the next time around.

"What was she talking about?" Troi asked, giving Guinan—back behind the bar and talking to another officer—and then Riker each a curious look. Her most curious look. The one that was only slightly less scary than it was mischievous, her black eyes even more beguiling with that spark behind them.

"I'm never really sure," Riker said, evading the question as neatly as possible. And he wasn't. He'd have to think about it some more. He sighed, sipped the tea—bland, to his tastes, but if Dr. Crusher said "restorative," then restorative it was—and found, among the jumble of his thoughts, one reasonably safe conclusion.

If nothing else, it seemed certain that after his time with the Legacy carnivores, baby-sitting Data's cat Spot would be—as Data himself would say, in his current colloquialism-hunting state of mind—a breeze.

Riker closed one eye and thought briefly back to previous experience with Spot. Thought of the cartiga. Thought of Spot.

Maybe not.

Doranna's Backstory . . .

After obtaining a degree in wildlife illustration and environmental education, Doranna spent a number of years deep in the Appalachian Mountains, where she never actually saw a sholjagg. When she emerged, it was as a writer who found herself irrevocably tied to the natural world and its creatures.

Doranna, who has published seven fantasy novels and won the Compton Crook Award with the first, figures that she was destined to write a *Star Trek* novel, given the names of her two irrepressible Cardigan Woloh Corgis—Carbon Unit (Kacey) and Jean-Luc Picardigan. We won't mention those preadolescent scribblings of *Star Trek (TOS)* stories, and yes, they've been burned, so don't even try to find them.

You can contact her at:

T&C@doranna.net

or

PO Box 26207
Rochester, NY 14626
(SASE please)

or visit *http://www.doranna.net/*

Look for STAR TREK fiction from Pocket Books

Star Trek®: The Original Series

Star Trek: The Next Generation®

Star Trek: Voyager®

Star Trek®: New Frontier

Star Trek®: Invasion!

Star Trek®: Day of Honor

#1 • *Ancient Blood* • Diane Carey
#2 • *Armageddon Sky* • L.A. Graf
#3 • *Her Klingon Soul* • Michael Jan Friedman
#4 • *Treaty's Law* • Dean Wesley Smith & Kristine Kathryn Rusch
The Television Episode • Michael Jan Friedman
Day of Honor Omnibus • various

Star Trek®: The Captain's Table

#1 • *War Dragons* • L.A. Graf
#2 • *Dujonian's Hoard* • Michael Jan Friedman
#3 • *The Mist* • Dean Wesley Smith & Kristine Kathryn Rusch
#4 • *Fire Ship* • Diane Carey
#5 • *Once Burned* • Peter David
#6 • *Where Sea Meets Sky* • Jerry Oltion
The Captain's Table Omnibus • various

Star Trek®: The Dominion War

#1 • *Behind Enemy Lines* • John Vornholt
#2 • *Call to Arms...* • Diane Carey
#3 • *Tunnel Through the Stars* • John Vornholt
#4 • *...Sacrifice of Angels* • Diane Carey

Star Trek®: The Badlands

#1 • Susan Wright
#2 • Susan Wright

Star Trek®: Dark Passions

#1 • Susan Wright
#2 • Susan Wright

Star Trek® Books available in Trade Paperback

Omnibus Editions
   Invasion! Omnibus • various
   Day of Honor Omnibus • various
   The Captain's Table Omnibus • various

Star Trek: Odyssey • William Shatner with Judith and Garfield
    Reeves-Stevens

Other Books

    Legends of the Ferengi • Ira Steven Behr & Robert Hewitt Wolfe
    Strange New Worlds, vols. I and II • Dean Wesley Smith, ed.
    Adventures in Time and Space • Mary Taylor
    Captain Proton! • Dean Wesley Smith
    The Lives of Dax • Marco Palmieri, ed.
    The Klingon Hamlet • Wil'yam Shex'pir
    New Worlds, New Civilizations • Michael Jan Friedman
    Enterprise Logs • Carol Greenburg, ed.